TONIGHT WE RULE THE WORLD

ZACK SMEDLEY

PAGE STREET

PUBLISHING CO.

PAGE STREET
PUBLISHING CO.

To Brodie Spade, Andy Zhao, Paige Nelson, Jackson Kotch, Alex Al-Jazrawi, Allison Basiley, and Olivia Benton— for our unforgettable time in the neighborhood.

Long live Old Friendship.

AUTHOR'S NOTE

WELL. I PICKED A BAD YEAR TO WRITE A BOOK WITH heavy subject matter.

The year 2020 will go down in history as a year that took a great deal from us as a whole: lives, jobs, sanity, perceived decency, and personal joy. While I have no right to complain about my incredibly fortunate circumstances throughout the COVID-19 pandemic, there's no other way to say it: This book was written during a year that I should never have picked up a pen, and almost every minute spent at my keyboard was thoroughly joyless.

I always say that my books aren't about protagonists experiencing trauma, but rather, about them conquering it. When I wrote my debut, *Deposing Nathan*, this worked because I was a college kid who felt on top. Words poured out of me, and when the content got tough, I could step away to enjoy the beauty and exuberance of the world outside my window. This time, though, I felt entirely unqualified: Who was I to rattle on about overcoming obstacles when I was regularly losing afternoons of writing to hypochondriacal panic attacks? How was I supposed to shine a light on human decency when every headline screamed the opposite? Couple this with the countless hours I spent inhibited by this book's heavy topics—which I was determined to portray properly—and the whole process felt insurmountable. I'd lie awake at night, dreading the morning when I'd return to it.

Yet, eventually, I always would. Because every week, I would get letters from readers who told me how much *Deposing Nathan* had helped them. Those letters went up on my wall, and they became the light that wound up guiding me (however gruelingly) out of my maze. To those readers: Please know I did my best to pour everything I could into this book, during a year when I— like so many others—had almost nothing in the tank to pour. I can honestly say I'm satisfied with the result, so now, it goes properly from my hands to yours.

Excellence was described by Aristotle as "the result of high intention, sincere effort, and intelligent execution." I can't speak to whether I achieved that last one, but I can tell you this project was born from the first two. Because you deserve nothing less than an excellent book.

I hope, from the sincerest place in my heart, that I've given you one.

—zs

12/14/2020

STORY
ONE

THE BOY WITH THE
BROKEN ARM

ONE

OF ALL THE THINGS I LEARNED IN MY YEARS GROWING up, the most important one was to never get in the crosshairs of Lily Caldwell. Lily: the sweetest angel you'd ever meet—as long as she liked you. And in fairness, she liked everyone by default. It was a tall order to wind up on her shit list; but if you did, you had serious problems.

I saw this firsthand more than once, being her boyfriend and all. And don't get me wrong; we had some wonderful years together. But trust me when I say I know what I'm talking about.

Snapsnap. Snapsnap.

I stretch and release the bracelet around my wrist, letting the wooden beads flick my skin in sets of two. *Onetwo. Onetwo.* When I was younger, I had more conspicuous forms of stimming when I was on edge—clicking my pen, rocking back and forth in my chair—but then Lily made me this fidget bracelet for my fifteenth birthday, and I've used it ever since.

Our school's Rent-a-Cop stares at me from his chair. The glint of his badge in the sunlight stabs the edge of my eye. I look away.

Snapsnap.

"Did someone die?" I ask the floor.

"No."

"Did someone get in an accident?"

"No."

"Is someone hurt?"

"It's easier if the other folks explain."

That's a yes. "Was it my mom, or my dad?"

"Your parents are fine, bud. We should be called in any second now."

The Rent-a-Cop (identified by his badge as Officer Mat Hewitt) is a skinny blond guy who looks maybe a couple years older than me. When he first knocked on our classroom door, I thought he might be another student. Then I saw the badge and the Glock 22, and had four thoughts in this order:

Shit—somebody's in trouble.

Shit—he's saying their name.

Shit—that's my name.

Shit.

He's been ducking my questions ever since he walked me down here to the admin lair. He's not exactly unkind, but he's clearly keyed up by whatever this is. The two of us are waiting to meet with someone—I'm not sure who—so all I can do is sit here tugging my bracelet and wondering what the hell I did.

Snapsnap.

"You can go on back. First door on the left," says a secretary on the other side of the room.

Officer Hewitt leads me into an office I've passed every day but never set foot in. One of the visitor's chairs is already occupied by a short, ripped Latino man in an athletic polo shirt—Mr. Yacenda, the cross-country coach and my guidance counselor.

He's a laid-back guy; always assuaging my nerves with, "Hey man, I'm not worried about it if you aren't!"

(He looks worried.)

Officer Hewitt closes the door, then takes a seat. All eyes swivel to the woman seated on the other side of the executive desk, dressed in a turtleneck the color of dried blood: Principal Felicity Graham, PhD.

Principal Graham is the human version of a textbook—aggressively attempting to be relatable and fun, but with a no-nonsense core constantly leaking through the mask. She's probably mid-forties at most, but something about her stiff persona makes her seem two hundred years old. Her pale skin is practically translucent under the harsh lights, and her hair is pulled back in a pristine bun.

She leans forward in her black leather throne, thin fingers laced together, and smiles.

"Here we are," she says, like I'm a package she's been waiting for at the foot of her driveway. "Hi, Owen—good to see you again. We chatted for a few minutes at the last senior assembly, but that was a few months back."

She reaches out to shake my hand but backs off when I squirm a little.

"What's happening?" I blurt out. I snap my bracelet again, a faster tempo this time. I don't like feeling crowded, and right now there are four of us stuffed in an office the size of a bathroom. I fix my gaze on the window behind her, where a fierce rain hammers against the glass—the kind you could feel if you touched your fingers to the surface.

Principal Graham's face tightens. "Why don't you have a seat?"

I do as she says, then dig a notebook and pen out of my backpack. Early on growing up, my father taught me the first rule of being in trouble: Whether or not you know what you're being accused of, take notes of everything you're told.

"Owen, I know you do best with directness," Principal Graham says. "So frankly, I want us to drop the HR lingo for a second and just talk to each other here. We're going to go over this step by step, then we'll answer every question you have— I promise. To start off, are you familiar with the ERAT system we have?"

She says it like "air-at." When I shake my head, she explains, "ERAT is short for Electronic Reporting and Tips Service—it's a website the county rolled out in schools a few years ago. Students can use it to anonymously report incidents they've become aware of concerning their classmates."

"Incidents?"

"Things like bullying or harassment," Officer Hewitt jumps in. "Even potential crimes."

He looks like he's about to say more, but Principal Graham cuts him off. "Owen, earlier this morning, this system received a report that was filed about a potential incident that may have taken place last month."

I'm in the middle of writing out the acronym when my pen freezes.

"Keep going," I murmur. An ugly chill works its way from my stomach to my chest to my throat. I'm not religious, but I start saying a vague version of a prayer—hoping for a scenario where this isn't what I suspect it is.

"Alright." Principal Graham's voice is aggressively even-tempered—each inflection meticulously controlled. "The report that was filed on our site stated that, during the senior class trip to Lanham University last month, you were sexually assaulted by one of your classmates. This would've been during spring break, so just over a month ago."

It's like when you spend all night working on a paper and

your computer crashes without saving it—all your work vanishes. It's so quiet, so instant, that you never react right away. There are always those few seconds of overwhelming denial: *This isn't happening.*

The next few seconds feel like that.

Principal Graham tries to meet my eyes. "Owen?"

Snapsnap.

I tug the beads farther back each time, snapping them on my skin with increasing sharpness. Officer Hewitt leans to steady me, but Principal Graham taps his arm, like, *let him do his thing.*

"I didn't write that," I tell them. "I didn't submit that, I swear. You can check my phone or whatever if you need to prove it."

"So . . . a few things, to start off," Principal Graham says. "The first is that you're not in trouble."

"Why would I be in trouble?"

"Owen, please. The second thing is that our response here is guided by a lot of different policies. Which . . ." She holds up both hands as though cutting off an audition. "I promise we'll go over all that, but we need to wait for a parent to be in here."

Parent? Oh, God.

"No," I say, forceful. "You can't tell them. Not allowed."

"I already gave them a call—Owen, you're still seventeen; I had to," says Mr. Yacenda. The rain against the window feels like it grows more violent—increasingly agitated.

We all sit in silence for a minute, maybe two. I spend it saying another small prayer to myself, urgently hoping that it's Mom who shows up, and not—

Down the hall, footsteps thunder so loudly that it's like they echo through the classrooms. The room damn near shakes. Some woman is saying the word "sir" a bunch, but the steps only grow more menacing, and the door flies open with such force that Principal Graham jumps to her feet. Me—I scoot back in the chair, taking myself as far out of the way as possible. That's always what you do when he's pissed.

"Everyone *freeze*," Dad orders, a notebook and pen already in his hand. "Owen, not another word."

My bracelet snaps apart.

TWO

September 5th—Freshman Year

Dear Diary,

My first day of high school began with a mandatory icebreaker and ended with me getting hit by a Ford F-250 pickup truck. In the grand scheme of things, it's difficult to say which experience was worse.

The icebreaker was more drawn-out—a boilerplate question posed by my new geometry teacher, Mr. Adler: "Tell us something interesting that happened to you lately." I didn't have an answer, but that didn't stop him from egging me on while several dozen pairs of eyes trained their crosshairs on my chest for a full minute. The pickup truck, on the other hand, was quick but painful: ten seconds of stupidity on my end after the bus dropped me home.

Old Friendship Landing—aka my home neighborhood since middle school—is a perfectly symmetrical community my family can barely afford. (The HOA likes to pretend it's just another 'burb, but the entrance is protected by an iron gate and security guard. That's fuck-you money.) The buses either can't or won't go in, so they drop everyone off at the roundabout in front of it. The dozen-or-so kids then march into the neighborhood in a uniform pack, making their way past the gym and the pool so they can split off to their respective houses.

I can't stand crowds, so I always try to wait by the gate until they disperse.

While I waited today, though, I realized one of the girls on my bus had hung back too. She stood frozen on the other side of the road, staring at me with her head tilted. Like she was studying my face.

The details of the next few seconds are a little fuzzy, if I'm being honest. I remember her raising her hand to wave at me. I took one step forward—another, I think—and I was raising my hand to wave back.

Then . . . *WHAM!*

It was less dramatic than I'm making it sound, but a pickup truck hit me—mainly the right side of my body—as I stepped into the street toward her. The air was knocked out of my chest, the girl screamed, and as I plunged to the pavement, I only had one coherent thought among the subsequent searing pain and screaming and blackness: *Crap, those fingers are backward.*

So all in all, today was not a very good start to high school. But at least I have an answer for Mr. Adler's ice-breaker now.

Sincerely,
Owen

September 6th—Freshman Year

Dear Diary,

I had to cut yesterday's entry short because it's very hard to type. But I forgot to mention that the girl who waved to me is named Lily Caldwell, and she stayed by my side until my dad showed up to take me to the hospital.

I mention that because she came and visited me again this afternoon. I was sitting out on my front stoop, listening to my music and watching some of the older kids play basketball in a nearby driveway. On the other side of the street, one of the boys from my bus—a Latino guy about my age—was sitting on his stoop opposite to me. His jet black hair fell halfway over his glasses, and he didn't look especially friendly, but our eyes kept running into each other as we watched the game.

Then: a tap on my shoulder.

"Oh my God, how's your hand?"

Lily's voice made me jump, and I think I squeaked a little too. If so, it didn't matter to her. She just sat right down next to me, staring at me like I owed her something. As I got a closer look at her, I realized I'd seen her around the halls back in middle school. Her ordinary appearance— wavy blond hair, ice blue eyes, lopsided smile stuffed with braces—was always offset by her socks, which ranged from odd to zany. She was like a reverse chameleon: always changing her colors and spots to stand out.

Today she was wearing neon yellow leggings, a purple blouse, and a concerned look on her face.

"How's your hand?" she repeated, nudging me.

We both looked to the cast entombing my arm. My

right hand had nine broken bones. I didn't even know there were that many hand bones to break. It turns out there are twenty-seven, and apparently you need every single one in order to type, brush your teeth, or jerk off. (Go figure.)

Well, I told Lily, *it's broken.*

I didn't mean it to be funny. But she laughed, so I was proud of myself regardless.

"That guy is staring at you," she said. She nudged her elbow toward the boy sitting on his stoop. "Do you know him?"

I shook my head.

"He's *not* nice. I keep inviting him to hang out with my friend group, and he just ignores me. Watch." She gave the boy the same vigorous wave she'd given me yesterday.

He made eye contact, got up, and went back inside his house.

"See?" Lily crossed her arms. Then she noticed that I still had earbuds in. "What're you listening to?"

The answer was "Ascent" by Brian Eno, my favorite song of all time. But I was embarrassed to tell her that because that song was just ambiance . . . basically a soothing melody without a rhythm or words. Not cool. So instead I said, *nothing.*

"Tell me! Come on, I want to know," she said, giving me a smile surrounded by freckles. She leaned toward me, filling my nose with the synthetic smell of cotton candy, and reached for my phone.

PLEASE don't touch that, I snapped, wrinkling my nose.

That got her attention. She put up both hands, clearly spooked. "Am I allowed to ask what genre it is?"

I got the sense she wasn't going to let it go, so I mumbled that it was sleep music.

"Yeah? Neat," she said. "Have you heard of the Killers?"

I don't think so, I said, truthfully.

"Oh my gosh, really? Yes you have—everyone has. I'm obsessed with them. Can I see this?" She reached for my phone again, more cautiously this time. I gave in and let her show me some of their songs, a few of which I recognized from the radio. We shared my earbuds, leaning close together. (The smell bothered me, but our knees got to touch, so I decided the pros outweighed the cons.)

She tapped my cast and bit her lip, like she was embarrassed. "Does it hurt?"

I wasn't sure how to answer that, so I didn't.

"Can you still do assignments and stuff?" she asked.

The school's getting a tutor, I told her. *To write down stuff for me.*

"I can do it!" She said it in a heartbeat, like she was waiting for the cue. When I frowned, she said, "No, seriously, let me. I feel really bad. You don't have to pay me or anything."

I just shrugged. She took that as a yes.

"Great. Oh, and . . ." She reached into her backpack, brandishing a red marker. "I love signing stuff. Hold up your arm."

When I raised it above my head, she giggled and said, "No—down here, smarty."

She took hold of my cast, leaned against me, and signed it:

Feel better soon and I'm sorry for directing you into traffic ☹
-Lily.

It's midnight now, and I'm still looking at it. She put
it right along the side, so it's always in view.

Sincerely,

Owen

September 21st—Freshman Year

Dear Diary,

I've seen Lily Caldwell *every* day of high school so far.
That's two whole weeks!

I told her early on that I live and die by routines (not
literally), so we developed one of our own: Every day
after school, we walk from the bus stop to the playground
and do my homework together at the picnic tables under
the pavilion.

I don't tell her this, but our sessions are my favorite
part of the day. Never mind the fact that I'm drained
from classes, and that I have to talk more than I'd like . . .
I get to spend time with someone besides my parents. I'm
always itching to get off the bus so we can exchange heys
and complain about our teachers, or cafeteria food, or
freshman assemblies.

There's no such thing as a bad day with her. Whether
she's doodling on my backpack or playing tic-tac-toe in
my notebook . . . she makes her own fun. I don't even
mind the nauseating smell of her perfume anymore.

Today, though, was extra special: She introduced me to something called magnet poetry. It's a game where you take a bunch of random printed words and rearrange them without any intention, usually with humorous results. It got its name because the words were attached to magnets that could be rearranged on a refrigerator, but Lily used an app on her phone.

She set the phone down between us, generated a list of random words, and scribbled one down on the paper:

mountains

Then she told me, "Pick a word from the list." So I did:

wander

We went back and forth until we had a full sentence, which Lily then read aloud for us both:

Mountains wander among their filthy corduroy pineapples.

"It's the 'filthy' that really does it," Lily said, the corners of her mouth dancing. Then, in a crusty voice: "*FILTHY corduroy pineapples!*"

You should have heard how loudly we were laughing! The three elementary schoolers on the swings gave us weird looks, and that only made it worse. It was a simple moment, but one we got to enjoy together . . . just the two of us. When she took a picture of the notebook page and said, "This is going on my blog," I didn't feel shy about asking her where to find it, and she didn't hesitate to tell me.

"Just promise you won't read my old poetry," she

added. "Or short stories."

Short stories? I asked.

"Oh, yeah." Lily pursed her lips in an I-guess-I-haven't-mentioned grimace. "I'm not published or anything. I'm trying to be, though. I wrote this whole book of poems that I worked on since I was . . . eleven? I think. It started when my mom moved out."

I wasn't sure what to say to that. But I must've looked worried, because she said, "It's not a big deal anymore. This was like, years ago. And even before then, she was always doing her own thing. She'd wake up one morning and tell us she was taking a trip to Hawaii or trying some new healing retreat in the mountains. And she kept changing jobs. No joke, a few days after my dad asked for a divorce, she just up and moved to a different state."

Moved? I murmured, fiddling with my glasses.

"Like, overnight. So he couldn't even finalize their divorce for a year. Yeah, it was *bad*. My dad just kept saying that her head was somewhere else." Lily made a face, turning red. "I got way off-track; sorry."

That's okay, I assured her. I wanted to encourage her to keep talking, because I loved that she was being so open with me. Things between us thus far had been friendly, but sort of formal, you know? Her phone was always buzzing nonstop with messages . . . she had a whole other life that didn't extend here. For all I knew, she tutored dozens of other guys just like me. But I had a feeling that she didn't tell a lot of people what she was telling me now.

"My dad has been great about it," Lily continued. "Last year he helped me email a publisher to ask if I could visit their office for a day; then he drove me to New York when they said yes. Yeah, my dad's awesome. I think my mom made him all paranoid that I'm going to ditch him too, so he turned into one of those parents that acts like your best friend."

I nodded. Not like there was much I could tell her to relate to that.

"But some of the kids in middle school made fun of me for the writing because—I don't know why. There was an article with a few of my poems in the school paper. Yeah, that didn't help." She played with a blond strand of hair, shrugging.

I got made fun of in middle school too, I told her.

"Aw, why?" Then she flashed a smile that made me feel ten feet tall and said, "What's there to make fun of?"

My appearance, usually, I said. (I inherited some of my dad's height, but none of his broad muscle. Couple my twig-like stature with my matted mess of hair, and you get a walking mop. The thick wire glasses don't help either.)

"Wait, like, your face?" Lily asked. "That's so mean!"

And my clothes, I clarified. My default wardrobe is sweatpants and a baggy T-shirt, so the sleeves don't bother me. My feet are size nines, but my shoes are twelves because it's less constricting.

"You'd look cute in jeans. Dark ones," Lily said. My face got so hot that I had to turn away, but she said it casually. Like it was no big deal. Then she added, with a little more hesitation, "Is that why you don't talk a lot? Or is there some other reason?"

The question itself didn't throw me (a lot of people ask); I was just surprised it took her this long. As soon as she said it, she started tracing a "U" on the picnic table with her pen.

And I wasn't sure how to answer, to be honest. Back

in sixth grade, I talked nonstop—always butting into people's conversations, going on and on when no one was really listening. Even the teachers stopped calling on me, because they seemed to know it would trigger a five-minute exchange about trivial stuff.

So I took the hint: talk less, and maybe people would like me more. As the months went by, no one treated me any differently, so I kept leaning into it harder. The worst part was when the nice kids tried to help me out, and I botched it even further. Like when one boy passed me in the hall, gave me a smile, and said, "What's up, dude?"

All I could do was respond with an uncomfortable laugh. You know what it sounds like.

By eighth grade, I was talking so little that it started to scare my parents and teachers—all of my answers were barely more than a sentence, and always in a whisper. It's how I've handled myself ever since.

I don't remember how I answered Lily's question, and I don't remember how she replied. But as soon as I got home, I went to her blog and started scrolling through it. It looked like a professional website: simple, red and white, with a picture of her signature in the footer. A filtered photo of our magnet poetry was up top, but I kept scrolling to try to find her writings. Unfortunately, most of her posts were just re-shared quotes uploaded by other users. One from yesterday read:

People come and go in life. But the right ones will always stay.

And before that:

Be your own upgrade.

Lots of stuff about self-care and being kind to others. But then I found one original poem called "My Town with Two of Nothing." I won't copy it here, but it was basically a lament about how our town is so small that we only have one Starbucks, one library, one movie theater, etc. It was strange to read, because I always loved our town for its quietness. Lily and I were polar opposites: She wanted to tear through life headfirst. I wanted to move as little as possible.

Her blog had a quote pinned to the top of her page, credited to French writer Victor Hugo:

A writer is a world trapped in a person.

She added a caption to this one:

What does it mean to be remembered? My goal is that regardless of where I go, what I do, or who I meet, people remember me. I want to change lives. I'm not just going to be a small author who sells a hundred copies . . . one day I'm going to write a bestseller. Everyone will see my name, and everyone will know it.

Hello, Readers: My name is Lily Caldwell. I'm a world trapped in a person, and one day, I'm going to matter for real!

I'm still thinking about those words. And it makes me wish I wasn't so spineless, because if I wasn't, I'd tell her that she does matter for real, to me. This may have been easy to guess based on my entries so far, but I've never had a friend before.

Sincerely,
Owen

THREE

EVERY ROOM MY FATHER ENTERS WAS BUILT TOO small for him. At six foot five, he's already tall physically, but his sheer presence adds another two, maybe three feet. His head always seems like it's in danger of ramming right through the ceiling—silver military buzz cut and all. A mountain of a man. He walks with a limp from the arthritis in his knees, but he never slouches.

I watch as he shuts the door behind him, then holds up his hand for complete silence.

Once he gets it, he says, "Anyone here familiar with the term 'BOHICA'?"

Dad and his goddamn speeches. Anytime he's pissed, it's the same routine: His eyes narrow, his jaw unhinges, and he spends the next ten minutes sucking up the spotlight. No salve can soothe Steve Turner's temper like the sound of his own mouth in fourth gear.

"It's a phrase that was cooked up by U.S. Military guys during the Vietnam War, okay. In 1981, it becomes the code word for Operation Grand Eagle—an ISA paramilitary mission where a group of Green Berets get sent to Laos to collect intel about POWs. Six years later, it becomes the title of a book claiming the mission's findings were falsified. The Senate Committee on Veterans' Affairs holds hearings, and the whole thing becomes a headache for everyone involved. Red tape out the wazoo. The phrase stuck around ever since, and it's one of the first ones I learned early on in the Marines—my buddies and I used it all the time. I've been out for the better part of a decade now, but the thing about BOHICA, see, is that I find it still applies to a lot of everyday life. I say it every time I get stuck in traffic; I say it before going to the DMV; and . . ." He sniffs. "Looking around here, I'm thinking it applies. See, BOHICA is an acronym. Know what it stands for?"

"Steve——" Principal Graham starts.

"'*Bend Over . . . Here It Comes Again.*'"

Dad claps his hands together once, looking around the office. Nobody smiles.

My head is in my hands. Officer Hewitt is leaned forward, jaw slightly agape. Mr. Yacenda sits frozen, midway through a sip of his coffee, while Principal Graham is still half-extending a gesture for my father to take a seat. Caravaggio couldn't have created a Renaissance painting this chaotic.

"Steve," Principal Graham repeats.

"You know something, Principal Graham," Dad says. He has this way of talking where everything he asks is part of some statement he's making, so his questions never really sound like questions. "Most of the people who call me 'Steve' are friends, family, or coworkers. You, however, are the person who's trying to arrest my son for some trumped-up BS he had nothing to do with. So how about we stick with 'Mr. Turner,' yeah?"

Principal Graham neither responds to that nor looks like she knows how to.

"Sir, we're *not* arresting your son," Officer Hewitt interjects.

"Who're you?" Dad sizes him up.

"Officer Matthew Hewitt. Or, just Mat," he says.

"With one T," Dad notes, sticking a meaty finger at the officer's name plate. "You old enough to drive at night, Mat With One T?"

Mat With One T does not respond.

"Alright," Dad says, then does what he always does: He seizes command of the room. "Folks, let's reel this in. We're going to go back to the beginning and break this down Barney-style: What, exactly, is this about?"

Principal Graham opens her mouth, but he isn't done.

"Start with the BLUF—give me the big picture," he continues. That's another thing about him—since he's former Military, half his vocabulary is acronyms. BLUF is short for "bottom-line up front."

Principal Graham kicks into gear, telling my father everything she's told me. He sinks into a chair, scribbling at the speed of light in his notebook. I keep waiting for him to interrupt her—to scoff and say things like, *What? No way, you've got the wrong kid*—but instead he just lets her explain everything.

Once she's finished, all he says after a long pause is, "Who reported this?"

"I can't say; I'm sorry," Principal Graham tells him.

"Was it Luke?" I blurt out. As all eyes turn to me, I kick myself for not even knowing his last name—then again, I only met him once. "Luke someone. He might go by Lucas. Was it him?"

"Guys, even if I were allowed to say, we have no way of knowing," she explains. "The ERAT system was designed to help students feel more comfortable coming forward, so it's completely anonymous."

Dad draws several forceful lines on his paper.

"Just so I understand: In order to encourage reporting from students who might otherwise be afraid of tattling on their classmates . . . you made a system," he says, "called e-*rat?*"

"Air-at," Mr. Yacenda tries, already cringing at himself.

"I take it quicksnitch.edu was unavailable?"

"We didn't pick the acronym."

"Well, there's a relief," Dad deadpans. "Here I was worried my tax dollars were getting pissed away."

(Steve Turner is the Western world's Sisyphus. Chained to the eternal hell of rolling a boulder up the hill of everyone's incompetence.)

"You know . . . here's the thing, okay," he continues. "About that overnight trip last month: I have a pretty good idea of when that was. Because if memory serves me right—and we can check this—that's the night my son came out as bisexual on social media."

No one speaks. I rub my eyes until stars fill up the room.

Dad leans forward. "So if you're telling me he was picked out and attacked on that same evening, we have one of two situations on our hands. Either that is the world's *biggest* coincidence—"

"Dad," I try to say.

"—*or*, we're dealing with a hate crime." When no one responds, he continues, "Now, I'm not saying that's the case. All I'm saying is if it were, it'd potentially expand the scope of this to action on a federal level. We'd be talking about a possible FBI investigation; we'd be talking about prosecution under DOJ authority. To say nothing of the civil suits that could be filed against the school, its leaders, and the county Board of Ed. *That's* what we'd be talking about if this were a hate crime, is all I'm saying."

Principal Graham is writing very fast.

Without looking up, she simply says in a small voice, "We will absolutely make note of that."

"Great. Let's talk next steps," Dad says. "Here's what I haven't heard yet: What do you plan on doing about this?"

Principal Graham's face loosens in relief—we're back on book.

"A few things," she says. She looks directly at me instead of him. "First we need to fill out a new School Incident Investigation Form, based on the ERAT tip and any new information you'd like to add, Owen. That gets sent to Mrs. Sondergoth, the Title IX coordinator for our school district."

"Title IX?" I repeat.

She nods, lips pursed. "Since the alleged incident is a sexual assault, it's what we call a Title IX incident. That means we need to take a few extra steps per the Office of Civil Rights. Mrs. Sondergoth is our contact for that info—her job is to help guide investigations like these."

"Investigation?" I squeak, as Dad says, "*That's* what I like to hear."

I shake my head. "I don't want an investigation. I don't want anyone to do anything."

Principal Graham gives me a small grimace.

"I understand," she says in a wooden voice. "And trust me, no one in this room wants to make things worse for you—"

"Why would anyone want to make things worse for me?"

"—*but*," she continues, pressing down on an invisible piano, "since your alleged attacker was a classmate, this could all make us partially liable or even extremely liable. And, you know what—heck, put *all* that aside for a minute." She leans forward on her elbows like she wants to scoop me up. "We care about every one of you guys. Keeping you safe . . . that's the whole gig."

"Sometime today, please," Dad snaps, drawing circles in the air with his pen.

She dances around it some more, but what it boils down to is that the school—specifically guidance counselors and Mat With One T—is required to talk to everyone who was on the school trip to find out if they saw or heard anything. She notes that the school will be required to send notices home to parents to let them know about the students being questioned.

"Your name will *not* be used ever, at all, period," Principal Graham assures me. "Within thirty days, we'll put together a report of any findings, which we can use to take appropriate disciplinary action."

"Disciplin—" Dad scoffs, cutting himself off as his eyebrows shoot up. "Pfft! *'Hey Joe Schmo, so we've concluded you're a violent criminal—knock that off right now or you can kiss senior picnic goodbye, buddy boy!'*"

"Mr. Tur—"

"I mean, sure, my kid may have been violently attacked by one of your students, on your watch, at your school, during your event, but at least we can be comforted in knowing you're bringing that nice, long hammer down. Can you tack on a few weeks of clapping erasers while you're at it?"

Mat With One T jumps back in. "This is only what's required on the school's end of things. If, on top of this, you wanted to file a report with the state police—"

"The real cops, you mean. Let's compare apples to apples here."

Mat With One T goes to correct him, then gives up. "I— sure. I'm able to make arrests as an SRO, but if you wanted law enforcement to lead a criminal investigation alongside the school's, we could help you meet with them to get everything synced up."

"Also, Linda," Mr. Yacenda pipes up.

Dad and I sit there scrawling in our notepads. I run out of paper and flip to a fresh page as Principal Graham clarifies, "Linda is our school liaison—a Student Services employee who communicates directly with law enforcement and DSS on a need-to-know basis for cases of abuse."

"Is Linda Mrs. Sondergoth?" I ask, still scribbling.

"No, two different people. I doubt this'll get kicked over to CPS, but let's loop Linda in too just to be safe." Principal Graham seems to realize she's basically talking to herself, because she leans forward to look directly at me again.

"Owen," she says. "We've all been doing a lot of yakking here. Do you have any questions?"

I swallow, setting down my pen.

"Well," I say. "You don't have my permission to do any of that. Like, any of it. I don't want anyone talking to my classmates, or asking around—"

"If you're worried about retaliation—"

"My girlfriend can't find out." I stare at my knees, clamping my arms together. "Lily Caldwell, my girlfriend, can't find out about any of this. So you're really screwing that up."

Mr. Yacenda makes a small noise that sounds like he's sucking in air through his teeth. Beside me, Dad folds his arms but stays quiet.

"You know what, I hear you," Principal Graham says. She throws up her hands, glaring down at her desk like it's covered in parking tickets. "Let's call it what it is, sure. Absolutely. But as I said, our job here is to keep all of you safe. And as part of that, this allegation isn't something we can ignore. Whether it was you who sent it in—"

"It wasn't!"

"—regardless of who it was, we're required to take action on it. We can't just pretend we never heard it."

"Does it count for anything that that's what I want to happen?"

"We just aren't allowed to do it, I'm sorry."

(Ugly pause.)

Dad closes his notebook. "What else for now?"

"For now, your job—and Owen's—is to take a beat and regroup. Take all this in," Principal Graham says.

"In other words, 'hurry up and wait,'" he says.

She ignores him. "Owen, I'm going to tell Mrs. Sondergoth to set up a meeting with you once she's back in next week. We'll go from there."

Dad gets up and motions for me to follow him out. Before he closes the door behind us, he stops to survey the office one last time.

"Get this right," he tells them. But he says it like he already knows they won't.

FOUR

November 3rd—Freshman Year

Dear Diary,

I survived!!! I made it through all eight weeks of having my wrist in prison, and after school today, a doctor used a small saw to cut that infernal hunk of fiberglass from my arm. And now I have my hand back! I've spent this whole evening doing everything I used to do, including tying my shoes, brushing my hair, brushing my teeth, and (TMI alert) the most monumental jerkoff session since the day I discovered porn.

And now here I am, typing with both hands again! Woohoo!

TYPING! IS! SO! FUN!

Cheerfully,

Owen

November 21st—Freshman Year

Dear Diary,

What a terrible month. I'm re-reading my last entry, and I just want to kick myself. I was so excited to have my arm back, I didn't even consider that it would be the last day I got to spend time with Lily Caldwell.

The worst part is that I think I'm the one who screwed it up. When I told her I wouldn't need her help anymore, I realize now that I was too blunt about it. (I do that a lot.) I remember she looked a little caught off-guard, and basically said, "See you around." We haven't met up or talked since, not even on the bus ride home. She has her own set of friends there.

I love having my hand back, but I feel less excited about life than any of the days when it was in the cast . . .

Sadly,

Owen

November 27th—Freshman Year

Dear Diary,

You'll never believe this! Last night after Thanksgiving dinner, I went to my room and decided to send Lily a text:

Hi—I don't mean to be intrusive, but would you mind if I emailed a few questions about writing?

(Yes, this was my way of getting to talk to her again, but I was also genuinely curious about her thoughts on writing.)

Twenty minutes later, my phone buzzed with her reply:

Intruder! Intruder!

Then: three siren emojis.
Then:

Kidding!! YES send me the questions, I don't mind. You can use my school email :)

What followed is too wonderful for words, so I'm just going to paste the exchange below.

To: Lily.Caldwell@Edgecome.edu
Date: November 26, 9:36 PM

Dear Lily,
Thank you very much for agreeing to talk to me. Here's what I'd like to know:
Do you have tips for fiction writing? I ask because I started trying it a few days ago.
Do you have a particular writing routine you'd recommend?
Thank you for your time and I hope your break is going well.
Sincerely, Owen

To: Owen.Turner@Edgecome.edu
Date: November 26, 10:03 PM

Owen,

You don't need to thank me! I could talk about this for days, and a BUNCH of my family is over for a party, so I'm just hiding in my room. So thank YOU for the distraction :)

WHAAAT you tried writing?? Show me!! To answer your question, I think about this a lot too. My tip would be to just use your imagination—don't be afraid to get weird! You can create people and kill them (always fun!) and make them do whatever you want. Go, go, go!

I never thought about a 'routine' until you asked, but I sort of have one . . . this is weird, but it's all about coffee for me. If I get a rush of inspiration, I need to be like, "we're making lots of coffee tonight!" Haha. Here's a picture of the brands I like.

I hope these answers help? I'm sorry if they don't!

-LC

P.S. My break is going okay . . . how's yours been? :)

November 26, 10:47 PM

Dear Lily,

Thank you for your fast response. As for showing you my writing, I'll consider it sometime.

Thank you for the coffee suggestions. Your answers are very helpful!

Sincerely, Owen

P.S. I'm sorry to hear about tonight . . . that doesn't sound fun. I've spent most of break hiding from my family too. Lots of staying in my room and enjoying the ability to use my arm again ;)

November 26, 10:56 PM

Dear Lily,

I don't know if you're asleep by now, but I just re-read my last email and wanted to clarify that the last sentence was NOT meant to be a sexual innuendo. I was referring to WRITING, which I'd assumed was clear, but I now realize the winky face can sometimes be suggestive.

I'm going to keep an eye on my inbox in the next hour in case you're awake, in which case I'd REALLY appreciate a response because I'm a bit worried now. But if you're already asleep, that's fine. I feel like I made it weird and I'm sorry about that :(

Sincerely, Owen

November 26, 11:08 PM

Owen,
*" . . . I'm mostly hiding from my family and enjoying the ability
to make use of my arm again ;)"*
So in other words, what you meant to say was . . .
FURIOUSLY MASTURBATING
Oh my gosh, dude—CALM DOWN! You're fine :) I'm not
mad at all . . .
. . . under the condition that you now have to send me that
piece of writing you did. Sorry, I don't make the rules.
-LC

November 26, 11:21 PM

Dear Lily,
My laughable attempt at describing an erratic game show
host is attached.
Also, your email made me laugh so loudly that my dad
knocked on my door.
Sincerely, Owen

November 27, 12:13 AM

Owen,
This is pretty good! I added a few comments :)
Are you close to going to sleep?
-LC

November 27, 12:19 AM

Dear Lily,
Thank you so much. I prefer bluntness, so this is great. I kind of want to keep working on this.
And no. Are you?
Sincerely, Owen

November 27, 12:32 AM

Owen,
Let's do it!! Did you mean now? If so, I kind of want to make myself some coffee.
And no ;)
-LC

November 27, 12:41 AM

Owen,

It would appear that I owe you an apology. Upon re-reading my previous correspondence with you, it has come to my attention that my use of what today's youth call "winky faces" may not have been entirely appropriate for our discourse. I would like to offer my assurances that I in ABSOLUTELY NO WAY meant the use of this emoji to imply anything SEXUAL in nature.

-LC

November 27, 1:03 AM

Dear Lily,

Okay, I'll admit I fell out of my chair laughing at that one.

Well played.

I'll try to make coffee too.

Sincerely, Owen ;)

November 27, 1:42 AM

Owen,

I'm glad!! :) Here's picture proof of me drinking my coffee . . . ignore my hair, the bags under my eyes, and my dirty T-shirt. I started on the doc . . . sit tight! Don't fall asleep!

-LC

November 27, 3:02 AM

Dear Lily,
Here's my latest addition . . . our main character is Caesar, a man who hosts screwed up game shows.
Also, is my heart supposed to be beating faster? Coffee is weird.
Sincerely, Owen

November 27, 3:34 AM

Owen,
Okay so you're like REALLY good at dialogue?? You should try screenwriting.
And to answer your question: It's coffee, silly :)
-LC

November 27, 4:01 AM

Dear Lily,
I LOVE the screenplay idea. I researched the format really fast and turned this into that. See attached.
Sincerely, Oven Turner

November 27, 4:03 AM

Owen,
Not going to lie . . . I think I'm crashing, and I think you may be too. Are you still alert?
Follow-up question: Are you aware you signed your last email "Oven Turner"?
-LC

November 27, 4:06 AM

Dear Lily,
Whoops. I think I'm crashing too. We should probably go to bed, but I would love to continue this later. This is the most fun I've had probably ever, and I'll admit I've been dancing around in my room on-and-off for most of this evening.
Thank you. Seriously.
Sincerely, Owen

November 27, 4:07 AM

Owen,
Sounds like a plan. And that dancing is just the coffee at work :)

You're so welcome!!
-LC
P.S. Before you go. The "Oven" thing made me think . . . do
people call you "O" for short? Can I?

November 27, 4:07 AM

People don't, but you can.
Goodnight, Lily.
-O

November 27, 4:08 AM

Night, O :)
-LC

FIVE

DAD TAKES ME STRAIGHT HOME FROM PRINCIPAL Graham's office. The front desk administrator tells us we need to sign out in order to leave. We don't.

The minute we're inside his SUV, I squeeze my arms against my chest and keep them there.

"They can't do that," I say. "What the hell is wrong with them?"

"Just stop for a second," Dad says. "Let's put together a *preemptive plan* here."

I rub my eyes, groaning. Dad and his military precision. Steve Turner couldn't spread butter on a bagel without a Preemptive Plan to extract the knife from the goddamn drawer.

"First order of business is to get home, okay," he says. "I've already texted Mom; she's going to meet us at the house. We're going to fix this."

"How?"

"Give me a second, please! Christ."

When I was twelve, Dad and I established our secret rule: We're both allowed to curse in front of each other as long as Mom doesn't find out. This has proven to be a long and fruitful arrangement for the both of us.

Rain hammers on the windshield.

Dad looks at me, grunting in his gravelly voice, "You good?"

I nod.

"Okay. I'm sorry I yelled back there." But he says that loudly, too.

We nearly ram through the neighborhood gate on our way to the house. The minute I step into the front hall, Mom hustles toward me like the building's on fire. Normally she works as an HR rep for an engineering contractor on the other side of town, but apparently work let her take leave for the morning. A petite redhead, her two most defining traits—her perky smile and the electric glow in her eyes—are both missing for the moment.

She wraps me in her arms. I can tell it's taking all her resolve to not crush me (she knows I hate that). Dad plants himself on the couch without saying anything.

Mom steps back, keeping her hands on my shoulders. "Hey, kiddo. I hear you got to see what Principal Graham's office looks like. Is that place stuffy or what?"

Out of the thousand things I love about Mom, my favorite is her ability to seamlessly switch gears. At home she's reserved, gentle: reading by the window or teaching herself the violin. But outside these walls, her go-to spot is the front line of the nearest protest. Whether it's an annual march in D.C. for gun control or a local demonstration about funding for special ed, she shows up and makes her voice heard. Dad and I can't go because of our shared crowd aversion, so Mom is loud enough for all three of us. She's made of steel but doesn't drown out the room when she doesn't need to. And right now, she's doing the same thing she does anytime there's an issue: Instead of falling to pieces or getting emotional like Dad, she's playing it cool.

"Her desk is way too big," I say.

"Right? I thought the same thing." Mom lets go of me and beckons toward the living room. "So, how about you take off that backpack and sit down with us for a second. Want me to get you some tea?"

I slip off my bag, shaking my head. I'm supposed to be embarrassed by her coddling, but she's such a pro at sneaking it in.

She brings out two cups of coffee, handing one to Dad as she tucks herself next to him on the couch. I collapse into my armchair on the side wall. (Technically it's Dad's, but this is the place I always sit in the living room, so we call it my armchair.)

Dad shakes his head like he's already disappointed in me. "So. Is the report true?"

"Ut-dut-dut-dut," Mom shushes him, holding up a finger. "Let's back up."

"We need to know, Jen."

"But we—"

"Yes." I say it clearly and without reserve, staring at my knees as I bounce them both. "It happened. It's true."

"Okay," Mom says, measured. "Just out of curiosity, when did this happen? Ballpark."

I tell her the truth, which is that it was at the senior trip last month. Every spring break, our school takes the seniors on a trip to Lanham—the only university within a hundred miles of our tiny town—so they can get a taste of their upcoming college life.

Dad's notebook is back out. He squints at it. "You mentioned a name in there. You asked if the person who reported you was someone named Lucas, or you said maybe Luke."

I picture myself putting Luke's head through a wall.

"Is that a friend of yours from school?" Mom tries. "Have we met him before?"

"No." I bite back the first fifty answers that try to jump out. "No to both."

Dad cuts to the point. "What's his role in this?"

(Silence.)

"Owen." Dad closes his notebook. "You have two people on your side in this thing, and you're looking at them both. Your friends, or Lily . . . they're nice and all, but they can't *help* you."

"You're not helping me."

"We're trying to, bud," says Mom. I can tell she's fighting to keep her voice level. "That's all we're trying to do."

"Then let this go. Please."

"How about we take a break?" she offers.

"Okay, listen. Both of you." Dad climbs to his feet, sucking up all the light from the window. He stops, swivels, and points his line of sight at the corner directly between the two couches. "No one is taking a break until we figure out how to get the school handled. What we need to do—"

"Handled?" Mom cuts him off, shaking her head. "If we try to bully our way in there, it's just going to piss them off—"

"Let's assume I'll find a way to live with that."

"Steve—"

"*HEY!*" He shuts his eyes, and his palm snaps up in a *be quiet* gesture. Three full seconds pass—silent except for him sucking in air—and he restarts. "What we need to do—if you'll let me *talk* here—is all get on the same page about what's going to happen next. If I have to be the guy who warns you about how ugly all this is about to get, fine. I don't mind being Mister Gloom-and-Doom if I need to. Because here's what this is going to look like." Now he turns to face me directly. "First of all, since everyone and their brother is glued to their phones these days, I'd be amazed if rumors didn't start circulating among the students soon."

"The school is required to keep the report private," Mom reminds him.

"I don't care if they're required to keep the report locked in the Cheyenne Complex, okay. Come Monday morning, kids are about to start getting yanked out of class by the boatload. Each one will be marched down to the admin wing, where Officer What's-His-Nuts is going to roll up in his Columbo costume, wave his plastic badge, and ask, *Hey there, Mary Sue, do you know anything about a violent crime that happened to one of your classmates on a field trip?* If you think Mary Sue doesn't *immediately* text her fifty closest friends about that, boy do I have a wonderful bridge to sell you."

"You don't know—" Mom tries to interject, and I can tell Dad is about to shush her again when I say, "He's right."

They both turn to look at me. I hate not backing up Mom when she's looking out for me, but he's right.

She just sighs.

"It's not 'if,' it's 'when.' So that's item number one," Dad says, counting on his fingers. "Item number two is that the school's going to write its report, which will get kicked over to a gaggle of higher-ups during their weekly OFAT."

That one is a favorite of his—Obligatory Fucking Around Time.

"From there it'll get brought up at board hearings, where I guaran*tee* it'll get turned into a whole song and dance. Item number three is something we need to get squared away immediately, and by immediately, I mean in-*the*-next-hour. Before we do anything else, you need to get tested for STIs."

My mouth starts to work, but Dad's hand snaps up a second time.

"Whatever you're going to say, save it. Doesn't matter. Happened a while ago? Doesn't matter. You think the guy was clean? Don't know, don't care, don't want to hear it; doesn't matter."

"I'm not going to the hospital," I say. Sharply, this time.

"Your mother said you'd say that." He nods to Mom. She reaches for the grocery bag beside her—I hadn't even noticed it—and withdraws three different boxes. Testing kits.

"Brought the party to you," she says. Her grimace is infused with apologies.

I twist in my seat.

"Did you call the hospital like I said?" Dad asks her. "What'd they say?"

"They, uh . . ." She closes her eyes, snapping her fingers. "They said the window on DNA is around seventy-two hours, and five days for other forensic evidence. So we missed that. We can still get a kit done if we want, or they said Owen could follow up with his PCP for a general exam. Whatever he wants."

"Nothing." I say it automatically. "I'm fine. I'll do the tests tonight, but—"

"You'll do them right now," Dad says.

"I don't have to pee."

"You'll drink water. Two of them are spit swabs, anyway."

I yank the bag off the couch without looking at either of them. I go to open it when my phone starts to rattle, ringing facedown on the table.

"Can I go?" I ask, feeling my stomach flip over.

"We need to finish talking," Dad says. "Why don't you stay put."

"Steve, let him—Owen, do you want to answer that?" Mom asks.

Buzzz, my phone says a second time.

"*We're going to finish talking*," Dad says.

It's probably Lily, Mom mouths to him.

"And he can talk to her later."

Buzz!

"Can I *please* go?" I plead.

"No one is going anywhere."

Buzz!

"Give him five minutes—hon, you want five minutes to get that?" Mom says, talking over everyone.

"No, I want to *go*."

"How about you stay here but your dad and I step out for a sec; that way you can answer that and—"

"No—fuck, just *drop* it! *CHRIST, Mom!*"

I bite my tongue half a second too late, feeling like an asshole as soon as the words are in the air. I've never yelled at either of them before, and the realness of it—the stunned look on Mom's face and the wide-eyed rage in Dad's—is ugly enough to make me want to crawl into a hole. Instead I do the next-best thing and palm my phone, rubbing my eyes with shaky fists as I head for the hallway.

Once I turn the corner, I flip the phone over to look at the screen. Telemarketer.

SIX

November 28th—Freshman Year

Dear Diary,

I'm very scared!

Last night—forty-eight hours after my email all-nighter with Lily—she called me. Yeah, *called*. Who the heck does that?

"Owen, hey," Lily said, once I gritted my teeth and picked up. "What're you doing tomorrow night?"

I froze in place. It was one of those movie moments, those no-way-this-is-happening instances. Was she about to ask me out?!

"Um, are you free?" She was still waiting on an answer. "I'm doing a Friendsgiving dinner at my place with some of the other people in the neighborhood, so . . . you know. You should come."

Friendsgiving? I murmured. She couldn't hear me, so I had to say in a louder voice, "What's that?"

"You've never heard of it? Friend Thanksgiving. Except a few days late."

I scratched the side of my thumb. "I'm not sure.

I don't like strangers."

"The people are *really* nice. Beth Lieberman, Vic Parmar, Austin Lambert . . . know them? Even if not, trust me—you want to do this. Listen to Lily. LTL."

(LTL. And I thought Dad was the one with acronyms!)

"I just don't do well with new people," I told her.

"Hm." She took a long pause. "What if it's just you and me? Is that okay?"

I paced in small circles, swooping around my room. "Really?"

"Sure, it'll be fun. Is that okay?"

"I'm just surprised you want to . . . spend time with me."

"Oh my gosh, yeah, sure. What are you talking about? Silly."

I smiled to myself—I didn't say anything, but I felt invincible.

"Like, we're literally neighbors," she pointed out, yawning. "I'll text the address. See you tomorrow!"

I barely slept last night because I'm so nervous. I made myself a schedule for today, so I know when to start getting ready. I've done everything I can do to prep: I looked up the walking route to Lily's house, I picked out my clothes, I even listened to some Killers songs to distract myself. But I keep checking my watch, counting down the hours—equal parts exhilarated and terrified. It's a rush, but I'm also seeing a minefield full of problems. New setting. New situation. New rules.

This is where being on the autism spectrum gets in the way sometimes, especially with new people. Whenever I walk into a room, the first thing I'm doing is collecting information. It's like this: Imagine that you open your eyes, and you're in the middle of playing a complicated board game with a group of people you're eager to impress—classmates, coworkers, whatever. Now imagine you're the only one who wasn't given a rulebook. Panic, right? It's your turn to play. *Go on—it's your turn, dude!* So you make some excuse. "Skip over me for now." People give you weird looks, but they move on with their mysterious game. Strike one. *Okay, how does this game work? We can do this . . . let's figure it out.* It's not like you can't adapt, but it's an exercise in reverse engineering—like eating a cookie and trying to deduce the recipe. You're able to piece things together and basically participate in the game. But the thing is, it never feels like you're participating authentically. You're always on the lookout for some new twist you haven't seen before that'll require adapting.

And on the off chance all this goes perfectly, the whole exercise still saps the energy out of you. You go to bed drained, and you wake up every day to the same choice: fit in, at the price of doing this draining cycle, or stay isolated and enjoy some peace and quiet.

All this because you didn't get a rulebook. But here's the clincher: imagine, now, that everyone thinks you did.

I have to get ready now. Please, please let me have my rulebook tonight . . .

Nervously,

O

November 29th—Freshman Year

Dear Diary,

Oh my gosh!! You'll never believe how it went yesterday!

I was incredibly nervous during the walk over—it was thirty-eight degrees outside, but I was soaked in sweat. When I got to Lily's house, I heard the bustling sound of activity through the screen door—chatter, the TV going, the kitchen fan whirring and clanking of cookware.

(Don't screw this up!)

Just as I lifted a finger to ring the bell, Lily's father opened the door.

"Captain Turner on deck! How the heck are ya!" He held out a hand, which I firmly shook, as Dad taught me.

Mr. Caldwell, as I immediately learned, was the whitest dad in the history of white dads—like if a riding mower and a rotisserie grill had a human baby. Standing a head taller than me, he was wearing a cooking apron—the kind that had a spatula on it with the caption "This Guy Is Flipping Awesome"—over a pair of loose faded jeans and a Penn State sweatshirt.

As he led me into the house, I was hit with a million smells—the sweetness of yams, the yeasty scent of fresh biscuits, the warmth of gravy and lit candles. I'd never experienced the scent outside my own house before.

"Now, Owen, I've got a bone to pick with you," Mr. Caldwell said, raising his eyebrows at me.

I gave him a deer-in-the-headlights look.

"I said I've got a bone to pick with you," he repeated. "Because let me tell you something: no matter what day or time it is, that girl of mine . . . wherever she wandered off to"—he craned his neck before turning back to me—"does *not* stop running her mouth about you."

Oh, I murmured.

"Ah—I know, right! That's always what you want to hear, right, Owen!" he ribbed, clapping me on the back hard enough to nearly knock the wind out of me. "No, it's all great stuff. And don't worry about me getting in everyone's way tonight—I'm done in the kitchen, so I'll be upstairs. Out of sight, out of mind."

(Hold up—everyone?)

I entered the kitchen to find two girls—neither of them Lily—bickering. One of them was tall with pale skin, offset by shoulder-length hair that was completely turquoise. The other was Victoria Parmar—a short Indian girl with cropped hair and a nose stud—who I recognized from second period.

The one with turquoise hair was holding up a can of green beans and saying, "Vic! I told you to bring *fresh* green beans. *Fresh.*"

"These are! No, it says so right on the can, look," Vic said. She repeatedly stabbed the label with a black-painted fingernail. "*Made with farm FRESH goodness!*"

"I swear I'll kill you."

"Mommy, Daddy, please don't fight!" said Lily's voice, and she appeared on the other side of the kitchen with a can of soda in her hands. Her hair was pulled back in a French braid, and she was dressed in a dark green blouse with a red skirt. Holiday attire.

"Oh my God, hi!" she said when she spotted me. "Come here. Guys, this is Owen. He's a couple streets down."

The two girls gave me friendly greetings that I didn't respond to. Then a *third* stranger appeared—a guy our age with braces, thick-framed glasses, and messy red hair. His shirt—a long-sleeve blue one with the Super-man logo on the chest—had three labels for canned yams stuck to the back.

"Austin!" Lily called. "Say hello to Owen."

He saluted me. "Hello to Owen!"

I bolted out of the room without saying anything. My hands were moving around too much, so I folded them under my armpits.

"O? Hang on, where are you going?"

Lily caught up to me in the front hall, wide-eyed.

"Listen—okay, I'm sorry, I'm sorry," she said, step-ping close so she could lower her voice. "I felt weird telling them not to come when I already invited them, but I *really* wanted you to meet them. Come on—O! Come on." She took my hand off the doorknob and held it in hers. "Just stay for dinner. That's it. I swear."

I stared at the door. Lingered on how nice her fingers felt in mine.

Then I asked, *Why does Austin have canned food labels on his back?*

"We're seeing how many we can put on him before he notices," Lily whispered.

I cracked a smile, and she tugged my hand again. "Can you please stay? For me? We're about to eat; you can leave in twenty minutes if it's weird."

I was still shaken up by the change of plans. But she looked at me with wide eyes, and I felt doused in warmth by her concern: She did this because she *wanted* me here.

I said okay.

Cut to: back in the kitchen, a few minutes later. As I sat down next to Lily at the dinner table, she explained to me that Beth—the girl with colored hair fretting over the green beans—was an aspiring chef. For that reason, she supervised all the cooking for group events like these.

The table setup was fancy with folded cloth napkins and everything. Holiday decor had been brought out early, and the ledge decoration—a set of alphabet blocks that were supposed to spell "Merry Christmas"—had been rearranged to spell "Mrs. Creamy Shit."

Austin, Beth, and Vic sat facing Lily and I, heaps of food piled between us. Lily, at my request, gave me three small plates so I could separate my food. I expected someone to comment on this as we all served ourselves, but the rest of the group either didn't notice or didn't care enough to ask about it. Beth had included several side dishes her family normally made for Hanukkah—things like tzimmes and latke cups—and politely explained to me what each of them were.

"Hey, new guy—" Austin said to me.

"His name's Owen, dude," Lily said, giving him an *are-you-kidding* glare.

"Owen . . . my bad. I just wanted to say I hope we didn't wig you out too bad earlier. We can be a weird group."

I blinked at him, and he held up a hand to add, "I'm being serious; I'm not making fun of you or anything."

I tried to give him a polite nod. I murmured, *You can make fun of me if you want.*

Everyone swapped puzzled looks.

(Fuck I'm bad at this.)

"That's what we have him for," Beth said, taking Austin's hand and giving me a small smile. Vic reached to pat him on the back, depositing a sticker for jellied cranberry sauce.

"On that note, I'm sorry in advance if my girlfriend poisoned us," Austin said, jerking his head toward Beth.

She gave him a chef's kiss that turned into a middle finger.

"Hi, by the way!" she said, giving me a vigorous wave with her free hand. "I never said hi—so hi. I'm Beth."

"Well, now you've said it three times," Vic pointed out. Then she asked me, "Aren't you in my Geometry class?"

I nodded.

"Thought that was you." Vic shook her head at me, her face blank and voice flat. "Aren't those kids obnoxious?"

I chuckled quietly, not sure how to reply, but she gave me a wry smirk and added, "I mean, they're so obnoxious."

"You guys have Mr. Adler?" Lily jumped in.

"Yep." Vic tapped her temple as she took a sip of water. "He didn't just fall off the turnip truck, you know."

(Mr. Adler used this phrase five to eight times per week.)

"What's a turnip truck, anyway?" Austin asked.

"It's a truck," Lily explained, very slowly, "for turnips."

"Oh my God, *thanks*. I meant where does the saying come from?"

"How should I know?"

"You're the writer!"

She drained her soda, waving him off. "Hey, who's the other teacher that uses a really weird expression? Something about like . . . chicken dinner."

"Winner, winner, chicken dinner?" Vic suggested.

"Right, but like, she doesn't say that! Oh . . . this is going to bother me now."

"Ooh—no, I know who you're talking about!" Beth jumped in, almost knocking over her glass. "It's not a teacher; it's one of the librarians. Whenever she's looking for a book and she finds it, she—okay, I think she's trying to combine 'ding-ding, we have a winner' and the thing you said. So what she says is—"

Lily, suddenly remembering, finished the sentence as she pounded a triumphant fist on my thigh: "*Ding-ding, chicken dinner!*"

The whole table erupted into laughter. It felt like my face might not ever become unstuck from how hard I was smiling. I marveled at how easily these people could bounce off each other—like they already knew how the rest of the room would react to whatever they were about to say. I'd never seen anything like it.

Once we all finished eating, Vic said, "Are we ready to head down now?" Then, to me: "Are you joining for the fire?" Then, to Lily: "Did you tell him about the bonfire?"

"Hey, Owen, we're doing a bonfire down near the playground," Lily said through cupped hands. "Unless you want to go home."

I shook my head so hard it almost fell off.

"Called it."

Cut to: Lily's yard ten minutes later, where our group was marching down the driveway with armfuls of old magazines and a bottle of lighter fluid. I followed them across the street to the wooded part of the neighborhood playground, which had a fire pit I'd never noticed. Vic— honorary fire wizard of the group—got a flame going, and we all collapsed onto the stumps circled around the pit. Everyone was chatting, bantering, and I sat there soaking it all in.

I came to learn more about each of them: Austin was the comedian of the group, always smoothing moments over and rolling with anything that was thrown at him— even jabs about how obsessed he was with marching band.

Beth, his girlfriend, was pure bubbliness . . . someone who laughed way too loudly and hugged way too tightly, but would keep looking at you while you told a story to a group of people who weren't paying attention. Vic, Lily's best friend, was the polar opposite: She liked video games more than people (her words) and spent most of her evenings streaming from her gaming emulator until Lily dragged her outside. She was the coldest member of the bunch—the least talkative and often in anti-people mode—but it was obvious she and I shared an appreciation for bluntness, so I liked her the best. And at the center of it all, Lily: organizing hangouts, stirring up conversation . . . constantly conducting the orchestra.

I was already dreading the moment when I'd have to wrap this up and go home. It was an odd feeling—knowing that an hour from now, I'd be wishing I could have one more hour like this. It made me want to reach out a hand for my future self to take, to grab onto me so I could pull him back here like I knew he'd want me to later. Everything was just so *giddy*: Austin finally noticing the labels on his back, and me being able to laugh and high-five with the others because I was in on the joke. Lily repeatedly asking me how I was doing, and me telling her I was great even though my face and hands were frozen. All this electric air. The five of us chatting, bantering, swapping looks. The invisible cities that lived inside us were all lit up, shining side by side in that little patch of woods. And all the while, I just stared at the flames and thought one thing over and over: *I can't believe I'm here.*

"I meant to ask, how'd you meet Lily?" Austin said to me, when he noticed I hadn't spoken up for a while.

We're not dating, I said. Then I realized, half a second too late, that he hadn't meant the question like that. Luckily Lily came to the rescue, giving a little fake sob and saying, "It's *over?*" Which let me pass off the moment with an awkward laugh, even though I was blushing.

"No, he's my writing friend—I told you this," Lily said, grinding her shoe over a stray ember.

"Another writer," Vic said passively.

"He's *really* good at screenwriting," Lily continued, nudging me. "He's like a super genius with the stories we've worked on."

"Yeah? Like what?" Beth said with a smile.

All eyes swiveled to me, and I squirmed a little.

Then I said, *I don't really know.*

"God, Beth, get off his back," Austin said.

"You know what, make me." But she turned to me just as quickly and added, "All good."

"That's right, dude," Austin said, giving me a fist bump. He added with a knowing nod, "Owen *gets* it."

(I didn't, but I didn't correct him.)

We kept it up until the flames became embers, and Vic said she needed to head home. I tugged at Lily's sleeve. She leaned in and said, "What's up?" and I asked, *Can we get a picture?*

"You said a picture? Absolutely. Hey, guys. Picture." Lily snapped her fingers. They huddled together. As I raised my phone to take it, Lily said, "Dude! You aren't in it."

I don't need to be, I told her.

"Don't be stupid," she said, and as I turned my phone around and leaned toward them, Beth said, "Yeah, get in here." Two different arms yanked me in close, and it wasn't in the tentative, being-polite way. They pulled me right in, like I'd known them for years.

Lily added me to their group chat so I could send the picture to them. Beth waved her goodbye; Vic told me to subscribe to her gaming live streams; and Austin said, "Don't do school, eat your drugs, stay in vegetables!" Then the three of them walked back up the road to their respective houses, all calling, "Alright . . . 'night, guys!"

Lily and I watched them go, then headed back to our street.

"So . . ." she asked as we walked, her arms swinging to their own beat. "Did you have a good time?"

I worked my mouth a few times. Words came out on the third try.

You have no idea, I told her.

She laughed and said, "Welcome to the group, dude." Then pointed at me and added, "On Monday, don't be afraid to sit with us on the bus if you want."

I'd love that.

She stopped us so she could hold up her phone and take a selfie—just the two of us this time. I looked like someone who just ran ten miles. She was as pretty as always.

"Look at you," she said.

I did.

Then she propped an elbow up on my shoulder and said, "Look at *us*."

And I did that too.

I headed straight to my room when I got home. My jeans were caked with mud and dirt; my hoodie smelled like smoke, and my knees ached like I'd walked around for hours.

I collapsed onto my bed with an enormous grin on my face, and I started kicking my limbs. I know that sounds like a stereotypical ASD thing, but it wasn't even a quirk. I was just so ecstatic that I got to have *this* life.

Things finally worked out for Owen Turner.

Sincerely,

O

SEVEN

MOM AND DAD HAVE NEVER BEEN SO ECSTATIC TO SEE me pass a test before—that plastic, piss-soaked stick may as well be the goddamn Mensa exam. I can tell none of us want to address the outburst from earlier, so we don't. They just tell me we're done here, and I go to hide out in the Studio for the rest of the afternoon.

The Studio is the name for what used to be our standalone garage in the backyard. Up until I was twelve, Dad kept all his tools and construction projects in there. Then I was diagnosed with ASD—aka Autism Spectrum Disorder—and the counselor recommended I have my own space to work without stimuli. Dad pushed back on the idea—("He'll learn to deal with it")—but Mom held her ground.

The next afternoon, he sent a text to our family group chat:

No one is to come to the backyard under ANY circumstances.

For the next ten days, my father was a ghost that lived in the walls of our home. I heard traces of him traveling throughout the house, but I barely saw him in the flesh—every day, he was working in the backyard until my bedtime. Then one night after dinner, he brought me outside to show me that our standalone garage had been converted into a standalone study. He went all out, too: laminate floor tiles, drywall painted my favorite shade of blue, a dimmer switch to accommodate my sensitivity to light, and hand-restored furniture. A work desk. A bookcase in the corner. A couch next to the desk facing a flatscreen on the opposite wall. And a big wooden sign hanging up top, carved in Dad's own handwriting:

Owen's Studio

That was the first day I saw him for who he was: Steve Turner, the Builder. But the truth is that my father has been obsessed with building things ever since his medical discharge from the Marines. These days, he spends most of his mornings at junkyards and thrift shops in search of old furniture to restore. His goal is to take old, beat-up junk and make it pristine. "Not a millimeter off," he always says. If he's unhappy with something, he keeps working on it. Almost every piece of furniture in our house, and in the Studio, came out of his shop.

Soon that wasn't enough, so he bought a patch of land up in the Pennsylvania mountains and built an entire cabin on it. Soon that wasn't enough, so he goes up there a few times every month, disappearing for days. I've only ever seen pictures of it—Dad says he goes to his cabin specifically for the solitude. And I go into the Studio for the same reason: to get a breather any time I feel fed up with other people.

Now, for instance.

I have the urge to smoke the last of the weed Austin sold me—something I've been using to stay mellow since the Lanham Trip—but I already took my Adderall for the day. So instead I plant myself at my desk and start to zone.

Zoning (that's what I call it) is what I do when my meds turn my brain into a machine. Once I get absorbed in a task, it's like I can feel physical gears turning. I have three monitors at my desk—each for a different purpose—and I click between them at the speed of light, dozens of tabs open as I tackle the next five steps of my task at once.

Today, I sit for hours and download all the documentation I can find about school sexual assault investigations. I read old incident reports from the Pennsylvania General Assembly; I dig up summaries of old cases in the state; I even comb through federal memos from the OCR outlining Title IX guidance.

None of it makes me feel better, and all of it makes me feel sick.

I'm in the middle of reading through our school handbook when my phone lights up with a text from an unknown number.

> Hi Owen, this is Luke. I'm assuming you know about the report by now . . . can I come by? I swear I can explain, and I don't want to do it over text. Please just give me a chance.

I reread it twice, then start mashing out a reply. A two-paragraph essay packed with the most awful shit I can think of; every all-caps insult in the book, profanity that would make Steve Turner cringe; and then, then . . .

When I'm done, I backspace it all, curse under my breath, and start again:

> There's nothing you can say to make this okay. Don't explain it, don't come to my house, and don't text me again.

I get a reply in less than a minute.

Okay. I'm sorry.

I smack the phone against my palm.

The problem is, I really am itching for answers. None of Luke's actions make sense, and I'm fixated on finding a way to make them fit together. But I'm so livid over what he did, I can't stand to hear his bullshit justification about how he's actually the good guy here.

I'm still staring at his response when the Studio's garage door springs to life, making me jump. I rush to pocket my phone. All the light from outside spills onto the ground, gradually tracing over the silhouette on the other side of the door. At first I think it's Dad or Mom, but then I realize the shadow is too short.

It's her—shit.

Lily ducks her head under the door to let herself in, her bright eyes sweeping the room like a spotlight. When her gaze finds me, it unlocks a grin.

"He lives," she says, waving her phone at me with a smirk. "Man, you don't call; you don't write . . ."

I check my watch and see that it's almost 5:00 p.m. My butt hasn't left the chair for six hours.

"Sorry," I say. "Not feeling great."

"I figured when you weren't at lunch." She holds up a bag that I see is full of cough drops, antacids, pain relievers, and a box of my favorite coffee. "I have gifts. I wasn't quite sure what your symptoms were, so."

Lily always, always, gives me stuff—well, she gives everyone stuff, but I get the brunt of it since I'm her boyfriend. She's the girl who makes little bags of treats during the holidays and passes them out to all her classmates in the halls. Or I'll mention over text that I've been wanting to see some new movie, so she'll come over with the movie downloaded and a pack of popcorn.

"Aw, what happened here?" she asks. My blood chills until I realize she's pointing to my bracelet, still snapped apart and sitting on my desk corner.

"That was my fault. Pulled on it too hard," I say.

"Aw," she repeats. "I can fix it if you have a glue gun."

I can tell she won't leave until she does, despite the fact that she looks exhausted from the day. So I tell her sure.

Lily is the busiest person I've ever met. She takes the job of being class president with extreme seriousness, which means she's constantly organizing fundraising events or special projects. Her social media pages are packed with pictures of her at charity events. Like the Saturdays she spends volunteering at the local animal shelter, or the time she staged a class-wide walkout after the school refused to hold an LGBT Pride event. And don't get me wrong, it's sweet how much of a do-gooder she is. But the job also turned her into a grade-A perfectionist.

"There," Lily says ten minutes later, sliding my bracelet back onto my wrist. "Good as new."

She puts her hand over mine, and my skin crawls with the conversations from this morning—everything I'm keeping from her. Everything with Luke. I pull away a little, and she tilts her head.

"You okay?" she asks. She has a blinding smile that could win anyone over, but I've had trouble making eye contact with her since the Lanham Trip.

What's funny is that I actually did try to talk to her about the assault the morning after it happened. Part of the problem is we were on the bus ride back to the school, so I had to be careful how I phrased everything. But I beat around the bush way too much, because she didn't even understand what I was telling her. From there it snowballed to the point where I couldn't bring it up organically, so I made myself okay with just dealing with it on my own. Part of that has meant putting on an act around her for the past few weeks . . . dodging her invites to go on dates and making excuses for why I wasn't getting hard around her. It was ugly—Lily can't *stand* dishonesty—but I was able to keep it confined to my own head.

Now? All bets are off. The school is escalating this into something real, something I'm keeping from Lily. If she finds out I'm involved, there's no coming back from that curveball. We'd be over—that's a given. But even scarier is the hand grenade that that would toss on the friend group during our final months together.

Our days as a friend group are already numbered, and a fallout with her would toss a hand grenade on everything. Everyone would have to pick sides, and I'm not confident that anyone would be on mine.

This needs to stay contained, plain and simple. Even if it means I start telling lies here and there.

"Hey, you're in your planning hoodie," Lily says, pointing to my jacket—the one I only wear when I'm trying to zone. "What's up with that?"

"Oh," I say. "Only thing that was clean."

"Ah."

There's one.

EIGHT

MRS. SONDERGOTH—A SHORT BLACK WOMAN WHO looks no older than thirty—calls me down to the guidance office next Monday morning and introduces herself as our Title IX coordinator. She's warmer than Principal Graham, but all her talking points are the same.

She tells me that the school is required to question students and chaperones from the trip immediately.

She tells me a report of any findings will be put together in the next month.

She tells me I can give the school permission to forward its info to the police, so I only have to give one statement instead of two.

She tells me I can refuse to give the police anything, but this will tie their hands to take action.

She tells me no one can force me to say anything—the only exception being if the police decided to take things to trial on their own, at which point the state could theoretically subpoena me.

She tells me if I were to name an attacker and they were a minor, they would need to inform that person's parents, but I would be kept anonymous.

She tells me if I want my schedule changed in order to feel safer at school, they can make that happen.

She tells me the school's job, and hers, is to eliminate the hostile environment created by this incident.

She tells me that their goal, same as hers, is to help me.

She asks me, several times in several different ways, if I'm willing to tell them who did it.

I say no until she stops asking.

NINE

"YOU SHOULD REALLY SPOT YOURSELF IN THE MIRROR," Austin advises. He watches me curl with the free weights on my usual bench. "If it's crooked, you can screw up your wrist."

"I'm fine," I mutter between sharp breaths, my arms quaking. I squeeze my eyes shut and focus on the fire running up my biceps. I'm not exactly fun to look at in the mirror, especially while I do this.

It was Beth's idea for our group to start hitting the neighborhood gym last summer, back when she decided to do track and wanted to get in shape. The "gym" is really just a single room with a few treadmills and free-weights, but it's right in the neighborhood and always empty. So we don't complain.

"Did either of you pick up your graduation stuff yet?" Vic calls from her treadmill, pulling out an earbud.

"The gown?" Austin says. "Yeah."

"What's it look like?"

"A gown. Want to know what the cap looks like?"

She flips him off. She and Austin have a brother-sister thing going . . . they like to rib each other, but Vic is a total gamer nerd and Austin loves Pokémon, so they practically live at each other's houses.

"Hi hi," comes Beth's voice as she buzzes herself through the door. "Sorry . . . forgot my wallet. Owen, you should use a mirror for those."

Beth's double-hi greeting has been an inside joke ever since she did it by accident when we met. Her hair is different today—she doesn't completely dye it anymore, but she still sports a colored streak on the left side. She just got it changed to royal blue, our school color.

"I'm done with these anyway," I tell her, re-racking the weights. I shake out my hands.

"Just saying." She climbs onto the treadmill next to Vic's. "Where's Lily?"

"She's got the thing," Austin says. When Beth raises an eyebrow, I clarify, "Fundraiser."

"Oh. Has she heard from Lanham . . . should I ask . . . ?"

I make an ugly noise with a thumbs down. Lanham University released its early decision verdicts back in December—I got in; Lily wound up on the waitlist. It's a sore subject with her.

"When are they going to let her *know*?" says Beth.

"Waitlist is usually in May," Austin points out. "Didn't she get into another one, though?"

"Hillview. All the students hate it there, though," Vic says.

"Says who?"

She blinks at him. "The students."

Even their small exchange tugs a smile out of me. This group, I swear . . . spending time with these people is like cranking up your favorite song with your windows open. It doesn't matter what kind of day it's been, or how little I'm in the mood to do anything with anyone. Breathing the same air as them makes me come alive.

And don't get me wrong; my dependence on them scares the shit out of me sometimes. It's like having explosives strapped to your neck and trusting other people to reset the timer every morning. You're always checking your watch, waiting for when this perfect little miracle runs out of days. In our case, we have three months until everyone disbands. None of us will be on the other side of the country, but we'll all be hours apart: Vic will be down at Johns Hopkins for systems engineering, Beth will be starting the culinary program at Johnson & Wales in Rhode Island, and Austin—following in the footsteps of both his parents and older brother—is set to attend UVA with an undeclared major. I'll be at Lanham, and Lily will either join me there or stay down here.

"Tell us what's new with you, O," Beth calls to me from the treadmill. "You seem quiet. How's your week been?"

I shut my eyes and pick up the weight to curl it again. "Boring."

TEN

March 23rd—Freshman Year

Dear Journal,

I'm sorry it's been a while since I've written—I've been busy with my new FRIENDS!

The next time I hung out with them after the Friends-giving event was a few weeks later, when we got back together for a holiday celebration (Pancha Ganapati for Vic, Hanukkah for Beth, and Christmas for the others). The hangouts became weekly after that.

For the first time in my life, I felt things. I looked forward to waking up so I could see what morning meme Vic had put in our group chat. I was excited to get my homework done on a Saturday so I could walk over to Lily's house, where she was always organizing some activity for the group. School was *fun* now. Because even if it was an awful day—the kind where you miss your bus or get slapped with a reading assignment—I had people to roll my eyes with, to complain to, to bond in solidarity with. I had *friends*.

That's them calling me now . . . got to go!
Sincerely,
O

April 9th — Freshman Year

Dear Journal,

Lily and I just had our first date, and I can't sleep because I'm still thinking about it.

I asked her out via text, so I could lay out my thoughts. I spent about an hour on online forums, getting a general sense of what a good text would look like before I stitched one together:

Hey sorry if this is a little awkward but do you want to go out sometime?

And she said yes!!!

It was a very typical first date activity—dinner at one of the local sit-down restaurants—but I was a nervous wreck the entire afternoon leading up to it. I sat in the Studio all day counting down hours, just like before Friendsgiving back in November.

Then I got a message from her two hours beforehand, and my heart plummeted. *She's backing out*, I thought. The only question was whether this was a rescheduling or a cancellation. Then I read the message.

SO. FRICKIN. NERVOUS!!

I remember still smiling at it when she sent a follow-up.

AHHHHHH!!!

(Me, making Lily Caldwell nervous . . . unbelievable. Last year's version of me would be on the floor laughing at the thought.)

But the date went exactly as expected—neither a fairy tale nor a disaster. At the end of the night I stuttered out asking if she wanted me to be her boyfriend—me!—and she said YES. And five minutes ago, she re-posted a quote on her blog: "You have me. Until every last star and the sun all die. You have me."

I'm somebody's boyfriend now!

AHHHHHH!!!

Sincerely,

O

October 2nd—Sophomore Year

Dear Journal,

I'm looking back on my entries from ninth grade, and it's kind of astonishing how much I sounded like a little kid. Then again, I'll probably think the same thing next year when I look back at this . . . so beat that with a stick.

How to describe the past six months? It's like I've discovered fire. A year ago, a Friday night would involve me playing board games with my parents and passing out by nine o'clock. Now, it's all Lily. Weekdays are for hanging out with the group; Fridays are for her and I. Those are the ones I look forward to the most. Unsurprisingly, Lily—already kicking ass at her new job of class president—is constantly suggesting new activities for us to try. Always planning, organizing, setting things up. We've walked around parks I've never heard of. We've tried new coffee shops and attended a river concert and gone to a corn maze to pick out pumpkins. And when we're apart during the week, we're texting. At first I kept waiting for her to get bored with messaging me, but she hasn't yet. (Knock on wood.)

That's the part I love most about our relationship: how invested we both are. She's not just the popular girl going on a few pity dates with the quiet loser. She's *active*—she messages me good morning with cute animal emojis, and tells me how much she misses me, and continues co-writing dark comedy sketches with me because she knows we both love it. It's such a high to live out what I dreamed about for so many years . . . being in a real relationship. Knowing you're growing up and stepping into all those milestones you see on sitcoms and read about in books. The certainty that what's supposed to happen is happening. *This is happening!*

For the first time, I had some serious self-confidence. I talked more. I worried less.

Even two days ago, when my mom borrowed my computer and saw the extremely R-rated messages Lily and I had swapped the previous night. Obviously, this was mortifying. To say nothing of the stone-faced *be-smart-about-sex* speech I got from Dad, during which he grilled me with the basic questions: "Is this the first time you two sexted?" (no); "Have you done anything in person?" (not really); "Do you promise to be safe when you do?" (obviously).

But as embarrassing as it was, I was also a little proud, you know? It was invigorating to have a *guess-what-happened* story to share with the group, especially when it involved me getting (virtually) laid.

"How bad were the messages?" Austin asked, when Lily and I shared the story with everyone. We were walking around the mall, so I was a little on edge from all the crowds, but Lily's hand on my arm helped.

"Wait—oh my God, were there *pictures?*" Beth asked, covering a horrified grin with both hands. "That's illegal."

"No, no," said Lily, sounding none too remorseful. "No pictures, no videos."

"Thank God. Holy shit, I'd leave the country if my parents saw my dick," Austin said.

"*This* is why we save ourselves for marriage," deadpanned Vic. She held her fingers up in an X. "Harlots."

"So wait, was it just *words?*" Beth asked. "That's it?"

Lily and I shared a smug look, and she said, "These were really, really bad words."

"Like 'poop,'" Austin suggested.

"No! Ew, what is wrong with you?"

"That's such a writer thing to do," Vic muttered, then mimed typing a message. "*I loved exploring your ample bosom, as it . . . protruded in the moonlight.*"

"That's *not* what they said!" Lily insisted, as everyone else cackled. But she gave my arm a squeeze, and I grinned even wider.

Sincerely,

O

October 16th—Sophomore Year

Dear Journal,

It's 2:00 a.m., and I just got back from my first Home-coming dance. My heart feels like it's pounding its way out of my chest!

It's kind of funny to think about, because originally I wasn't going to go at all. Of course I wanted to spend an evening with Lily; but with my ASD, she might as well have been sticking me in a war zone. The crowds, I could deal with . . . it was a big gym. But bright lights and loud music are murder on my sensory overload.

I guess you could say we'd had our first fight about it—she explained to me why it was rude to suggest that she go alone, and my defense was basically, "Yeah, but I don't want to go." She came up with a compromise where she bought me a set of earplugs and sunglasses I could wear and promised we could leave if it got to be too much. I told her, but no way was I wearing that shit for the night—it'd feel like everyone was staring at me no matter where I went.

That pissed her off even more—because she was "trying to work with me!"—so finally I gave in and agreed. Earlier this morning, she dragged me to the mall to get dress clothes and a haircut. I tried to fight her on it, but she pulled the "Trust me—LTL" card again.

And the thing is, it became impossible to fault her wardrobe decisions once I'd gotten dressed for the dance.

There's no other way to say it: I looked *good*. My new short hair worked with my glasses to frame my face perfectly. My shirt was the proper size—hugging my body in the right places, the sleeves neatly rolled up. I wasn't jock-cool, but I was nerdy-cool—a guy who walked with a clean edge; someone who smelled good and wore a leather watch instead of a Velcro one.

Our group met up at Lily's house before the dance to get pictures. Her yard was all decked out in Halloween decor—remnants of the yard-decorating contest the five of us had held earlier in the month. I stepped around the light-up pumpkins onto the stoop and saw Mr. Caldwell, who gave me the usual as soon as I got inside.

"Captain Turner on deck! And whoa—look at that head of hair! Barely recognized you there, dude."

I was in the middle of saying hi back when Beth and Vic, both sparkling in their silver dresses, poked their heads in the hall.

"Hi hi—dude, your hair!" Beth squealed at me.

"Damn," Vic added. "Looks legit."

Lily had a similar reaction when I found her in the living room.

"Whoa! Oh my God—whoa!" she said. I took a second to marvel at how beautiful she looked—her eyelids glowing with glittery eyeshadow; her dress the same dark green as the tie we'd picked out earlier.

"You look nice," I told her.

"*Me?* How about you!" She stood on her tiptoes to prop an elbow on my shoulder. "Whoever picked out your clothes really knows what they're doing."

"This is true," I murmured. But as we all took pictures in her living room and piled into Mr. Caldwell's SUV,

I felt myself starting to sweat. I could either spend three hours getting my eyes and ears brutalized, or be the guy answering "why are you wearing sunglasses?" all night. Maybe I'd flip a coin.

Lily noticed how zoned out I was during the drive and put her hand on my leg. I put mine on hers, which helped distract me a bit . . . especially when she slipped her hand into my pocket. I made a little squeak, and we swapped surreptitious looks. It was dark enough for me to hide my boner, but Austin noticed Lily's hand and shook his head.

"Hey, Mr. Caldwell!" he called through cupped hands, and our fingers jumped off each other as he said, "Can you turn down the AC?"

Lily flipped him off as Beth and Vic snickered.

I tried to laugh with them, but I felt my anxiousness climbing. By the time we all piled out of the car in front of the school, I was squeezing my shoulders and covered in sweat.

"You have the stuff?" Lily asked, tilting her head.

I really started to get worked up—pacing, muttering incoherently, snapping the stim bracelet Lily had given me for my birthday. The bass from the music was pounding through the walls, people were pouring into the school, and everyone in the group was looking at me. I dug the sunglasses and earplugs from my pocket but didn't put them on.

"Hey," Lily said, watching me pace and trying to meet my eyes. "Let's get some more pictures."

I shook my head, muttering some half-assed version of "don't want to." God damn it, this was a mistake.

"Just one," Lily insisted.

"Stop—" I turned to her and was about to tell her

off when I saw her eyes. Or rather, I didn't. Because she was wearing a huge pair of pink sunglasses, and a pair of earplugs to match.

I started to say, "Wh—" when I looked over to Austin, Vic, and Beth. Each of them had put on a huge pair of shades and were in the middle of sticking in earplugs like Lily's.

"Wh—" I started to say again.

"Come on, dude, get your stuff on," Lily said impassively. When I didn't move, she laughed at the expression on my face.

Meanwhile, Austin turned to the others and yelled in an exaggerated voice, "AM I TALKING LOUDER THAN NORMAL?"

"NO YOU SOUND GREAT!" Beth shouted back through cupped hands.

"WHAT?" screamed Vic.

I wanted to say something, but my eyes welled up and my words got lost. Lily just pulled me in for a hug and whispered, "So, is this a little better?" and I nodded against her and said how much I loved her, and she said the same back.

It wasn't the first time I'd said it to her. But God damn, I'd never meant it more.

Sincerely,

O

ELEVEN

STUDENTS START GETTING PULLED OUT OF CLASS BY the end of the week. At first it's inconspicuous—a teacher getting a phone call here and there to send a kid to the front office. They're clearly trying not to make a big deal of it. But by the time it's happened four times in one morning, word gets around: The senior class is being interrogated.

They say there's a drug search coming.

They say a cheating ring was busted for the AP exams.

They say people were zip tied and hauled to jail in a paddy wagon.

No one in the group brings it up directly, but I still skip out on the gym with them for the next week.

My father, meanwhile, has started roaming the house at night. I hear him pacing around our main level for hours on end—lumbering from one room to the next with his distinctive, thunderous limp. The thing about Dad is that he's an attack dog. Everything is pure mission with him—he throws himself into every task he locks onto. Right now, it's this. Every day when I get home, the first thing he asks is if the school found anything yet.

One Sunday, I'm locked in my room when I hear his huge footsteps approach.

"Owen?" Dad barks from the other side, followed by two acute raps of iron knuckles against my door. *THUDTHUD.* "Car repair in ten minutes, remember. We have a lot of work to do."

I hear my mom shout from upstairs that he should give me a break and let me skip out.

"This was our plan, and we're sticking to it," Dad shouts so we both can hear him. "We agreed on this."

Saying that I agreed to help Dad replace his car's AC system is a bit of a stretch. It's more along the lines of, "Dad makes me work on projects with him to hone my life skills." As he likes to say, "You're not going to be one of those entitled college pricks who barely knows how to turn a wrench." So I don an old set of work clothes, he does the same, and we meet up at the hood of his ten-year-old RAV4.

"Before we do anything else, let's go over our *preemptive plan* here," Dad says. He leans into the hood and hooks his wrench on the axle of a small black disk. "Try and turn that for me."

I do.

"Go ahead, give it all you got."

It doesn't budge.

"Stuck, right? Therein lies our problem. That black cylinder —pay attention now—that's the compressor to the air condition-ing, okay. It's supposed to turn freely. It gets jammed, and the whole thing goes TU."

(Tits up.)

"Our task today is to replace this sucker. Now, this can either be work, or it can be a *lot* of work. It all depends on you, and how solid your strategy is." He frames his hands above the compressor like he's about to throttle it. "The trick is to be smarter than the item you're messing with."

After a few more lines like that, we roll up our sleeves and get to work. Dad puts on the usual classical music—you'd think a guy like him would put on hard rock or something, but he hates loud noises even more than I do. He almost never uses power tools—he even gets his wood pre-cut—and he only does his shop work to classical. So we're serenaded by an upbeat Tchaikovsky ballad as we disconnect electrical wires, pry off the fan belt, and drain fluid using Dad's homemade refrigerant recovery machine. ("Retail pricks'll charge you an arm and a leg to buy one. That's how they get you.")

I can't lie, there's something soothing about working on Dad's projects . . . at least at first. In the beginning part, when I'm only sweating a little, and the symphony is in full swing, and we're just going through the motions. All kinetic; all tactile, no thought. Dad's version of zoning.

"Don't forget, you start your driving practice in this thing next month," Dad reminds me. "I just need to replace the tires first—no one but me drives it until then. These ones are so bald you can see the air in them."

"Do I have to?"

"Yes, you have to. Don't forget, you're required by law to pass your driver's test before college."

"Wait, what law?"

"That'd be the 'You Live Under Our Roof' clause," he says, fiddling with the hose with a joyless smirk. "Under subsection, 'You Do as We Say Until You Pay Your Own Bills,' of the Turner Family Constitution. When you get behind the wheel, you're taking a two-ton hunk of metal and moving it at deadly force. That's a *weapon* you're driving, and you're going to learn how to do so safely. This isn't optional."

I've wanted to put off driving for as long as possible. For me, it's sensory overload. I'm constantly checking and re-checking everything that's going on. *When is your turn? Okay, one mile. What happens after that? Which lane do I need to be in? Stop grabbing the wheel so tight. Check your mirrors. Breathe.*

It's a lot.

"Damn it. This little shit." I think Dad's talking to the compressor. No—something next to it. "The power steering pump is in the way."

"Do you want a wrench?"

"What I *want* is to meet the brain-dead asswipe that engineered this."

It's important to understand that Dad wasn't always this perpetually pissed off. I have memories of moments from when I was little . . . like the time he brought a hand-decorated sign to my first-grade talent show, or when he pranked my mom on Thanksgiving by hiding the fancy plates. Somewhere under all that skin is a real human—or there used to be, at least.

I don't remember a lot else about back when he was in the Marines, but it feels like a whole different life. Groceries came from the commissary, not the store. An American flag flew proudly on our front porch. We sported all the military brat gear, and every birthday party of mine was at a bowling alley since that was the one thing every military base seemed to have. We moved around every couple years, and I'd have a meltdown each time. Around the house, everything was *yes, sir; no, sir; yes, ma'am; no, ma'am.* Each evening meal was preceded by an inspection to ensure I'd cleaned my room and made my bed.

It all changed one night when I, at age seven, did something I was told never to do: I came into their bedroom at night without knocking. I'd had a nightmare that made me wet the bed, and I couldn't stand sleeping in it, and I forgot to knock. I just walked in—the lights were off, and the TV was playing infomercials. Dad was closest, so I started shaking him. When it didn't work, I shook harder.

It happened all at once. It was like the last shake I gave his shoulders ended up being one too many, and as his feet hit the floor, my father transformed into a monster—a beast of a man that erupted into a killing machine, swinging his tree trunk arms at lightning speed: a hurricane of human force. The first punch landed squarely on the side of my head. That's all it took. My body flew backward like it had been nailed by a Brink's truck, and I *SLAMMED* into the wall; crumpling, seeing stars, stunned.

The noise woke up Mom, who woke up Dad, who saw what he did; and as soon as he saw he started screaming, "Holy fuck! *Holy fuck!*"

He kept yelling it as he wheeled around and started punching again, this time with full purpose and directly into the wall. Drywall dust kicked up in all directions; Mom yelled at me to run, and all the noise hurt my ears even more than the punch had, and my father screamed and screamed and I sobbed and sobbed.

The next morning, Dad went out and didn't come back for days. I don't know where he went, but when he finally returned, he had a box of my favorite donuts. He didn't apologize for what he'd done. None of us said a word about it. But he finally reported his PTSD, got a disability rating of thirty from the VA—later bumped up to fifty for his knees—and was medically discharged from the Corps.

All of the old Dad—the pride, the patriotism, his spotlessness—started to slip away until it was a hollow shell. He walked around angrier. The flag came down. He yelled at people more—never without reason, but always with unwarranted intensity. He became a man who assumed the worst in everyone he met . . . walls built overtop torn-down trust.

And all the while, he's been trying to sink into this new life: We moved into Old Friendship Landing, rated the safest community in the state. We would die in this house before he ever made us move again, he said. He turned to classical music and furniture building at his cabin up in the mountains. He always needed to be *doing* something, because he'd never known anything else. He became Steve Turner, the Builder.

I asked him what war was like, once. He told me: "It's boring."

"Hold this," he says, handing me a flashlight. I lean in with it while he wrestles with the bolts on the steering pump, veins bulging on his sweat-soaked forehead. My whole body is aching at this point, and I'm covered in sweat too, but I know better than to ask for a break.

We get the compressor out just as the sun goes down, and Mom pokes her head out to let us know that dinner's ready. Dad snaps at her that we'll reheat it once we're done. Steve Turner has never once, not ever, taken a break from getting his ass kicked by a project.

"Hold the light steady, Owen. Steady . . . never mind; God damn it." He wrenches the flashlight from my hand as more classical music floods the garage. "Take this hose—that's the refrigerant line. Stick a paper towel on the end so no gunk gets in."

"Can I use the bathroom?" Anything to get out of the humidity for thirty seconds.

He sighs hard. "Can you *hold* it? Fine, go. *Quickly*. Get bug spray while you're in there . . . getting eaten alive out here."

As I walk through the house, Mom says brightly, "All done?" I don't answer.

Half an hour later, Dad and I are leaned back against the car, watching the vacuum pump suck out residual moisture. We catch our breaths, eyes shut.

Then he says, "I want to start doing weekly email check-ins with you."

"Huh?"

"I'm reading this book."

"Okay?"

"It says you're supposed to check in periodically with the survivors of sexual assault, to see how they're doing. So that's what we're going to do. Doesn't need to be weird, doesn't need to be too personal. Just every Saturday, send me an email to let me know how you're doing. If it's the word 'good' with your signature at the bottom, fine with me. But we're going to do it."

"I don't—"

"You don't get a vote," Dad says, when I open my mouth to object. "One email a week won't kill you."

"The school said they can manage whatever counseling I need."

"The *school*." He says it like it's the name of a universally hated baseball team. "Yeah, that's funny. I got news for you, bud. Those jokers couldn't manage their way out of a cardboard box if it had an exit sign taped over the goddamn flap."

"They said there are rules for how they handle it."

"All beside the point. Do you have any idea how many times someone's made me a promise to take care of something only to turn around and fuck it up?"

"No."

"Yeah, me neither; I lost count a couple decades ago."

"Mom keeps saying things will work out."

"Your mother is what we call *overly optimistic*, okay. Wonderful woman, but she could walk into a room of shit and she'd start looking for the pony." He wipes the sweat off his brow. "The pump is done. Help me transfer the faceplate."

The two of us spend another hour kneeling in the driveway, working via flashlight. Mom sticks her head out the door to let us know our dinner is in the fridge, then goes off to bed. Dad doesn't say a word, but I can tell he's in pain—his knees shouldn't be tak-ing this kind of punishment for five minutes, let alone an hour on the hard ground. But he sits there and shakes and keeps doing what he's doing, all the way until the new compressor is primed with oil and its faceplate is secure.

"There," Dad says, giving it a test wiggle. "See? That's not going anywhere."

He tries to get up, but grunts and keels to the side. His hand smacks against the side of the car to steady himself—with his size, it rocks the whole vehicle. He belts out one crisp, "*Ouch*," through gritted teeth.

"I can help, hold on," I say, rushing over behind him. "Lean back."

"I'm fine; just protect the compressor, will you."

I watch him as he holds onto the car, pulling himself up as he blows out air slowly. His face is twisted up, but he's not going to stay down. Not him; never him, no sir.

The day I broke my arm back in ninth grade, Dad gave me a talking to in the hospital room about pain.

"I broke a few bones in my day," he said. "Most of 'em when I was younger and being an idiot. Your grandpa Bill would always tell me, 'Tough guys don't feel pain.'" He did the imitation in a mock-deep voice, then mimed chucking something over his shoulder. "Buncha BS, man. Of course tough guys feel pain. Everyone feels pain. I've had any number of things that hurt like hell; I bet that arm hurts like hell too. But what really makes the difference, I've found, is that tough guys don't show it, okay. They take all that pain and crush it. In the Marines, we had this thing we'd yell anytime something hurt . . . SITFU. Know what that stands for?" Then he said with a wry smile, "*Suck it the fuck up*. You try."

"SITFU."

"Anytime it hurts, just say that: SITFU!"

I know he was trying to help, and I get what he meant. But all I know is that none of his advice made my arm hurt any less. It just made it feel like my fault that it hurt so much in the first place.

TWELVE

August 31st—Junior Year

Journal,

Guess who lost his virginity today? (Hint . . . this guy!)

Yeah, I can't believe it either. Someone check if hell's frozen over yet.

It happened after the end-of-summer pool party hosted by the neighborhood. Lily and I were supposed to walk there together, but she texted saying she'd meet me there.

I tried not to be pissed during the walk over. Honestly, she and I had been in a rough patch for a bit now. It started toward the end of last year, when the pressure of finals had our stress levels going overboard. I thought things would get better over the summer, but she got a job at the local coffeehouse that sucked up the last of her free time. And the past few weeks of gearing up for junior year—"the most important one for college!"—started bringing all of the school bullshit back. Gone are the days of us going to the playground every day when we get off the bus. Now it's us looking at universities we want to apply to, and me fending off my Dad's nagging to pick a career other than screenwriting.

But out of all of it, the thing that's caused the most friction is how absorbed Lily has gotten in student government. Back when we were underclassmen, all her focus was on her writing. She harped on her whole thing about wanting to matter, and she poured all that into her poems—not to mention our joint projects. But then she redirected all that energy into SGA. Now, it's like she's out to win a service award. She started all these new initiatives—charity events and even town halls—so the class can give her feedback. People love her for the job she's doing, and she eats it all up.

Don't get me wrong, I'm happy for her. But I can't stand the moods it puts her in. It's given her a real edge—one that wasn't there when we were younger. Her perfectionist brain is in constant overdrive, and she expects the most from everyone. And the more stressed she is, the more we're at each other's throats.

When I met Lily, I thought she was damn-near perfect. Then we had our first rough patch, and I thought things were ruined. And soon we grew a long enough history where there was no absolute good or bad anymore; it was just her and me, with our own weird little collection of moments and makeups and memories of every kind. We learned to both take a step back and remember that we're on the same team. Our magic phrase is the one Lily likes to use: "Look at us." Remember why we're here—remember that we love each other, and we can get through this because it's *us*. We say that, then we resolve things, then we kiss and apologize and say "I love you" before we leave.

Anyway. I walked to the pool alone.

Austin was already in the locker room along with two other guys: David—our neighbor, who was home from college—and a boy whose name I didn't know, but I recognized him as the odd guy who refused to wave to Lily and I on the day I met her.

"There he is," Austin said when he saw me. He and the others were showering in their suits. The air smelled like chlorine.

"My fault. Left the house late." I set my backpack on one of the benches. "Lily had to do some posters. I was finishing them for her."

"Does she at least let you pick out your own collar?" David asked as Austin gave a mock sob. The boy in the corner smirked but didn't say anything.

I flipped them off. The "Owen is wrapped around Lily's finger" jokes have been in full run since the start of our relationship.

I stripped off my shirt and took a second to study myself in the mirror, flexing a little. I started going to the neighborhood gym this past summer with Austin and Beth, and it showed. My arms had some actual shape to them, and my shoulders were more filled out. Lily had also talked me into getting contacts—no more '90s Dad glasses.

"Hey," called David from the other side of the locker room. "Are you about to jerk off to yourself or something?"

I realized I was still posing for the mirror. I dropped my arms and dug my board shorts out of my bag.

"Is that a thing?" he continued, frowning. "Jerking off to yourself?"

I squinted. "Well . . . hold on. Do you mean picturing

yourself doing stuff with other people? Or do you mean like, having sex with a clone of yourself?"

"I'd fuck myself," Austin said.

"Amazing, I've been telling you to do that for years."

"*Whoa*—good one. Fucking incredible joke, dude."

I pretended to throw my flip-flop at him. He flicked water in my direction.

"I'm talking about like, where you look in the mirror while you do it," David said, shutting off the shower and drying himself off. "I feel like that's not weird. I've definitely done that before."

"Jerk off to yourself?" I said. "That would make you autosexual."

"What's that?"

"It's where you jerk off to yourself."

"Yeah, dumbass, weren't you listening?" Austin said.

The two of them headed to the pool, clapping me on the back as they walked by. I realized I was alone with the nameless stranger, who was rubbing sunscreen on his legs.

After a minute, the guy said, "I didn't expect to learn a new word when I went to this thing."

It took me a second to realize he was talking to me. "Huh?"

"Autosexuality," he said, pulling off his shirt. "Haven't heard that one before."

"Oh. Yeah."

"The million dollar question: Is it gay to enjoy your own dick?"

It seemed like he was trying to joke around, but he stumbled over his words, so it was hard to tell.

"That's a tough one," I agreed. "I guess 50 percent of

your brain is like, 'Dude, there's a dick in your hand.'"

"When I was younger, I didn't see a problem with that. But I'm also bi, so I'm not a great test subject."

"Oh." I turned away as I wiggled out of my shorts and underwear. The guy did the same behind a makeshift towel curtain he draped over the locker door, which hid some things but not everything. Suddenly I felt half-shy, half-invigorated at being so exposed. When it came to my sexuality, I'd probably known for a couple months now that things were . . . flexible. My recent porn searching had taken me some interesting places, and while there was no doubt I loved everything with Lily, I didn't really hate the idea of stuff with a guy, either. Especially not with this guy, and especially not if we were going to keep talking about our dicks.

I waited until he left, then turned the shower on cold.

Once I found Lily and got in the pool, Beth and Austin quickly engaged us in a game of couple vs. couple chicken. I wound up losing on purpose because the feeling of having Lily's legs wrapped around my neck started to make my shorts tent.

She poked me in the side and grinned at the noise I made.

"What?" I asked, wiping my wet hair out of my eyes when I resurfaced.

"Just you," she said, pecking me on the cheek. I shot a nervous glance over to the picnic benches under the pavilion, where my parents were chatting with Mr. Caldwell.

"What're you thinking about?" Lily asked, giving her dad a wave.

I shrugged, shimmying my shoulders to the beach music from the speaker system. "Not much. Everything's a little loud."

"Is it the music? I can ask them to turn it down," she said, her smile slipping.

"It's more the people." I flinched at a crowd of little kids screeching and splashing on the other side of the pool.

"Got it." Then, keeping her arm snaked around my shoulders, she said, "We could go somewhere with . . . fewer people?"

I wondered if she meant that the same way I heard it, but then she grinned at me and her hand trailed south, and I knew it for sure.

Cut to: Her and I racing across my yard toward the Studio, towels billowing over our shoulders. The minute we shut the garage door against the sun, we were kissing and touching and peeling off each other's bathing suits, her hands running through my damp hair as we wiped each other's skin dry. Then she asked about the condoms we bought last month but hadn't used yet, and I asked if she was sure, and she asked me the same thing.

In a blink we were on the couch, me telling Lily I was nervous in my trembling voice with a trembling laugh, and her saying how cute I was and to just follow her lead. Don't think about it. Don't calculate. Don't focus, just feel. Then she started doing things that made me feel everything, and she just completely let herself go, egging me on and kissing me with her wicked grin. And I sat there torn in half by how much I loved this and how much I didn't plan to be here. Doing this. But it was her, so we worked it out like we always do. We took it slow. I stopped at one point to say, "This is so *fun!*" and Lily laughed and shushed me. We got on the couch, and when that was too awkward we tried the floor with pillows, then that hurt my back and butt, so we went back to the couch, laughing with each other and making love in the patch of sun from the Studio skylight.

I needed to pick something to look at to last longer, so I fixed my gaze on the shell of my cast sitting on my desk hutch. Lily's red name on it. I looked at us—the boy with the broken arm, and the girl teeming with too many words. Her and me and me and her. Teetering on the precipices of our hearts.

I thought back to the first time she gave me a hug—it was during one of our tutoring sessions, when we were talking about our middle school "firsts" and I admitted to her that no one besides my parents had ever hugged me. She'd said, "Aww, I'll hug you!" then did it. I remembered I loved the security of it. Safety, stability—an anchor.

It was like a film reel. I saw her and me going from sitting in my yard studying, to laying in it watching the clouds, to running around in the rain. I blinked and we were kids—a girl giving a boy his first hug. Then I blinked again, and we were adults—a man and a woman both glowing with the intimacy they just shared and holding each other the same way they used to.

Look at us, man.

Sincerely,

O

THIRTEEN

THE RUMORS ABOUT THE SCHOOL INTERROGATIONS level off over the next few days—once people realize no one is getting jailed on the spot, they all go back to studying for finals. That doesn't make me any less jumpy, though. The whole issue is like an untamed animal that lives inside me, constantly clawing at its cage and keeping me awake at night.

So I put all the focus on group activities. The last week of April, the five of us have a cookout in Lily's backyard to celebrate Vic's birthday. Lily hangs a sign up in her living room—a plain white one that simply reads "Birth"—and we play the game Taboo. Essentially it's a game where someone has to get their team to guess a certain word but can't give clues that explicitly state what it is. Except in our version, the other team shouts out gibberish to try to throw everyone off.

"Alright," Vic says. "Uh, Beth's hair is . . ."

"Long!" says Beth.

"On fire!" says Austin.

"Greasy!" says Lily.

"Wow, *thanks*!" Beth shouts at them. "Blue!"

Vic spins her hand.

"Navy! Turquoise!"

"YEAH!" Vic high-fives her.

"And your hair's gorgeous, Beth," adds Lily.

I grin, holding up my phone to take a picture of the scene. If there's one thing I could do all day, it's watch my friends hanging out with each other. Every time they do, I look around and try to capture the scene. What it's like to turn to my left and see Austin there, holding hands with Beth. Vic's snide remarks and Lily's giggles. It's the magic of everyone being under the same roof—the air crackling with all our joy and teasing. During these moments, I feel completely at ease: totally in tune with life and just being my plain old self.

"Your turn, O," Lily says, passing me a card. I smirk at it—my word is "pencil."

"Last week I gave Lily my . . ."

"Autism!" shouts Vic.

"Bisexuality!" yells Beth.

"Those aren't it, but they win," I say.

"Food!" Lily tries, her face scrunched up.

"Nope."

"Dick!" Austin says.

"Dude, you're on my team!"

"That answer's plausible!" he protests.

"You think the answer's 'dick,' Austin? You think that's the word on his card right now?" Vic chews him out.

"Just, in all caps—DICK." Beth traces her finger in the air.

"That one's not plausible anyway," Lily says between gritted teeth, throwing the game into pause as everyone yells, "Ohhh!" I do my part, giving a good-natured laugh and accepting her apologetic kiss on the cheek, but deep down it makes me want to break a window.

The timer goes off, and I throw the card down harder than normal.

"There's the goddamn word," I mutter, instantly regretting my tone. I've flipped the lights off everyone's smiles. I cough, then force a grimace to erase the awkwardness. "Wow, this game causes a headache."

"Yeah, buddy," Austin says, buying it. He hesitates, then takes his turn. As soon as he reads the card, he says, "Oh, perfect. This week at school there was a huge . . ."

"Exam!" says Lily.

"Hemorrhoid!" shouts Beth.

"Assembly!" I pipe up.

"Gangbang!" says Vic.

The timer dings—everyone groans.

"*Austin*," Vic chastises as she gets ahold of the card and looks at the word on it—*interview*. "That's not even the right category, you fucking mistake."

"Way to go, Austin!" says Beth.

"Way to *go*, Austin!" I echo.

"Yes it is!" he calls over a chorus of slow claps. "Wait, yes it is! Hold up, hold up—didn't the cops talk to you guys?"

Everyone stiffens.

Snapsnap.

"They talked to you, Owen?" Austin asks, noticing the way I shift in my chair. All eyes train on me. For the first time in living memory, I feel uncomfortable around these people.

"Ah. Erm." God damn it. "Was it the school cop or the real cops?"

"Who's the school one?" Vic asks. "That young guy, always looks like he's holding in diarrhea?"

As everyone laughs, Vic goes, "No, have you seen him? He always has this look on his face." She sits up straight, staring into the distance in wide-eyed panic.

"Yeah, I think it was him," Austin says. "So did he talk to you?"

I try to turn it around on him. "Did he talk to *you*?"

He thumbs at his glasses. "Well, yeah. He asked about you, actually."

My fingernails sink into my jeans and squeeze until it hurts. ". . . Me?"

"Yeah." He leans forward. "They said, 'We're looking for a guy who caused a traffic incident three years ago when he got hit by a truck waving to a girl.' Sorry, man. Had to throw you under the bus."

"Or truck," Beth snickers.

Everyone relaxes. I muster a scoff. "Ha ha. Asshole."

"Nah, I'm playing. They just asked about the trip to Lanham last month. Apparently some shit went down there."

"That's what I heard," says Lily, scooting closer to me.

"What else?" I ask her, way too urgently.

"Literally just that."

"*I* heard a girl got assaulted," Beth says.

"Whoa, what?" Lily's eyebrows arch. "Did someone talk to you?"

"That's just what I heard—no, nobody talked to me. Some girl in my Latin class—Kayla someone—she said the school questioned her or whatever, and they asked if she knew about any incidents that happened on the trip. When she said, 'Hey what do you mean by incidents,' that's when they basically said they were looking into a sexual assault. I don't know."

"So do they mean like . . ." Austin lowers his voice, unusually serious. "Like, what exactly happened?"

"I *don't* know; that's what I'm saying." Beth raises both hands. "That's all she told me."

"Jesus," Vic says.

"Shit," Lily adds, shaking her head. "Can you *imagine*? Just imagine being that girl, and you've got to come to class every

day knowing the whole school is all over your shit. I'd kill someone, man."

My blood boils.

"Yeah, poor girl," Beth says quietly, munching on a potato
chip.

"That has to suck," Vic agrees.

"Yeah," adds Austin.

"Poor girl," I croon.

Snapsnap.

When I go to sleep that night, I dream that I'm lying in a dark
and shapeless world. A deck of cards labeled *Taboo* sits on my
chest, but it's heavy as an anvil. It crushes the air out of my lungs
and presses me into the floor, so I pull the deck apart. My name
is on every card, penned in permanent red.

FOURTEEN

April 21st—Junior Year

Journal:

I'm writing this as I sit in the Studio in the middle of the night, listening to the sound of rain on the roof above me. My ears are still ringing from Junior Prom earlier tonight, and as a footnote, there is a possibility I'm still a bit stoned.

We didn't get high at the dance, obviously. It happened afterward, once the five of us got home and had the chance to change out of our formal wear. We met back up at the playground shortly after midnight, where Austin distributed the banana bread edibles his older brother had snagged.

Lily, who decided to abstain, became babysitter.

"Okay, show of hands," Austin said as we all raised the bread to our mouths. "Who here has never been high before?"

Everyone's hands went up, including his own.

"Jesus Christ," Lily said, snapping a picture of us.

"Hey, delete that! That's evidence of *criminal activity*," Austin hissed.

"It looks like regular bread in the picture, dumbass," Vic said.

I spent the next hour rubbing my hands together, invigorated. This had been Austin's idea, but I was excited to be part of it. (After doing research to know what to expect, of course.) It was the type of new experience I didn't mind trying.

Sometime later—I can't quite remember how I ended up there—the girls were swinging on the swings in their pajamas, Austin was sitting on a stump with his tie draped over one shoulder, and I was saying to him in a serious voice: "You aren't listening. I'm not asking if you'd have *sex* with a vacuum; I'm asking if you would try sticking your dick in one."

"Okay." Vic held up a hand mid-swing. "Normally I'd think you're weird for asking that, but that's a *good* question."

"Hey, I wonder if it's kicked in yet," said Lily.

"Oh, it has, all right," Austin declared.

"God damn it's right," Vic said.

"What is?" he asked.

"You know, man . . ." She lobbed her head back and forth. "That one is a *bad* question. First Owen asked a good question, then you asked a bad one. You ruined it; good job."

I remember making a joyful squeak, letting my head tilt so I could look up. It was just one of those *nights*, you know? The air was perfect—alive with the chorus of crickets, blending with the ringing in my ears and banter of the people I love. I sighed, taking a deep breath of being alive next to them.

The next hour was a little fuzzy, but I know everyone

started getting hungry. At one point, I asked Vic how she was doing. She just gave me a light, rare hug.

"*I*," she said, "am like the stars in the *sky*. Do you know *why*?" Then she leaned and hissed, directly into my ear, "Cause I'm *hiiigh*."

Someone suggested we go back to the Studio and hang out there since it looked like rain. Then Beth floated the idea of us spending the night in there.

"YES!" I screeched it loud and shrill, jumping to my feet.

"Hey—dude, calm down," Lily said, hugging me close to keep me still and putting a finger over my lips.

"That idea makes me so *happy*," I murmured in a more contained voice.

"I know it does. Here's what we're going to do." Lily held up a hand to shush us all. "You guys walk with Owen back to the Studio, and I can bring over snacks and sleeping bags from my place. Remember to text your parents."

"Do you have chips?" Austin asked, looking like he'd just won the lottery.

"Chips sound *so* good right now," Beth crooned. "With Cheez Whiz!"

"Is the Cheez Whiz critical?" Lily asked.

"YES! Just call me the Whiz Queen."

"Or the Cheez Wizard," I piped up.

"Someone look up 'Whiz Queen,'" Austin said.

"I wouldn't," Lily advised.

The next part I remember is one of my favorite images ever: the five of us, chilling in the Studio in our pajamas. Lily brought ice cream with her, prompting a giggly group hug. I inflated a spare air mattress, triple-checking if anyone needed extra blankets. God, what a

RUSH! This was happening! We shut the garage door, the lights were dimmed, and the TV was turned on to some late night talk show.

"How're you doing?" Lily asked me, leaning her head on my shoulder.

"The air feels good!" I said.

"Hold on, wait . . ." She lost it in a fit of giggles. "What exactly do you mean by that?"

"The air feels good!" I said.

"You know what? It does," said Vic, patting me on the leg. "I'm with *Owen* on this one."

"Love me some good air," Austin chirped up. He was taking a video on his phone. "God, Lily, you don't even support your own boyfriend!"

"I *support* him!" She clutched my shoulders, sounding horrified. "I support you, Owen!"

"Wait, guys," I frowned. "I feel like I was saying something before? Like way before."

"Vacuum cleaners," Beth reminded me. When that didn't help, she clarified, "You were asking Austin if he's tried having sex with one."

"I haven't, by the way!" Austin yelled, pumping his fist.

"Have *you*?" Lily asked me with an openmouthed laugh, and I shook my head.

"No, no . . . my sexuality's not that fluid."

(I stopped myself just in time. Over the past school year, I've definitely confirmed to myself that I'm bisexual, which isn't a huge deal, but it's still one of those things that I haven't told the group yet. Not that I'm afraid to, but I figure, why go through the hassle? I'm with Lily; it shouldn't matter anyway.)

"Now I'm wondering what inspired the question,"

Lily said, joining the other girls on the couch with a mock pout. "What're you trying to say, O? You prefer a vacuum over your own girlfriend?"

"In his defense, vacuums have that fancy tank where it power sucks everything into, like, a vortex," Austin pointed out. "You got to give him that torque power drive swirl action."

"Sounds like a job for the Whiz Queen," said Vic.

"Listen," I told them. "In my defense, I didn't ask if you'd fuck the whole vacuum."

"An autobiography by Owen Turner," said Lily.

"I was *just thinking out loud*, wondering if it would feel good. *How* do you know it wouldn't feel good, Austin? That's all I'm saying is how do you know? Oh wait, you don't. It could be like a blowjob."

"OR A SUCK JOB!" yelled everyone else almost in sync, and we lost it again.

The five of us carried on like that for I-don't-know-how-long . . . another couple hours, at least. We dimmed the lights more as the TV shows turned into shitty info-mercials, and the clear night outside morphed into a steady drizzle on the Studio exterior. Inside, though, it was inebriated anarchy: The couch got moved for reasons I can't remember; Beth and Lily drew doodles all over the whiteboard I use for my weekly planning; Vic rambled to Austin and I about the gaming emulator she'd just built; and he and I listened while splitting the old pack of candy corn that had fallen out of the couch cushions.

"The forbidden corn," he whispered to me with a knowing nod.

We giggled about this until Beth found his clarinet— which he'd left in the Studio after our last gym session—

and we took turns trying to play it while he gave us pointers and took video.

Eventually Vic and Beth were lying on the couch, Austin was on the air mattress, and Lily and I were snuggled in sleeping bags. The weed started to wear off, and the others conked out one by one. But I wanted to capture this while it was fresh, so here I am. Writing this and looking at all of them.

God *damn* I wish I could exist like this forever. Such pure joy. The five of us lying around in our pajamas, inebriated, listening to the pitter-patter outside against the steel door. Pure resplendence of being. I'd sell a piece of my soul to stay here awhile, sitting in my favorite spot with all the people I love.

I think about a video Lily recorded and posted online earlier tonight, captioned, "Look at this cutie patootie!" In it, I'm in the middle of the dance floor just completely letting myself *go*—hips moving, clothes close-fitting with my tie thrown over my shoulder and my sleeves rolled up. Hair matted with sweat and sunglasses crooked, but wearing a huge at-home grin. And I think about how wacky it is that time can just fly by, and we can all look older but it feels *so clearly* like we were just doing these same things one, two, almost three years ago. And I feel myself wanting to tell my friends I love them, but when I whisper it, all that comes out is, "I love." So I just say that over and over again. "I love. I love. I love."

I really do.

Sincerely,

O

FIFTEEN

"IS YOUR SEAT UP FAR ENOUGH?" DAD ASKS. "ARM CHECK."

I lean back in the driver's seat of his SUV and stick both my arms in front of me. My wrists can just touch the steering wheel.

"Perfect. That's where you want it." He hands me the keys.

Driving practice is something I've put off as long as possible—Dad and I have never graduated from parking lots. When I'd told him I wished I could stay off the road indefinitely, he offered me his version of practical advice.

"Wish in one hand and shit in the other and let me know which fills up first."

So here we are.

"Your first drive on the main road. This is going to be exciting!" says Mom from the backseat.

"Nooo," Dad says in an impatient singsong, like, *we know better*. "Driving isn't supposed to be 'exciting'—don't put that in his head. I guarantee no one's premiums ever went down over something *exciting*."

Mom volunteered to come along to help "manage tempers." It isn't working so far.

My father, meanwhile, looks like he hasn't slept in a decade. According to Mom, all he does is refresh his email every few hours to check for updates from the school. He's acting like we're on critical lockdown, waiting for a reprieve so we can start living again. By night he still roams the halls, limp-pacing back and forth like he's trying to sweat out an illness.

"Okay. Let's go over our preemptive plan here," he says. "Are you paying attention?"

"Yes, sir."

"We're going to make a right-hand turn out of the driveway onto the street—remember that it's two-way, so you may pass other cars. If that happens, just let it happen. We'll go past the playground, left onto the main road—don't give me that look; I'll help you through it—and make a right turn into the plaza past the field. Say that back to me."

"Right turn onto street, left onto main road, right into plaza. Got it."

"Do you have any questions?"

I shake my head.

The thing is that Dad's actually a great driving instructor when he's calm. I love Mom, but this is one area where I prefer Dad's no-nonsense approach. He knows exactly what kind of information I need—lane info, landmarks, hazards—and reliably rattles it off with military precision. I eat it up. For all his faults, he's one of the most important things a person can be: consistent. We don't exactly have a warm father-son bond that involves us winning any three-legged races together, but for things like this, we function well as a unit.

"Remember: Any time you change directions *or* lanes, you use this first." He points to the blinker arm. "That's your turn signal. An important fact to make peace with upfront is that about 10 percent of the fuckweasels on the road couldn't find this if it were duct taped to their firstborn, okay. Don't ask me why; I've given up trying to figure it out. Seven percent of the people in this country believe chocolate milk comes from brown cows. Not jumping to any conclusions about the overlap of those two groups; all I'm saying is, let's add a chocolate milk question to the driver's test and see if the problem doesn't work itself out. But. Until that happens, we deal with it."

"Steve?" Mom interjects, leaning forward. "Remember what we said this morning."

"This mor—" Dad's lips peel off his teeth, and he looks ready to detonate. But then all at once, his face floods with a sugary smile.

"Fine," he says. He turns to me and says, still beaming, "Owen, I forgot to ask. How are you *feeling* today?"

"Uh," I stutter. His shit-eating grin is unsettling to me, and I immediately start looking for the trap—Dad is never like this. Try watching a Pixar movie with him sometime and do a shot every time he smiles. You'll be able to drive home afterward.

"Doing good?" he asks. "Ready to hit the road? Metaphorically, of course."

"Are you okay?"

"Do I not sound okay?"

"You sound like you're about to tell me my call is very important."

"Ah, no, no no no. Your, um, *mother*"—he raises his eyebrows at his own lap—"had a talk with me this morning about how in order for these lessons to be productive—which we all want, obviously—I need to be more . . ." He searches for the word.

"You know. Perky. Upbeat . . . *Shh, you're doing great, don't worry about the road, just do your best.*"

His tone immediately pisses me off. It puts me at center stage of the theatrical production going on in his mind: that I need to be coddled, or given a participation trophy, or that I can't handle someone being irritated with me. He's putting the kid gloves on.

"You don't have to do that," I tell him.

"I just want you to feel relaxed, and above all, know that I'm not pissed."

"Okay, *why* would you be pissed? We haven't started the car yet."

"I said I'm *not*—I'm *not* pissed."

"Okay, please . . . just, stop acting. You can be your . . . normal you." I turn to Mom and say, "Tell him he can stop."

"Hey, hey, Owen?" Dad leans close to me, his voice slipping a notch as he mutters in a melodic growl, "Let's just *try this shit*, please."

We both lean back in our seats. I catch my own reflection in the rearview mirror and adjust it so my face is out of the frame.

"Lights, camera, action," says Dad. He knows how much I appreciate patterns, so during our early sessions, we came up with a startup routine and drilled it until I could do it in my sleep: lights on, parking brake off, shift into gear. Each time I do it, I say, "Lights, camera, action"—one word for each of the steps—under my breath. Dad rolls with it.

"We're going to exit the neighborhood the usual way," he says as we pull out of the driveway. "Remember not to gun it near the playground. That's how you turn the neighbor's idiot kid into road pizza."

"Got it."

"We make our turn, let the wheel come back . . . good. You've got this part down," he says. "Next, we're going to pull up to the intersection at the main road. I'll give you plenty of warning."

"Thanks."

"You're welcome."

"Feeling more relaxed now, sweetie?" asks Mom.

"*Let him focus, Jen!*" Dad barks, his smile vanishing. Mom

gives him a look, and his mask slips back into place.

My hand slips for half a second, and I squeak. This is another thing that gets me on edge about driving—the sheer amount of control in your hands. When I picture passing another car, the thought floods my head: I could jerk this wheel five inches and end three lives. That's all it would take—half a second of motion. Less effort than it takes to lift a spoon to your mouth. The thought makes me scared of my own strength.

"Now, this is the hairier part," Dad warns as we approach our turn. "We're going to pull into the shopping center at the opening in front of that sign, you see it?"

"Yes," I say. It's approaching. Meanwhile, I look in the rearview mirror and grunt—the entire back window is full of blinding white light that hurts my eyes. "There's something behind us."

"I see them. Just stay focused."

"What the hell is so *bright?*"

"They're called LED headlights, and they're the sole reason capital punishment should exist. Ignore them."

"*I can't goddamn see behind me!*"

The car is right on my ass. I check my speed—we're going thirty-eight in a forty-five.

"In point-four miles, your destination is on the right," the GPS rattles off.

"Slow down, please." Dad's smile is back. "We're going to turn right up here—don't be afraid to slow down; ignore whatever the person behind—"

"*BEEEEEP!*" says the car behind us. I jump.

"—we're ignoring them, we're ig-nor-ing them," he chants like a mantra, his shoulders seesawing with each syllable. Steve Turner has been reduced to song and dance.

"Now they're flipping me off," I say.

"That motherfucker," he says through a tight, toothy grin. "Owen, I said slow down."

"But that red car—"

His face melts.

"That red car can go FRONT-FUCK THE BERLIN WALL, you understand? Now, *for this turn*—"

"Steve!" Mom admonishes.

"Be quiet, Jen!" says Dad. "*For this turn*, the curb is sharp, so you need—*are you listening?*"

"Destination on the right!" says the GPS.

"So you need to take it slow—*slow-er*—Owen—THE HELL ARE YOU DOING?" Dad roars.

THUMP—the front of our car slams the curb head-on.

The front goes up.

The front crashes back down.

A deafening *BLAST*—like the bang of a cannon; or, as I would soon learn, the sound of a RAV4 tire blowing out.

We're wrenched to a stop. Horns blare. An expensive-looking symbol illuminates the dashboard warning panel.

"*Shit!*" I say.

"Oh *no*," says Mom.

"Low air pressure in front-right tire," says a voice from the dashboard.

"*TSSSSSSSSSSSSSSS!*" says the front-right tire.

"Arrived," says the GPS.

"MOTHER OF *FUCKING CHRIST!*" says Dad.

SIXTEEN

IT'S DAD'S SCREAMS THAT LET ME KNOW WE'RE ABOUT to die.

"GET OUT OF HERE! ALL OF YOU GET OUT OF HERE! GO, GO! GET THE FUCK OUT OF HERE!" He yells it at the top of his lungs—smacking the dashboard, tugging at his seatbelt, thrashing like a caged animal. His voice chills my blood—he's not angry. My father is *terrified*.

"Steve! Steve. SteveSteveSteve." Mom is shouting now too. One of his fists flies back, nearly taking my head off, and she yells, "Owen, GET OUT!" When I hesitate—stuttering without moving—she says, "RIGHT NOW, GO!"

I rip my seatbelt off and throw myself out of the car, calling for my parents to follow me. Holy Christ, is the car about to explode? *Why aren't they coming?* Are their seatbelts stuck? Am I about to watch my parents die?

The driver's side door hangs open. Dad is still losing his mind, but he's not getting out. Mom has squished herself against the backseat, as far away from his swinging arms as possible. She's not leaving . . . she's talking to him. Not yelling, not panicking, not rambling—talking. Clearly and in a controlled manner.

I hear the sound of screeching brakes from a thousand miles

away, and it isn't until I feel a hand on my shoulder that I realize someone in a white truck has pulled over and is trying to talk to me.

"—ambulance? Do I need to call an ambulance? *Hey, do I need to call an ambulance?*"

I look to the stranger—a grizzled guy built like a lumber-jack—and work my mouth without saying anything.

Snapsnapsnapsnap.

"Alright, I'm calling," he says.

"No!" I spit out. "I mean—I don't know. I think it was just a tire, but—I don't know if it's about to explode."

"Explode!"

"I don't know! I, I—shit. I have no idea. I don't know."

Mom eventually extracts herself from the car and takes over. She orders me to go into the shopping center and gives me money for the food court.

An hour later, after manually installing the spare tire and driving my father home, she comes back and gets me separately.

I don't ask her what happened on the ride home, but she brings it up on her own. It's important, she says. It's important to tell me what I'd already suspected—that this was the same thing as what happened when I was little. That the sound of the tire blowing out sent my father to somewhere other than the inside of the car. That when he was yelling to get out, the reason he said "all of you" instead of "both of you" is because he wasn't talking to us at all. She tells me the same thing she's told me since I was ten: "The only people who completely understand PTSD are the ones who have it."

The words tumble around in my head as I go to sleep that

night: *GET OUT OF HERE*. The urgency—the terror. It makes me understand why he never told me what shit he saw overseas, and I realize how much scarier it is that I'm left to imagine.

I remember this picture Dad took with me: eight-year-old me dressed as Buzz Lightyear for Halloween, sitting on his lap as he wears the helmet on his head. It was the first time his smile looked different. Strained. Impatient.

I think about how my father has buried these awful things that happened to him—the war that lives in his head and his heart—instead of talking to someone about it. I think about how desperate I am to erase what happened to me, just as he's desperate to erase whatever happened to him. Two men carrying ourselves as though we're okay—concealing our scars from the world. And my heart aches for how much my dad and I have in common . . . how much we would have to talk about, if ever we talked about anything at all.

Owen,

Here is the spec sheet of the tire that needed replacing. No need to reimburse us—it was an easy mistake to make. Your mother is going to handle driving lessons from now on.

I apologize for raising my voice.

-Dad

SEVENTEEN

January 25th—Senior Year

Journal:

Came out to Lily today. Not intentionally—I think I really screwed it up.

We were down at the playground putting the finishing touches on the snowman we built. My face was frozen and my nose had started to drip, but I was having a blast. Lily and I have been starved for some one-on-one time for the past month, and when she hit me up this afternoon, I put off all my homework to say yes.

"Can I say something mean?" she asked me. Then, before I could answer: "I love Austin. But how the *hell* did he get into UVA?"

"His parents, probably. They both went there."

"Maybe." She brushed a bit of snow off my jacket. "Apparently he's officially going there. Like, for sure, definite, signed-the-paperwork official. Which is neat, but now he and Beth are starting to have that conversation—do they do the distance thing or not—and—"

"They have different opinions?" I guessed.

"No, it's not even that! He won't even have the conversation."

"Ah."

"That's the issue, yeah." She nodded at me knowingly. "And then he's all, *Chill out, babe, why do you want to plan our breakup, blah, blah.*"

"Flawless Austin voice, by the way."

I tried to keep it light, because I knew college was an especially rough topic for Lily at the moment. I got into Lanham early decision right before winter break, which of course was great—Mom started crying when I read it, and Dad showed his support by buying me professional screenwriting software for Christmas. But Lily wound up on the waiting list, despite her gold-plated resume. I felt so bad that I didn't even tell her I'd already accepted my enrollment to the English program.

"I think this is done. What do you think?" She pointed to our snowman—a misshapen lump with two rocks for eyes and a baby carrot for a nose.

"He looks cold."

Lily stuck her tongue out at me, pecked me on the cheek, then took off her hat and tugged it over the head. We took a few selfies in front of it, then snuggled at our old picnic table under the pavilion.

"Hoo," she said, shivering and rubbing her hands together.

"Cold?" I asked, then yelped as she pressed her hands to my neck. (She knows I hate that, but she loves hearing my noises, so sometimes she can't resist. I deal with it.)

"We should go somewhere warm. Maybe a coffee shop?" she suggested, pulling my arms around her. "I can drive."

Lily's car—an old Passat that she got used this past summer—was a game changer as far as being able to spend time together outside the neighborhood. It also meant she'd become our group chauffeur.

"It's polite for taxi drivers to ask how you're doing first," I quipped.

"I will *smack* you."

"No you won't. Okay, stop!" I laughed out another, "Ow!" as she slapped me on the shoulder and said, "Fucker. Let's find a place."

We huddled around my phone.

"I'm making you try something new this time. Not just plain hot choc—" Lily started to say. That's when it happened: I opened the internet browser on my phone, which started to auto-play the last tab I had open. Which, in this case, was a video of two college guys having sex with each other.

"Whoa, what the *fuck?*"

Time froze.

I closed out the window and stuffed my phone back in my pocket, but the damage was done.

Lily got to her feet, yanked her hand out of mine, and said, "Owen!" in an *okay-dude-what-the-hell* voice. For once in her life, she had no idea how to react. The girl who always had an easy retort had a hand to her mouth, her eyes wide. She shook her head and started to say, "Oh my God," under her breath. She said it over and over again, like it was a mantra. Oh my God. Oh my *God*.

Finally I wrenched myself out of my stasis and said, "It's not what you think!"

"O—"

"Please—"

"Are you gay?"

"*No.*"

"You can tell me if you are."

"I'm bi, okay?" I blurted it out just like that . . . this thing I'd been contemplating telling her for over a year.

I remember she blinked at me, slowing to a halt. Then she sat back down and said, "Oh." Then, "Wow."

Then, nothing.

"I was about to tell you, I swear." I tried to put a hand on her shoulder, but she wriggled away, so I backed off. "The reason I didn't say anything is because it doesn't matter. *Honestly*. Nothing here—not our dates, not our relationship, not the sex; *none* of it—is affected by this. It is a completely separate thing."

Lily got to her feet, looking at me with new eyes. "I need to go home for a bit."

"No, please stay." I started to panic, but all she said was, "I don't like how I feel right now," and booked it past me.

That was five hours ago, and she's not answering any of my texts.

Like I said. I think I really screwed this up.

Sincerely,

O

January 27th—Senior Year

Journal:

I finally convinced Lily to finish our conversation from a few days ago. I was afraid it would take longer, but after giving her a letter I typed out explaining things, she agreed to meet back down at the playground.

Our snowman was half-melted.

We greeted each other with a short "hey" and sat down at the same picnic table as last time. I handed her a thermos that I'd filled with her favorite coffee, which got her to smile. A tradition we recently developed whenever we sit down to resolve fights: start with coffee.

"I swear I was trying to figure out how to tell you," I said to her, once we got into it.

Lily said, "Okay."

"It's not one of those things where it's because I like you any less. That's not how it works, I promise."

Lily said, "Okay."

"It'd be like, if someone liked blonds and redheads. They wouldn't find you, a blond, less attractive or anything just because you're not a redhead, even if they sometimes watch porn at home that has redheads; say, if it's an off day, and—"

"Hey, O? I said okay," Lily said. My heart scooched up as I realized that she was smiling, albeit a little warily. "Learn to take yes for an answer."

"You're not still pissed?"

"To be clear, I was never pissed about you being bi. Who gives a shit, right? But you didn't talk to me about it. You were covering it up."

"In my defense, you never asked. So I didn't technically lie."

She gave me a *come on* look, and I abandoned that track. "Sorry—point taken. You're right."

Lily folded her hands, squishing them between her knees. I expected her to say the usual stuff you see in books and movies—"I won't tell anyone" or "you're still the same person to me"—but she didn't linger on any of those platitudes. Instead she asked, "Have you told anyone else?"

(I haven't, and said so.)

"Have you thought about it?" she asked.

"Not really."

"You should."

"Think about it?"

"Tell other people. If that's something you'd be comfortable with."

I leaned my head against hers, staring at the grungy wood of the table surface. "It's not that I'm not comfortable; I just don't know if there's a point. We have, what . . . seven months until we all leave forever?"

"I think it would be good for you," she pushed. "And I think you'd regret it if you don't. I really do. You could tell the group first!"

Her gears were turning—she was in planning mode. And as much as I appreciated it, *this* was why I didn't want to tell her. To me, being bi was such a non-headline. It's not that I was ashamed, but the idea of turning it into a huge ordeal made my skin crawl. It felt cringey, disingenuous.

This was the double-edge sword with Lily: I loved how full her heart was, but she never heard you when you asked her to go small. Lily didn't do small, ever.

So I said, "I'm not going to tell anyone for now."

Her face fell a little, and I could tell she was disappointed that I wasn't on board. But she said, "Whatever you want. Just think about it." Then she pulled me into a tight, strong hug—the kind she knows I like—and murmured to me, "Hey. I'm really proud of you."

"I'm proud of me too," I quipped, and she giggled. "So we're good, right?"

"One condition," she said, then whispered in my ear, "We watch the rest of that video together later."

I felt my jeans tighten at the zipper, and made a noise that got her to beam.

"Uh," I verbalized, "yes please."

As we got up to head back, Lily tilted her head and said, "Huh."

"What's up?"

"Just thinking. This is the same table where we used to do homework together."

I grinned, loving that she remembered that. "And?"

"That's it. I was just thinking about that."

She leaned forward and used her finger to write in the snow on the table:

Owen likes butt sex :)

As I cracked up and kissed her, she said, "Look at us now."

"I am," I told her, drawing comfort from the old line. "I am too."

Sincerely,

O

EIGHTEEN

VIC IS QUESTIONED A COUPLE OF DAYS INTO MAY. Nailed right after AP exams start. Beth and Lily have their turn the next day. They confirm that the incident was definitely sexual assault, but that's about all they get from it.

"The questions were really vague. Every answer was basically 'I don't know,'" Lily tells us at our next gym session. I resist the urge to snap my bracelet, but she doesn't seem hung up on it. In general, Lily has been more easygoing the past few days . . . earlier in the week, she got the news that she'd been accepted to Lanham for next year. Obviously I went through the motions and congratulated her along with the rest of the group, but secretly, I hate how mixed my feelings are on the subject.

Six months ago, I would've been ecstatic knowing that at least a piece of the group—the most important piece—was going with me. I couldn't imagine a future without Lily in it. But now, everything between us feels condemned. All of it is hinged on us avoiding honesty; not talking about why it feels so slimy when she tries to touch my hand, or other parts that I used to love her touching.

My last exam of high school is my AP English final. I walk out of it with my head held high, twirling my Finals Pen. (My special pen that—you guessed it—I only use for final exams.) I'm so absorbed in my relief at being done with it that I trip on the doorjamb and drop the pen.

"I got it, man," says the guy in front of me. I start to tell him, "Not like I need it again anyway—" but then he turns to face me, and I freeze.

It's him.

"Whoa. Hi," says Luke. He looks as stunned as I feel. The sound of his voice sends me back in time. My jaw locks. Behind me, a cluster of people bitch at me to get out of the way.

I book it down the hall.

"Can we talk?" Luke calls after me. His footsteps follow me until I'm forced to say over my shoulder, "No."

I'm boiling over, but I can't articulate anything.

"Two seconds. Just two seconds!" he says. I wheel around to find him raising both hands, his eyes huge with concern. He stares right at me, like it's important he say all this to my face. "Whatever you need to call me, or tell me, is completely, 100 percent fair."

I squeeze my eyes shut, regroup, then open them. "Just tell me this: Did you report it yourself? Or did you tell a classmate, and they did it?" My anger kicks into overdrive the longer I look at him. It feels like the only thing keeping me from knocking him out is my need to get information.

"Wh—of course I didn't tell our classmates. Why would I do that, Owen?"

"*Why would you tell the school?*"

"I shouldn't have. I thought I was helping you—but you're absolutely right. I screwed up."

He's trying to sell it—his eyes are sad, maybe even a little teary behind his glasses. His chest heaves with panicked breaths. What makes me want to strangle him isn't even the violation of trust. It's this *oh my God, I didn't realize this would backfire* routine. It's aggressively ignorant, and I don't feel like explaining that. I don't know what I want from him, but I know I'm not done yet.

"Owen," he says. "I get that nothing's going to fix this. . . . Hate me all you'd like. You have every right, no question. But I just need to tell you: I'm so, so sorry. For whatever that's worth—"

"So, nothing."

"I figured." He brushes a strand of black hair out of his eyes, his shoulders sagging. "I'll leave you alone now. I can tell you're angry."

"Like that's the worst crime in the world."

"No one—"

"Like I don't have *excellent* reasons to be fucking angry these days."

"*No one*'s saying you don't." He takes a half-step toward me. "If you want to beat the hell out of me because it'll make you feel better, you have my full permission to go ahead. I'm serious."

I raise my fist and swing it at his head, faking out at the last second. He winces, and his arms twitch, but he keeps them low. I do it a second time, and he stumbles backward, tripping over his own feet and falling to the floor on his butt.

Now I'm done.

NINETEEN

March 9th—Senior Year

Journal:

I'm sitting here on Lanham University campus, look-ing out at all the buildings with all their lights, and I can't believe how peaceful it is. How to describe this feeling? I hate that my words always fail me when it feels like I need them the most.

(Some screenwriter I'll be, indeed!)

This morning a bus took me and fifty other kids from the senior class to visit campus during our spring break. That's right: We're on break, and voluntarily spending it by visiting another school. We are nerds incarnate.

Normally this would be something exciting—typing up my little personal itinerary the night before, laying all my clothes out. But I spent the whole day on edge because of the plan Lily and I put together: Today, I was coming out.

Lily noticed how quiet I was being during the campus tour and asked, "How're you doing?"

The other three were within earshot, so I took Lily's

phone and typed out for her to read: Nervous about later.

She gave me a warm smile, squeezed my hand, and typed out: You've GOT this. You're going to do great!!

By the time our group was eating dinner in the dining hall, I was checking my watch every two minutes. My heels hammered against the floor. No one seemed to notice except Vic, who raised an eyebrow and asked, "You good? You seem like you're trying to achieve liftoff."

I felt Lily's eyes on me. I sent her a quick text under the table: ASK THEM NOW!!

She rolled her eyes at her lap, and I got a reply within seconds: Chill out, my dude. I heaved a dramatic sigh in her direction.

"So apparently there's this really chill rock garden on the north side of campus," Lily eventually said to the group—offhandedly as we ate dessert—and I realized she was doing it. "We should check it out when we're done eating."

"We have to be back at the dorms," Vic said.

"Not until later, though."

"I was going to get my phone charger," Beth said. I felt my stomach plummeting, silently screaming at Lily to get a handle on this.

Like always, she had it under control.

"So let's do this. We check out the rock garden, chill there for a bit, then we'll have time to head back afterward. That sound good?" Lily asked.

Everyone answered, "sure," including me. I told her *thank you* with my eyes, and she put her shoe over mine to quiet my nervous foot.

As we made our way outside, I felt myself relax a bit. A breeze followed the five of us as we wove through the rows of buildings, up the stairs toward the highest point on campus: me, Lily, Austin, Beth, and Vic. All of us in our spring outfits, making our way through my future home. And as we reached the top and took pictures of the sunset, it was time.

I remember I watched everyone chattering about nothing—Vic lounging on a bench as Austin and Beth leaned back against an enormous rock—and the thing happened where you're trying to say something big but can't find a good opportunity without talking over people. I clenched my teeth, counting, trying to find the courage to open my mouth, and I felt like I was falling when Lily said, loud and clear, "Hey, guys."

The others quieted down. Then they looked to me and I was seized with the sensation of being at the end of the diving board, unable to take the plunge. All I could do was awkwardly turn to Lily and say—with a hopeless laugh to break the tension—"I don't think I can do it."

"Yeah, you can," she said.

"Do what?" Austin asked, swinging himself around on the rock.

"Don't think so," I told Lily with a manic grin, just desperate to get out of this.

"Owen," she said.

"Are you okay?" Beth asked me, her eyes apprehensive.

"He's good, just—" Lily hissed in a hushed voice. Then she said to me, "Would it help if we turned around?"

I shrugged. "Sure. Sorry."

"Don't apologize—I get a killer view!" Austin said to the rock in front of his face.

There we all stood for the next fifteen seconds, in complete silence: everyone facing away, and me, working my empty mouth.

I tried once, twice, three times, then choked it out: "So I'm bisexual. That's it. That's literally it. Yeah."

All four of them turned around.

Lily said, "*There* we go."

Beth said, "Oh, wow," in a neutral voice.

Austin belted out, "Dude!" as he grinned behind one hand.

Vic, completely unsmiling, walked up to me and said, "I'm just going to hug you now . . ."

"That's fine!" I yelled, way too loud, and she just said, "Seems like the thing to do. Get over here, yep." I started laughing as I hugged her, exhaling at the feel of it. Mountains moving off my back. A net lifting itself off my limbs. Lily joined our embrace, then Austin and Beth, and I started to tear up.

"I . . . this isn't like, sad crying, okay!" I insisted, a little pitifully, collapsing onto a bench and laughing into my hands once our hug broke apart. "It's just, I like, I . . . I *love* you guys."

The girls cooed, "Aww!" as Austin said, "We like-love you too."

"And I was so, *so* nervous about this, and this feels so nice, and—" More noises. Then I yelled as loud as I could, right into the sun. "THIS FEELS SO GOOD!"

(Yeah. I was a mess.)

Beth said, "Would a picture help? Let's take some pictures. Let's do that," and the five of us all piled into each other.

Cut to: now.

It's dark out, the sky is sparkling with stars, and I'm alone on this rock overlooking my new home. The others went back to the dorms, but I told them I wanted to stay for a bit and write this down. Moments ago, I sent my parents a text I've had typed out and saved in drafts for weeks now:

Hi Mom and Dad. I'm sorry if this is random, but I just wanted to let you know a thing about me, and that thing is that I'm bisexual. We can talk once I get home. Love you.

Then, just before powering off my phone, I posted a portion of that—specifically the second sentence—on all my social media profiles. No going back.

Here I am.

I'm fixing my eyes on the top of the library building in the distance. It has a red ring of lights lining the roof, casting the whole area in a warm glow. I can't believe how peaceful I feel—completely at ease. Is this what college will be like? Shit, if so, I can't wait. Just me being able to sit looking up at the night sky, totally alone with my thoughts and feelings.

It's so *quiet*.

I wish I could stay here longer, but I just got a text from Lily saying that Austin is over at Beth's room, so she and I have the dorm to ourselves. I'll try to enjoy all this night air on my walk back. With all this beauty, how could I not?

Sincerely,

O

TWENTY

THE ARTICLE GOES LIVE DURING THIRD PERIOD AND IS circulating by fifth. Beth posts the link in our group chat with several exclamation marks.

A twelfth grade student in Middleham County, Pennsylvania, has accused a fellow classmate of sexual assault during a school event.

The alleged incident reportedly took place this past March during an annual overnight trip for the senior class. While SRO Matthew Hewitt confirmed to WTOP that an investigation into the matter is ongoing, he emphasized that the questioning of any one student is in no way indicative of their ties to the allegation.

"We're talking to everybody, plain and simple," Officer Hewitt stated.

Due to the ages of the students involved, none of their names have been made available for public release. No arrest has been made at this time.

It's only a tiny piece—a few paragraphs buried on a local news site that six people read—but it's confirmation. It's talk about me, in print.

I cut the rest of my classes for the day. I debate faking sick so my parents can pick me up, but I don't want to raise any red flags. So I just hide out in different study halls.

The front office calls for me over the intercom about ten minutes before the final bell. When I get down to the admin office, Mat With One T is waiting for me.

I raise an eyebrow at him. "Going to cuff me for skipping calc?"

"Not today, bud." He tries a smile but doesn't quite pull it off. "Principal Graham wants to see you."

"Should I call my dad?"

"Already here."

TWENTY-ONE

NOT ONLY IS DAD IN PRINCIPAL GRAHAM'S OFFICE, HE'S already in the middle of a speech.

"There's this saying down in Texas . . . are you from Texas?" Dad asks her.

"No, I'm not."

"How about you?" he asks Mat With One T as we step into the office. "You from Texas?"

"No."

"Yeah, me neither; I'm from Missouri. But there's this saying down in Texas." Dad holds his hands in front of him. "It goes like—the saying goes, *They couldn't pour water out of a boot if instructions were printed on the heel.*" He shakes his head at Principal Graham. "Now, I'm not saying that's the case here . . . but, well . . ."

"Mr. Turner."

"—I'm just saying, if the boot fits." He folds his arms. Without looking at me, he continues, "Owen, I'm going to take the wild guess that you already saw the article from this morning."

I sit down next to him. "Yeah."

Dad opens his arms at Principal Graham and Mat With One T,

yielding the stage to them. "You two want to explain that one to my kid?"

"Owen." Principal Graham faces me, hands folded—no notepad in front of her today. She gives me a grimace that looks glued on. "First of all, how've you been holding up?"

"Let's stay on target, please," Dad snaps.

She closes her eyes, then launches right into it: Some of the students and their parents—no, she can't say who—started throwing a fit over everyone being questioned during school hours between finals, which is the only time it's allowed to take place. One of the parents knows a guy who knows a guy who likely helped feed this to the local press.

"Obviously we can't know for sure, so please don't quote me on that, but that's my . . . off-the-record guesstimate about how this happened. I wanted you to know that, frankly, it's as much of a headache for us as it is for you two."

"I *sincerely* doubt that," Dad says.

Principal Graham is aggressively massaging the back of her own head, like she's trying for a self-induced aneurysm. She clears her throat. "The other reason we called you down here— do you want to wait for Mrs. Turner?"

"I don't know where she's at; go ahead," Dad says.

"The other reason we called you down here is because we've finished looking into things," she continues. "The report is being written—it will be seen by *none* of the students or parents, but we can get you a copy by end of day tomorrow, if you'd like to read it."

Now Dad gets a whole new look on his face—like Principal Graham is here to write him a lottery check.

"Well, there you go!" he says, exuberant. He smacks his own thigh. "So you found the guy! Let's talk about what you're going to do to him."

My heart climbs. My hands have come loose, flopping around me like they're trying to escape my arms.

Principal Graham's eyebrows arch, and I can immediately tell she doesn't have good news. "It's important you both know we did talk to a number of students—believe me when I say we left no stone unturned."

"*Let's talk about what you're going to do to him.*"

"Mr. Turner, I'm telling you right now that we weren't able to make any determinations about who was responsible for this. I know that's not what you were—"

"Now, *wait*—"

"—*not what you were hoping to hear*, but please listen. In the interest of managing expectations, I'm going to just let you both know—and again, you can read all this yourself—as far as we can tell, no one who was on the trip saw or heard anything, nor did anyone hear about anything. And I mean anything at all. Which of *course* is not to say it didn't happen, Owen," she says, giving me a nod. "I want to be clear on that. But given the scope and constraints of this, we feel we've done all we can."

"So what I'm hearing is, this is a big ol' CYA maneuver," Dad says. (CYA—*Cover Your Ass.*) "Am I getting warm?"

"Mr. Turner—"

"Don't get me wrong, it's a *hell* of a magic trick," he continues. "The local media chucklefucks throw some fairy dust, yell 'abracadabra,' and suddenly—poof!—you've all disappeared up your own assholes." He claps his hands to his face, feigning wide-eyed wonder.

"This whole thing has had its peaks and valleys," Principal Graham says, even-tempered. "We gathered a lot of information except the name—"

"Oh, oh—that's *all* you missed, is it? There's the ringing sound of success." Dad unclicks his pen against his knee. "*Other than THAT, Mrs. Lincoln, how'd you enjoy the play?"*

"I understand you're frustrated—"

"If I have to hear one more time that you're just as upset as we are," he says, "I will physically leave."

She tries to placate him by getting into the boring logistical stuff: the fact that the findings won't be public and that guidance counselors are available anytime if I need them. She explains that the report will be stripped of any identifying info, then sent to the State Board of Education and General Assembly, and eventually its data will become part of a larger report for two congressional committees. All this mess reduced to a few numbers and components for colored bar graphs.

"But this won't be a part of Owen's educational record in any way," Mat With One T adds.

"Why would we care about that? He's a month away from graduation," Dad snaps. "As is, by the way, his attacker. A competent administration would be slapping the guy with an indictment, not a diploma. He's in your database; he's in this *building*, and I seem to be the only person left in the room who feels that should make him easier to apprehend than goddamn D. B. Cooper. So I'm not leaving here unless, and until, you can answer me: What else are you going to *do* about this?"

"What I've just told you is the extent of what we can do," Principal Graham says. "Protocols are in place for how we do our job—"

"I'm not telling you how to do your job; I'm telling you how everyone else does theirs, and asking you to do the same exact thing. If the state police were taking the lead on this, they'd take the mind-blowing step of continuing their search until the guy is caught. But you're telling me if we ask for the same effort and accountability from the folks actually in charge of the students, teachers, and chaperones who were a part of the incident, all we get is the investigative equivalent of smacking a pipe with a wrench?"

"Mr. Turner, what more would you have us do?"

"For starters: *Don't set down the wrench.*"

"To be frank—this is coming from the powers-that-be. I know that's not what you'd like—"

"What I'd *like* is at least one idea that the powers-that-be didn't yank right out of their rear ends. We're dealing with something that only gets reported one out of five times," Dad says. "You all are doing a wonderful job of demonstrating why."

Principal Graham doesn't make eye contact with me, but I know the part she isn't saying: that they can't do anything more to help me if I'm not going to tell them who it was.

She says, "If you want to file an appeal, that's an option—"

"Oh, more red tape—yeah, perfect. I need that like I need assholes for eyeballs." Dad climbs to his feet. The dismissal bell rings over the loudspeaker. He opens his mouth again when there's a knock on the door.

Mom peeks her head in.

"So sorry I'm late," she says.

"Don't be." He wrenches the door open and gestures for me to follow him. "Come on, let's go."

"Dad," I say, antsy. He's tearing his way out of the admin wing, declaring, "I can't be back there right now."

In the front lobby, students are emptying out all around for their buses. I'm horrified to spot Austin, Vic, Beth, and Lily gathering near the far bench. At first they all wave, but their smiles peel off when they see the circus spilling out of the front office: me, my mother, Principal Graham, and Mat With One T, all chasing after the raging bull known as my father.

Mom swats at his shoulder, stopping him. "What's going on? What's the school doing?"

"The *school*," Dad says, "as a consolation prize for our pain and stress, is handing us a big ol' heaping bucket of fuck-all. They couldn't find anything, so they're giving up. Whole thing's a wash."

"They're what? Oh, come on——"

"No no no, if you *think* about it, it makes sense, okay," Dad says, slapping his hands together. "See, when they started this whole goat rodeo, they were on the right track. Granted it was only to cover their rear ends, but still. . . . They accidentally got something right. So naturally the Board of Education stepped in to make sure a thing like that never happens again."

His voice is thundering halfway across the lobby. I tug at his sleeve. "Seriously, can we talk about this somewhere else?"

"Yeah, come on, let's——" Mom starts to say, but then Principal Graham steps up.

"Steve, please, let's go back inside," Principal Graham says. You know things are out of control when she looks panicked. "I understand you're disappointed, so why don't we——"

Dad bursts out into an empty, joyless laugh. The hallway chatter softens.

"Okay." He decapitates the air with his hand. "Just so you're aware—first of all, I can't tell you how unimpressed I am by the customer service routine right now. Talk to me like a person, please. I don't need hand-holding, I don't need the dog-and-pony show; I just, *just* need action. I need you to do the thing you've been mandated to do by the Department of Education, the DOJ, the OCR, Titles One through Nine, Pennsylvania state law, and me."

People are staring.

Phones are out.

My legs are made of stone.

"Let's go," Mom urges Dad. She turns to the others and says, "He and I should go."

"Please accept my personal apology," Principal Graham says to her, unflinching but more urgent now.

Dad stiffens.

"Are you—that's—holy *shit*." He takes a half step back, looking her up and down. "For eight hours a day, we trust you with our child. Then I find out he gets attacked—*sexually assaulted*—under your care, and I'm told to let you fix it on your own. My job was to trust the process, and your extremely simple task was to find out which of his classmates did this. Instead, what happens? You all roll up the clown car, put my kid through hell—he's spent five of his final eight weeks of high school getting an extremely public vivisection—and now we're sitting here with bad ideas, bungled execution, and a grand total of no fucking results. And given all of that, your *best possible* version of an acceptable response is to say, *Hey, don't get too worked up, because we found a lot of information... except for the one thing we needed to fucking find?!*" He gapes at her like she's grown an extra head. "*No*, I don't accept your personal apology!"

I want to melt through the ground.

Dissolve. Disappear. Disintegrate.

Instead I stay right here.

Here.

People watching and people listening and people recording.

Not everyone, but most of them.

(*Shitshitshit.*)

Then I hear it from across the lobby. The nightmare chatter. Surreptitious exchanges between my classmates.

"Is that him?"

"Oh shit, I think that's him."

"Wait, hold on . . . it was a guy?"

My classmates are saying it to each other softly, but it's all I hear. It drowns out my father, who's now being physically led out of the front lobby by my mother, and Principal Graham is barking at everyone to go to their buses, and I'm tearing out the front door of the school—not following my parents but splitting off as far away as I can get. I hear people calling after me . . . lots of them. Mom. Principal Graham.

Lily.

I keep running.

It's drizzling and mucky out—I don't care. I sprint around the side of the school until I hit the fence bordering the football field, leaning back against it and sliding to the ground.

Soon Lily is standing on the other side of the parking lot, about the same distance as on the day I broke my arm. This time, though, she's staring at me with a face I'll never forget: It has the rest of our story written all over it, and there's nothing left but anger and endings.

TWENTY-TWO

LILY STARTS RUNNING AS FAST AS SHE CAN TOWARD the football field—right past me. I climb to my feet, wiping the wet mulch off my butt as I chase after her.

"Do not *fucking* follow me," she warns, but she slows down enough that I catch up to her.

"Lily, come on, let's just talk. Let's talk!"

"*God!*" She grabs my wrist, dragging me toward the bleachers until we find a dry patch under them. Garbage is littered all around our feet. She backs away from me so we're almost ten feet apart, facing each other like we're stepping into a cage match.

"Tell me right now: Is it you?"

I bullshit her: "Who?"

"Holy shit." She clamps a hand to her mouth, shaking her head. Her huge, shocked eyes are fixed squarely on my face. "It is you."

"Listen to me—hey, *listen.*" I snap at my bracelet, my fingers fumbling. My whole body shakes; my mind is in damage control mode, but every page inside it is blank. Finally I manage: "I'm not the one who told the school. Okay? I *swear*, I didn't want this to get out—"

"Well, you told somebody!" Her hand drops. "Who'd you tell?

Austin? Vic? I swear, if the entire group has been covering this up . . . oh my *God*."

Lily starts to pace, arms tucked close to her chest—the same thing I do when I feel cornered. She looks disoriented, like she just woke up somewhere strange.

"No, I didn't tell them; no one's been lying to you—"

"*You have*, dude!"

"I didn't want this to get out." I repeat it like it helps somehow. I grab my own head—everything inside me feels upside down. "The only person I told was this one guy, and I barely even knew him—"

"Are you *kidding* me?" She gapes. "You never said a word to me, but you went to someone you barely knew and said—"

"I promise, it's more complicated than that—"

"—on that note, what *did* you say, exactly?" She looks me up and down. "Let's talk about this."

"I don't feel like going back over the specifics—"

"Wh—*wow*." Lily shakes her head again. "So after a month of lying about this—talking to a *stranger* about it without saying a word to me—you don't want to go over it the first time it comes up because you don't *feel like it?*"

Thunder rumbles in the distance, rolling off the treetops. I put my finger to my ear to adjust to the noise. My boiling panic is re-condensing into irritation, anger—I want to fix things, but I'm getting fed up at the web Lily is spinning.

"Just so we're clear," I snap at her, in a harder voice, "I tried to talk to you about it."

"What does *that* mean? When did you ever once say something about this?"

"*Right* after it happened!" I try to pace, but there are only a few inches of dry space to my side, so I just shift my weight.

"Right after?" she asks. "Really? So what time of the night was that?"

"Okay, it wasn't *right*-right after, but on the bus ride home the next day!" I stab a finger in her direction. "No—do *not* tell me you don't remember that."

"So . . . okay. Let's recap." Lily clenches her arms together, staring at the wet ground. "You were there on the trip, the— *thing*—happened . . ."

"The *thing*?"

"—*after it happened*, you hung out with me, with everyone, for the rest of the night, right? And you didn't say anything!"

"I was acting off! No, no—you can't tell me I was being my usual self. Something was off! I was quiet; I didn't talk—"

"I thought you were just on edge because of coming out," she says. "I'm sorry I assumed, but you can't blame me for that. You just can't."

"You laughed at me." More anger licks at my insides as I step closer to her. "No—when I tried to talk to you about it on the bus, and tell you something happened, you laughed at me."

"I thought you were . . . kidding around, or something! You were being weird and kept saying things 'went wrong' and you were like, barely coherent—"

"Yeah, *that* wasn't a clue—"

"*I'M SORRY*, okay!" Lily balls her hands into fists, her wet hair sticking to her face. "I'm sorry I was confused, and zoned out from being on the bus for two hours, and didn't understand what you were saying—"

"I was trying to tell you I'd gotten hurt. *All* I needed you to do was listen to me—"

"That's not fair, O; not *remotely* fucking fair—"

"Jesus Christ—"

"Yeah, you can say that again—"

"*Jesus fucking Christ.*"

"You try to talk to me about something once, then you never

bring it up again—"

"What about later that week? Hm?" I take another step closer to her—I can't believe her version of this is so different than mine. No way is this her earnest, unironic take on how things played out. "A few days later, during spring break, I specifically said I needed to talk to you about something, and you immediately changed the subject. You knew, Lily, you fucking knew—"

"I *KNEW*? Are you for *real*?"

"You didn't know exactly what I was going to say; but you knew it was bad shit that we needed to discuss, and you didn't want to hear it, so you avoided it. God forbid I steer the conversation for once."

"So, what . . . you tried to bring it up twice, then dropped it forever?"

"Hey, at least I tried!"

"Try *hard-er!*"

"What for?" When I see the look on her face, I hold up my hands. "I'm really asking. I wanted to talk about it; I tried twice, but when that didn't work, I decided to drop it and move on. That was *my* decision. I should be allowed to forget about it, keep it to myself, whatever—"

"YOU TOLD THE *SCHOOL!*"

"No I didn't! You are *not* hearing me—I didn't." I smack my own hand. "I told someone else, who told the school, then about fifty-seven other things happened—"

"Do you have any idea—Owen—"

"*What?*"

"—do you have *any idea* how little *difference* that makes?" She shakes her head at me, her eyes on fire. "All the students know now, the police know now; me, Beth, Austin, Vic, and half the graduating class got interrogated; the local paper wrote a story about you; meanwhile I'm sitting in the dark for all of this, and after I learn about it, you're seriously going to stand there and think it's important to point out that you weren't technically the one who hit *send on the report?*" She glares at me, openmouthed again. "Let's not even get into the fact that I had to learn about this from a tantrum by your *dad*, more than a month after you're claiming this happened—"

"Okay." I cut her off, shaking my head. "*Stop.*"

"Don't tell me what to do."

"I mean it." I hold out both hands, fighting the urge to explode. "Stop doing that right now."

"Doing *what?*" Her mouth is open in a half-laugh, half-WTF expression.

"Talking about a thing that happened to me like it may or may not have happened to me. This isn't Schrödinger's cat; it is not up for debate."

"It is."

"Stop."

"It is!"

"I SAID TO STOP!"

TWENTY-THREE

March 10th — Senior Year

Journal:

~~I'm not sure how to start this.~~

~~This isn't something that I want to write down, but I~~ ~~think it's impor~~

I remember it started with the crimson light in the window.

It was hours after I'd come out to everyone, and I was laying in my dorm bed cuddling with Lily. She'd snuck over and Austin was out for a walk with Beth, so it was just her and I. The room was almost pitch black, but the fiery red light from the library roof reached through the window so it was spilled all over the bed, highlighting both our torsos.

I remember squeezing her, and her squeezing back.

I remember she said, with a smile in her voice, "I'm really proud of you for today."

I remember thanking her, and kissing her, and us making out with all our usual fun and familiar noises. We fell back onto the pillow, facing each other. Then she reached down to rub over my pants, and I shook my head.

"Not right now," I murmured.

I remember her asking if it was because she smelled or something, and I assured her it wasn't—I was just exhausted, and in more of a cuddly mood than a sex mood, and I hadn't brought condoms, and I wasn't comfortable taking clothes off when Austin could be back any second. Lots of offhand reasons.

I remember the relief I felt when she said that was fine, and we went back to kissing and laughing together.

Then, the chill of her fingers on my bare chest as I realize she'd unbuttoned my shirt.

"Hey," I said softly, in a *dude, come on* voice. "Stop."

I remember her pointing out, in her usual teasing manner, that we didn't have to keep our shirts on to make out. I remember I started to fidget, so she grabbed my wrists to calm me and told me to relax.

I remember the pressure on my chest.

The red light in the air.

Lily on top of me.

TWENTY-FOUR

THE WIND WHIPS RAIN UNDER THE BLEACHERS ONTO both of us, splashing our skin. Lily steps back.

"You need to stop yelling," she says, digging her heel into the mud. "You're not being rational right now, O; do you get that?"

"You raped me."

Finally, for once, I knock a beat of silence into the sparring match. And there we stand—staring at each other, stunned. Panting even though we've barely moved.

"That is *not* what happened," she says.

"What, so I'm lying?"

"You're . . . confused."

"I'm . . ." I work my mouth once, twice. Switches flying back and forth in my brain, blowing circuit breakers and sending mixed signals every which way. "You can't be *serious*. You're upset that I didn't talk to you about it, and now that I'm trying to, you're shitting all over this."

"Can I say something?"

"Is that not what you're doing right now?"

"Saying something?"

"Shitting all over this."

"*Can I say something?*"

"*No!*" I start to pace now . . . circling her. Trembling with vindication. I only realize now how much I was counting on her sympathy—for her to be completely broken up over this, begging to help take this pain away now that it was out in the open. I didn't expect a knife fight over the facts.

"You were *nervous,*" she insists. "I'm not trying to upset you. But what if you're wrong about this?"

"What if I had a dick growing out of my forehead?"

"Do you?"

"Way to take this seriously."

"You started it."

"You raped me."

"What if I didn't?"

"You did."

"No. Owen."

"Yes. Lily."

She grabs at the air. "Okay. Stop and think about this—"

"I'm going to blow your mind and tell you I've done that a time or two already."

"—*think about this;* listen to me and think. You were nervous, and . . . I love you, but you know how you get when you're nervous—"

"Assaulted?"

"*Finicky.* I thought you were okay with it—we were making out!"

"That happens all the time."

"You were hard!"

"That happens all the time too. Do you have a point?"

"You're being unfair." Lily repeats the line from before. "You've already made up your mind, and instead of hearing me out so we can sort through what happened, you're just yelling at me."

"What is there to go *over?* I said no, and you did it anyway."

I blink hard, beating back a pile of dark images. "Jesus Christ, did you need to have sex with me *right then?* We could've done it the next day—I said that! You could've had it any other time—"

"Whoooa." She bursts out laughing, but her face is filled with a scowl. She holds up a hand like a traffic cop. "First of all, bud, let's not talk about your dick like it's some gift from God—"

"You know that's not how I meant it."

"*Second* of all, you're missing the point!"

"Yeah? I think I'm a lot fucking closer to it than you are!"

"The *point* is, I didn't know you had an issue with us having sex that night. *If* I was aware of that, I wouldn't have done it; but I wasn't, so I did. *What part of that doesn't track with you?*"

"WHAT PART OF 'STOP' DOESN'T *TRACK WITH YOU?*"

"*It was you and me!*" She stomps her foot. "Dude! It was you and me."

"Who cares?"

"We've had sex a hundred times before."

"Who *cares?*"

"*Me!*" She raises her arm, glaring. "Am I supposed—you want to get into this? Fine. Am I supposed to believe that we've had sex without issue a hundred times, but that time on March ninth, it was *rape?* O—come on. This is murky. At *best.* I know you know that."

"Why?"

"Why *what*, dude?"

"Why is it murky?"

"Because it's you and me, and we clearly have different definitions of some of these terms. Given all that, who's to say if anything . . . *wrong* . . . even *happened?*"

"On March ninth, I did."

"You said it was rape?"

"I SAID NO!" Everything is pouring out of me: all my anger,

all my bitterness, all my stress, all my sanity. "I said *stop;* I said, 'Hey, Lily, get the *fuck* off me.' This isn't complicated. I'm so sick of this—"

"Okay, let's just take a minute—"

"Let's not!" I squeeze my arms, my voice tightening. "Do you seriously think you can spin this in a way that's going to make me go, 'Well, you're right, I guess this didn't happen to me'?"

"I'm not trying to—"

"Because you can't."

"—but if me explaining this can help you, O, then I want to do that! That's what I'm saying!"

"You can't! That's what *I'm* saying!"

We stare at each other, both out of breath again. There's nowhere left for either of us to go, and we can both feel it.

The rain comes down, down, down, down.

Lily sniffles. Then she looks at the ground and says to it, almost offhand, "Well. This relationship is over."

"Yeah." I say it to the ground too. I don't know what to feel about any of it . . . all I know is how much invigoration I get out of saying that. Out of taking the plunge, cutting the cord that's been wrapped around my neck for months now—feeling that festering urgency finally reach its tipping point.

Lily takes a step back from me.

I wait for her to apologize.

I wait for her to say she'll miss this.

I wait for her to tell me to go to hell.

But all she says is, "I can't believe this. I really can't."

Then, "I'm going to go now."

And she does.

TWENTY-FIVE

March 10th—Senior Year cont.

Journal:

~~I don't know if I can remember~~

I remember her telling me to relax as she pulled my jeans and boxers down.

"Not right now. Come on." My irritation gave way to mild panic—not because I cared about being exposed in front of her, but because she wasn't stopping. Why wasn't she stopping? I was about to tell her we could do it tomorrow, that I'd make it up to her; but then she was back on top of me, covering my mouth with kisses every time I tried to open it. I twisted my head away, but she got upset and asked me why I was being so weird. Except she didn't say it like a question. She wasn't really asking.

"Let's just do this," she whispered in my ear.

"Stop—come on. Lily, *seriously*. Get off. Li-ly." My voice climbed as I started to squirm under her. Saying her name like it was someone else's. Feeling like I was in a car barreling toward a brick wall, and the harder I pressed on the brakes, the more panicked I got when I realized they didn't work. The horrified realization that *this is happening, I am about to crash into this, and there's no stopping it.*

"Shh!" Lily covered my mouth between whisper-giggles. "O, you are *so* loud."

My breath came in fast through my nose, and when I tried to sit up, she slid up my chest and whispered R-rated things in my ear and cooed at how my body responded. She was naked now, grinning wickedly and kissing me and on top of me and kissing me and on top of me.

Cut to:

Cut to:

Cut to:

I was going to have to shove her off.

I raised my arm—except it didn't move. Why didn't it move? Had I been drugged? No, this was all me . . . my body was going numb the same way it did when I fell asleep: poisoning its own defenses when I needed them the most.

The room was smothering me on all sides, locking my limbs in place as my muscles shut down. I heard Lily say, "Come on, stop being dumb," as she moved and held my dead wrists against the bed frame. And now I was having sex I didn't want to have and kissing someone I didn't want to kiss; my body was made of cinderblocks, and everything was wrong.

Please get off, I said—it was more urgent than before, but my voice was softer instead of louder. Meek. A polite request.

"Come on, you want to do this," Lily said.

(I don't want to do this.)

"LTL," she whispered.

All I could do was latch onto the light from the window and whisper one thing over and over until it got smaller and smaller; down, down, down, down.

TWENTY-SIX

Stop.
Stop
Stop.
Stop.
Stop.
Stop.
Stop.
Stop.
Stop.
Stop.
Stop.
Stop.
Stop.
Stop.
Stop.
Stop.
Stop.
Stop.

TWENTY-SEVEN

I STAY UNDER THE BLEACHERS UNTIL THE RAINWATER finds its way into my shoes, soaking my socks. At first I flinch, then I wince and step into the downpour—one leg, the other, then my whole body.

It's that unwanted validation: the thing you dreaded happening has finally happened. And now it's done with, and the fallout is exactly as ugly as you were expecting.

I take the late bus with all the freshmen.

When it lets me off at the neighborhood gate, I rocket through the rain to the playground and lay down flat on the slide. My arms and legs hang over the edge. The metal is cold, my clothes are soaked, my head is stuffy, my body is numb. I keep opening my eyes every few seconds, waiting for Lily to appear . . . to break down and tell me how sorry she is for everything. And the reality leaves me drained and disgusting.

TWENTY-EIGHT

Fucking disgusting.
Look at us.
Oh my God, look at us!
Stop it.
Disgusting.
Us.
LOOK AT IT!
Oh my God.
Stop it.
Stop Us.
You.
Stop.
STOP.
Me.
Disgusting!
Disgusting
me.

STORY TWO

NAIL BY NAIL

ONE

LIMBO.

That's what everyone at school is calling it. It starts with the fact that our teachers tend to schedule senior final exams for the first week of May, since the AP tests on that material are the following week. The backwards result is that, while we're required to keep showing up for another three weeks, the senior-level classes have no cirriculum left to learn and no exams left to take.

So: Limbo.

I'll give props to my classmates for one thing—they may be nosy and worship at the altar of rumor, but the majority of them aren't downright *dicks*. In a lot of places with your run-of-the-mill teenagers, videos of Dad's tantrum would've gone viral, and I'd be the subject of twice as much gossip as before. But it had this weird opposite effect—once everyone had a face to pin to the Lanham incident and the interrogations ended, people stopped giving a shit and went back to their lives.

(Limbo.)

In the immediate aftermath of my breakup with Lily a few weeks back, I started out in rough shape: I'd lay in bed for long stretches, tight-chested and saying to myself, "You're healing from an injury. This is going to hurt until it's better, so here's how we soothe the symptoms." Music. TV. Porn. Sleep.

But then I'd start distracting myself by zoning in the Studio, and I did research on everything we'd argued about—the fact that one out of three rapes are committed by a partner, and 15 percent of culprits are minors. After a few days, I found myself thinking, *good riddance.* She did this and she knows it.

But I miss the group.

They don't know why Lily and I broke up, but they know that it happened. She probably told them. In the days that followed, all three of them sent me some version of, "Hey dude, just wanted to let you know I'm sorry for all the shit you're going through."

I wasn't sure how to reply. *Thanks? Appreciate it?* Anything longer would have felt like I was trying to talk about it, which I wasn't. Eventually I got tired of thinking about it and just didn't respond. I haven't hung out with them since the fallout, because I don't want to see Lily if she's there, and I don't want to deal with their questions if she's not.

That's the part that kills me: For three years, I dreamed of this as being the fairytale era of my life . . . the part where I could kick back at grad parties, go to senior week with my girlfriend, and ride the high of graduation. A summer full of beach trips with my crew before we all hug in the rain and say our tearful goodbyes.

I watch a lot of TV.

Mom lets me wallow for a week, then takes matters into her own hands one Monday morning.

"Hey," she says, peeking her head in my room. "Sleep in."

"Huh? What about school?"

"You're home sick today. Purple cramps."

Purple cramps isn't an actual illness. It's a code phrase Mom and I came up with when I was younger: Every now and then, she'd take off work and keep me home from school so the two of us could have a mental health day together. It started during one of Dad's deployments and has since become a whole fixed routine: After sleeping in as late as we want, we go to the family diner in the plaza and split the Number 3 breakfast platter. Then we go to the department store and each get one thing we want. I was obsessed with collecting Tic Tacs when I was younger, so it was usually mega packs of those. But today it's a personal coffee maker for my college dorm.

"Which of these do you think you'd like best?" Mom asks, sweeping her arm out in front of the aisle.

I pull my spreadsheet comparing models out of my pocket— I always do my research in advance of shopping trips. "We're looking for the . . . K238 model. I think it's that one up top."

"How about this one instead?" she asks, pointing to the box below it. "Ooh, it looks fancier."

"And twice as expensive. It's because that one has brew strength control and stuff."

"Well, if it has *brew strength control*—"

"And stuff."

"—and *stuff!* I think now we have to get it."

"Mom, you don't need to spend that kind of money on me."

But she's already setting it in the cart. "You've earned it, college boy. College man."

(I haven't, but I don't argue.)

"How're you holding up with the Lily stuff?" she asks, pretending to read the label on a shelf unit. I'd told her that Lily and I broke up, but I said it was because Lily needed some time to process what happened to me. Not quite total bullshit.

"Not great."

"I'm sorry, bud."

"Thanks. Kind of sucks."

"Well, you know what? Sometimes, looking back, we're thankful that we didn't end up with what we thought we wanted at the time."

"I guess." As we head for the next aisle, I ask, "What about you and Dad?"

She stiffens a little at the mention of him. I'm not sure whether she threw him out or he left by choice, but all I know is when I got back to the house after my fight with Lily, he was gone. Left to stay up at his cabin for a few weeks, Mom said. As far as I know, he's still there, and as far as I care, it's where he belongs.

"When I met him?" Mom purses her lips. "Talk about jumping through hoops. Well, the first few times I talked to him, it was just to figure out when he'd be done with the treadmill—we went to the same gym."

"You guys met at the *gym?*"

"I never told you that? Yep. And one day we both got there and someone else was using our treadmill."

I smile a little. I have a special treadmill at the neighborhood gym too. Maybe I inherited that tendency from them.

"So we got talking during the wait, and that was that. But then, those first few dates—Good *Lord.* It was like I was being vetted. Your dad has a lifetime of trust issues, O. *A lifetime.* He views everything through the lens of the danger it could present. He's so sure that everything in the world is out there to let him down. If it hasn't yet, it will. So he tries to plan accordingly. Which means he feels even *more* upset when things still go wrong. Yeah, not a great system."

I don't tell her what I'm thinking: that that's exactly how I feel about the world sometimes.

"A couple years into the relationship," Mom continues, "this is around when I was expecting a ring . . . I had him do a month of inpatient treatment for his PTSD. Well, talk about a letdown . . . that didn't do anything for him. He tried pot—"

"*Dad* smoked weed?"

"Ohhh yeah." She closes her eyes and nods, blowing a raspberry. "Total pothead. I'm talking, contact high if you *looked* at the guy too hard, know what I'm saying?"

"Did it help?"

"Not how he wanted it to. It was only for a few months. Counseling was a non-starter, too. I tried to get him to look into prescription meds, but he got spooked when a buddy of his tried that and wound up dead by suicide. Obviously that wasn't the cause, but again . . . all possible dangers."

I wait for her to add something to that, but she doesn't.

"What's going to happen when he gets back?" I ask.

Mom stops the cart, thinking on it.

"We'll have to see," she says. "He still wants to find the person who—you know. That's really important to him."

"Important enough to throw a tantrum in front of half the school? Like a petulant fucking child?"

She studies the cart handle quietly.

"Sometimes I think he's a sociopath," I say.

"No, sweetheart, he's your dad."

"That's not the opposite of a sociopath."

"I get it. But with Dad, responding with equal aggression only turns the temperature up and makes it worse for everyone."

"But *why?*" I huff. I'm so sick of this shit. Why does Dad

always get to be the one who explodes but no one else can set a toe out of line? Why can't I ever be the one who's allowed to blow up at him, and he can find a way to deal with it?

I snap at my bracelet. "I wish no one ever found out."

"I know." Mom's voice tightens. "Have you reconsidered therapy?"

I shake my head. Mom's been on my back to see a therapist since I was twelve, but the closest guy is an hour north and I couldn't tolerate doing it over the phone. With everything that's gone on recently, the argument has resurfaced.

"Okay," she says. "But I really want you to consider it for college."

"I don't need to talk about it."

"But I want you to feel like you can, bud. That's the key. If you're ever in trouble—and this goes for college, too—I don't want your first thought to be, 'My parents are going to kill me.' No matter what it is, how much money it'll cost, however late in the night . . . Anytime you're in trouble, I want your first thought to always be, 'I need to talk to my mom and dad.'"

I let that sink in.

"And your dad . . . right now, he's just processing all this," she adds. "When he gets back, let me talk to him."

"Mom." I hold both hands in front of me like I'm trying to hand her something. "When has that ever, ever worked?"

TWO

March 10th — Senior Year

Journal:

Look what I did.

That was the mantra that turned around in my head as Austin drove me home from the school, the Lanham bus having just dropped us off. My attempt to confront Lily on the bus had fallen apart, and my stomach churned the whole car ride home.

I squeezed my eyes shut against a thousand images from only ten hours ago.

Squirming.

Saying *stop.*

Again and again and again.

Light the color of blood.

Can't breathe.

Breathe.

(Can't.)

"Here we are, sir," Austin said. We were in front of my house. He tried to meet my eyes. "Are you good? You seem quiet."

I slipped the mask back on and grinned. "Yeah, totally. My stomach's just upset."

"Probably my driving, sorry. Hey—so much respect for coming out yesterday, man. We've got your back. Obviously."

I nodded.

"You sure you're good?"

"I'm just tired." Always the lie.

"I feel that—get some sleep. Enjoy spring break. If you need anything, just say the word."

I stumbled through my front door. My parents sat blinking at me from the living room, and I remembered the text I'd sent them. My brain knew they were processing my coming out and all, but my body was waiting for them to offer help after what had happened to it.

How do you not see? How can you not TELL? I wanted to yell at them. I felt physically exhausted, like I'd spent all night hauling bags of cement. Worn. Surely I should've had some mark on me—blood caked around a wound or scars on my body.

(Nothing.)

Finally Dad said, "Are you in or are you out? Shut the damn door."

It happened all at once: I choked on my breath, then the contents of my stomach started to come with it. I swallowed hard to force it back down, but a bit of bile leaked its way through my teeth onto our living room floor. Both of my parents were on their feet now, and I was waiting for Dad to curse or yell about me ruining the goddamn carpet, but all he said was, "Buddy!" the same time as Mom saying, "Owen, sweetheart." Soon my throat was on fire, Mom was behind me with a glass of water, and my father was on his hands and knees with paper towels to wipe up my mess.

Look what I did.

"Let's get you upstairs, hon," Mom said. Her hands hovered near my shoulders. "Okay to touch you?"

My head whipped back and forth.

"Alright, no big deal," she said. There she was, same as always—the mom who's not fazed by the crisis in front of her. "Steve, have you got—"

"I've got *this* handled," he said definitively, his voice making me jump. He pointed at the stairs. "You get him all squared away. He looks like death warmed up."

I hated everything about this. Now they were here and fawning over me exactly as I'd wanted them to do two seconds ago but it was only because I threw up and

LOOK WHAT I DID!

I blinked and I was in my bed in my boxers. Mom was next to me asking, "Do you want me to get anything?"

I shook my head again.

"Buddy?" she said next, and it was in that tentative way she used before saying something risky. "I know you're not up to talking right now, and we can do that later. But before you go to sleep, it's important to me that I let you know I'm proud of you for sending us that text. And everything you're worrying about right now . . . it's all going to work out."

Thrashing. The hand over my mouth. Pressure on my chest. Paralysis.

"It really is. And neither of us are upset with you in any way—I'm not; your dad isn't—and we both love you. So much. Okay?"

Look what I did.

LOOK WHAT—
"Can you nod to let me know you heard me?"
I did.
"Okay, bud." She made a kissing sound instead of actually doing it.
I looked over to my dirty clothes.
It was my last thought before I slipped into a world of darkened, violent nightmares.
Look what I did. Look what I did. Look what I did.

I woke up disgusting: Vomit aftertaste coated my mouth. Sweat soaked my body and matted down my hair, sticking it to my scalp.
When I checked my phone, I had one text—it was from Lily:

Soo how'd your parents react?? :)

I wriggled out of my underwear, ripped the sweat-soaked sheets off the bed, and threw everything in the wash.

THREE

I GET LILY'S TEXT THE DAY AFTER COLLEGE SHOPPING with Mom:

Can I come over for a bit to talk?

I cycle through all the blistering responses I want to send. How I refuse to be her doormat. How I should've called her out on everything sooner. How what she did was wrong.

But I owe her a goodbye that doesn't involve us biting each other's heads off under the bleachers. Plus, there's one thing that I need to hear straight from her own mouth: an admission of guilt.

Lily finds me in the Studio, just as I finish writing about a boy who lives with flowers and on anniversaries they give each other bouquets of humans. I've left the door open so sunlight fills up the space. The air is humid and smells like a summer morning.

"Knock-knock," she says. She's in white shorts and a blue tank top with sunflowers all over it—totally dressed for the weather. Seeing her splashes my insides with ice water. I thumb my bracelet.

"Coffee—how'd I know you'd do that?" Lily asks, grimacing at me as I hand her one of the two mugs on my desk.

As we sit down on opposite ends of the Studio couch—
everything silent except for the cicadas in the yard—I realize I
have no idea how to begin. I try to let myself calmly drift through
the moment. Because I'm indifferent to this, right? This isn't
going to be one of those bullshit scenarios where she says sorry
for everything, and I fall on my knees like, 'That's okay, let's forgive and forget, see how cute we are!'

"What's that?" I ask her. I've just noticed a shopping bag at
her feet.

"Oh." Lily blushes. "This is your stuff. That you left at my
house."

Right.

"There's also a gift I was going to give you for graduation, but
don't feel like you have to keep it," she says. "I just didn't have
anything else to do with it."

"Oh. Thanks."

For a few long minutes, there we sit—sipping our drinks, scoff-
ing at the awkwardness of not speaking. We stare out at the lawn,
then to each other, then at the lawn again.

"It's good to see you," Lily blurts out. "I realized when I was
walking over, I think this is the longest we've gone without seeing each other. It was, what . . . eighteen days?"

"Yeah . . . wow. Nope, wait," I say, pointing at her. "There was the
trip you took to Boston a few summers ago. That was three weeks."

"Ooh, you're right. Damn, dude."

As much as I hate to admit it, there's an intense ache at seeing
her curled up on the couch in here again. Like if I could just wipe
my mind of what happened, we could return to being our happy
little selves and invite the others over for a movie night. But this
is where we are. Here.

"Okay," Lily says, grabbing at invisible rope. "Can we just . . .
rip the scab off?"

I tuck my knees up on the couch so I can face her. "Sure."

She mimes tearing off a piece of skin.

"I've spent a lot of time thinking about our argument," she continues. "I said some . . . really not-okay stuff to you."

"Yeah. You did."

She shakes her head. "O, I'm sorry. I'm so, so sorry, for everything I said, all of it. I'll spend the rest of my life saying that if that's what you want."

Nice try. "I wouldn't bother."

I wait for the return jab, but it never comes. Instead she nods along with me.

"That's fair," she says. "I've been thinking—first of all, are you okay talking about this?"

I fold my arms behind my head. "Am I okay with, like, talking about the Lanham trip? Sure. But to be honest, this whole thing has sort of screwed me up, and I'm not interested in you putting it under a microscope to try and explain why it shouldn't have screwed me up. *That* would be shitty."

"Wait. Is that what you think I'm here for?" She balks at me. "I'm not. Promise."

"I don't want to get back together."

"I'm not here for that either."

"Alright."

"But I wasn't okay with just . . . leaving things, you know? I want closure; I know you want it too, and that was important to me because, I mean . . . I love you." She winces. "I hope that's okay to say. You have no idea how much this has been weighing on me."

I nod, wincing back. Everything about this hurts.

She drains her cup, turning away from me. Then, "Your desk has the corner chipped off it."

"Yeah. It's a problem."

"Okay. Just making sure you knew."

God *damn* do I miss her—the old Lily. If only she were still in there.

She's not, idiot.

Shut up, I've got this.

"Question for you," says Lily, now talking to her fingernails. She bites one of them.

"You shouldn't do that."

"Ask a question?"

"Bite your nails."

"Oh." She stops for a second, then starts chewing on a different one. "Question. Other than the Lanham trip, do you think things were . . . going well? For us."

I snap at my bracelet again, mulling it over. "Mostly. But you never took no for an answer."

"That's not what I'm talking about."

"That's what I'm talking about. Not just the trip—before. No matter what it was, things always had to be your way." I point to the patch of wall above my desk. "Remember the wreath?"

A few Christmases ago, I bought my first holiday decoration for the Studio—this artificial wreath made out of green garland. It looked *awesome*. Lily said it looked tacky, and I said whatever.

Then we were doing homework in here a few days later, and I went inside to get us a snack. When I came back out, I found that Lily had taken the shiny wreath down and put up a newer, more expensive one she'd bought herself.

She wrinkles her nose at me.

"You were *mad* about that?" she asks. "The new one looked better! Everyone agreed with me."

"I didn't." I shake my head. "You've never taken no for an answer—that's the problem. And you didn't that night at Lanham."

"Just to be clear, this isn't me contradicting you, but I didn't *hear* you that night."

"Wait." That throws me off. "You didn't?"

"No! That's why I was so upset when you called it rape." Her voice buckles. "I wasn't trying to make light of it; of course that's valid. Now, I don't know how many rapes are committed by a partner—"

"I do: It's one in three."

"But my point is that, I think for it to be—*that*—it would mean the person intentionally did it. And I want to be really clear, what happened was still *not* okay, at all—"

"No, it wasn't."

"No, it wasn't," she echoes me, nodding. "But it's like murder: If it's not intentional, it's not murder anymore . . . it's manslaughter, right? It's just . . . the connotations of the word, that bothered me. That's all."

"Okay, well. Three things with that," I say with a scowl. "First of all, manslaughter is the name for third-degree murder, so yeah, that would still count."

"Alright, didn't know that—"

"Second of all, even if they were different, manslaughter's not a whole lot better—"

"Yeah, this analogy worked better in my head—"

"—*third* of all, no matter what it's called, you still fucking killed the guy!"

She doesn't respond.

"This is getting stupid," I say to the floor, putting my head in my hands. "It doesn't matter what you call it. It happened. I'm not comfortable sweeping it under the rug."

Lily gives me an upturned palm, like, *that's fair*. "It's intentions versus actions. It goes without—I *hope* it goes without saying that I didn't mean to upset you that night."

"No. I mean, yes. I guess."

"Doesn't matter," Lily says. "Whether I meant to or not, that's what happened."

I don't like how tepid the word "upset" is, but I nod.

"And *that's* our problem. Right? Because I can tell you a million times that I didn't mean to. But there's no way for me to prove it."

Don't let her derail this.

"That day under the bleachers," I say. "As soon as you found out I was the one who got assaulted on the trip. You didn't ask me who did it."

She blinks. "Huh?"

"You didn't ask me who did it." I force myself to stare her down. "You already knew it was you. How could you know that, if you didn't think you'd done anything wrong?"

Lily shakes her head, rubbing her eyes. "Because you spent the whole trip with me. Oh my God, wait—*did* someone else do something to you?" She looks horrified.

"No." I rub my eyes too, then regroup. "Okay. Fine. How about after the trip? We never had sex after that. I made sure we never got the chance."

"So?"

"You never brought that up either. You never asked me why it stopped; it should've been a clue, but you didn't say a word. It's like you already knew why."

"Wh—*or*, I could tell that you didn't want to, and I was respecting that! I didn't want to pressure you by bringing it up."

Silence.

Her airtight explanations have me all turned around. Ten minutes ago, I was prepared to nail her to the wall with an avalanche of evidence. But the thing is: Could I actually be wrong here? The more I talk about this, the more I realize how many of my conclusions were based off assumptions. I was never taught any of this shit. Maybe it's like she's saying, where it wasn't rape—wow, that is a strong word—but instead some wild miscommunication, a tempest in a teapot. It wouldn't be the first time I've been wrong about how the world works.

And that's just it: She's the one who *showed* me how the world works. Here she is, offering reasonable explanations for everything . . . and here I am, trying to school the person who wrote my rulebook.

"This is random, but before I forget, what's your plan for senior week?" Lily says. "Are you still going to go?"

Shit—I forgot about that. Our group was going to spend a week hanging out at a beach house owned by Austin's grandparents.

"I'm fine with you going," she says. "But don't feel like you have to."

I don't say anything.

"I think that's the worst part of the breakup for me," she continues. "That our group won't be the same, and these are supposed to be the best days. I don't know." She shrugs. "If there was one strong argument for staying together, that'd be it."

I study her for a long time.

"Is that what you're suggesting?" I ask.

She pauses. "I don't want to pretend I *don't* want to do that. Right? Like, being honest . . . would I love if I could just reach over and hug you, and catch you up on everything from these past few weeks, and we'd go back to normal? Obviously. Do I think this misunderstanding—which you have every right to be upset about—is worth how much it's going to suck spending the summer alone? No. But I'll do whatever you want to do. I want to be really clear I'm not trying to like . . . force you."

The feeling of her saying she misses me—that someone misses me—spreads warmth through my whole body. Because I associate everything with her. I associate snow days with her . . . curled up on this couch drinking hot chocolate and talking to my first friend in life. I associate summer nights with her—the rush of the end-of-year celebrations. I think of Christmas, and I think of her. She was the first person I ever gave a gift to, other than my parents. And the first person to ever give me one.

And most of all—above all else—at the end of the day, I *want* her to be right. I want this to be trivial enough to just forget about. I want Lily to still be that kind, golden-hearted girl I remember, the one who introduced me to the group and helped me come out and bought me shoes with her own money.

I want this erased.

Damn it. I'm trying to hold onto my resolve, that determination from when she walked in here. But I've forgotten what that angry voice in my head sounds like.

I ask her, "How would this work?"

She smiles her old smile. "Well. What *I* think we should do is just . . . wipe the whole slate clean. Which, I think is a good idea for two reasons." As always, she's got a plan. "The first is mostly for you. These next few weeks are going to be . . . well, hopefully amazing. I mean . . . our last day of high school is coming up, man."

"I still can't believe it."

"And I know you like things to go according to plan, so I don't want to screw this up for you. I don't want us to go to stuff where we're supposed to be having fun, and instead we're still going back and forth on this. So that's the first reason for my . . . I guess, call it, Relationship Reset."

"What's the second reason?"

"Honestly?" She looks right at me. "I miss you. That's all. I so, so miss you."

I feel my frown loosen.

"You and I both . . ." She hesitates. "We both said and did shitty stuff. And I was thinking about how we could spend hours going back over everything, and it was just like . . . fuck that.

You know? Because all I could keep thinking is . . . I *miss* you, dude. And to me, that's the important part. I keep wanting to find a wand I can wave that'll just take me back to before."

I swallow and add, "That's how I feel too."

"Right!" Her eyes light up. "So let's *do* that! There's no reason we can't just forget about it—not a word to anyone. Okay. So, correct me if I'm wrong, but it sounds like we're on the same page. Yeah? Relationship Reset?"

This is my window. The chance for me to tell her to go to hell with her little plan, to insist that we *do* spend hours dissecting exactly what each of us did wrong, because I'm almost positive I would come out ahead.

Relationship Reset.

"I *might* be okay with trying that," I say. Cautious. "But I have a condition."

Stay in control.

"Anything."

"You take 'no' for an answer. It doesn't matter what it is. Whether it's a wreath, or how I want my hair cut, or anything sex-wise, period. If I don't want to do something, it doesn't happen, and you don't make a big deal about it."

"*Done.*" She's grinning at me from ear to ear, sitting up on her heels now. She slides her way toward me on the couch, raising an eyebrow and saying, "Let's test it. . . . Is this okay?"

I nod.

"Is this okay?" She's straddling me now.

I nod. Then, I let her kiss me. And I kiss her back. We grab each other and moan into each other's mouths, releasing nearly three weeks' worth of pent-up feelings. And it's only a couple of hours later, long after she's left, that I realize: The only thing I set out to get—an admission of guilt—is the only thing I didn't get.

FOUR

THANK *GOD* LILY AND I HAVE WORKED THINGS OUT.

Come Monday, I rejoin the group in carpooling to school instead of taking the bus like I had for the past few weeks. For a minute, I'm nervous. I'm waiting for the questions, the side-eyes, the surreptitious glances exchanged behind my back. Instead, Vic says hi, Austin pats me on the shoulder, and Beth hugs me. Then they ask how my weekend went, and I sink back into everything immediately: the banter, the rhythm of talking with them, all of it.

We spend our last week of high school doing a whole lot of nothing. All around us, things are wrapping up. Beth has her last track meet. Austin quits his job at the frozen yogurt shop. We enjoy the catharsis of cleaning out our lockers, only to get nostalgic when we realize we'll never have lockers again. We feel our backpacks get lighter and spend evenings shooting the shit down at the playground. And me, I'm right back where I belong: enjoying the end of everything together and hanging on to all the little moments exactly like I want to. It's the group and me, ready to blow the hinges off the universe. I can just *feel* that this era of my life is lightning in a bottle—the kind of thing that you don't find everywhere or anywhere except here and now.

My last day of high school is on a Tuesday. I get up and I

put on my annual Last Day of School outfit: a red T-shirt with faded jeans and mismatched socks. When the five of us meet up to drive to school that morning, Beth's "hi hi" is in a voice that sounds like a grimace . . . excited, but wary. We're all bracing ourselves. Then we walk into school without our backpacks and go to first period for the last time.

I end up leaving lunch early to wander the main hallway. I laugh a little at the freedom of breaking the rules . . . what're they going to do, write me up?

All the things I felt in this building . . . the rush of walking to classes with friends for the first time. The good days; the bad days. The ordinary ones. From now on, if I ever walk this hall again, it'll be just like I used to, instead of just like I do.

When will I even walk through the halls again, anyway? What will it feel like?

"I'm graduating, bitch," I murmur under my breath.

"What'd you call me?"

I jump at Lily's voice, but I turn to see she's giving me her usual teasing smile. She reaches out and puts her hand over mine, swiveling so she's standing shoulder to shoulder with me.

"How're you doing so far?" she asks, in that *I-know-today-is-rough-for-you* voice.

"Not bad, not great. Everything's dialed up to eleven."

"Isn't it always for you?"

"Fair enough. Dialed up to fifteen, then."

"Fifteen. Oof." She pats my arm, pulling me next to her. And together, there we stand. Facing the empty hall.

"This might just be a me-thing," Lily says, "but it feels like we just started here."

"Definitely not just a you-thing."

"We're *old*."

And we smile at the sea of lockers, remembering.

Two hours later, the final bell rings.

I stumble through the main lobby in shock. None of us say much in the car ride home. Austin offers us the Italian ice in his freezer, so we pull up to the park and eat it in the back of his truck while I try not to cry.

"Saying goodbye to everyone is going to suck," Lily says, leaning her head on my shoulder as our legs dangle off the truck bed.

"I was just thinking that," I say.

"Keep in mind, it's not like any of us are dying or anything," Beth points out.

I nod, because she's right. "But we won't be here anymore."

"Yeah," she says, and she nods because I'm right too.

The five of us sit side by side in silence.

It feels like I can barely remember the simple days—the ones where I'd wake up excited to go to school to see everyone or run around the neighborhood. Exploring the thrills of new friends, a new voice, a new life. The early times where everything just felt *correct* in the world. Small and simple and pristine. Sometimes I close my eyes and try to slide into the skin of younger me—the guy who went to bed thinking about his new girlfriend with a stupid smile on his stupid face. God—first love. Beginnings. I'd take all this hurt all over again just to feel that little ache of being alive. Because everything morphs—so slowly you barely notice it—until you realize Christmases have become less about wonder and more about shopping stress. Birthdays lose their magic. You have more of those days when it's impossible to feel like the path ahead is better than the one behind you. So you listen to all your old music from when you were younger, and you're longing for the days when you first discovered those groups. You try to get a second helping of all that novelty, to convince yourself that it hasn't been extinguished from your life. But it's a smaller hit each time—like stripping out a screw. It feels like life adds more and more stipulations tacked onto simple joy until it's not worth looking for anymore. You get to go to prom and graduate high school, but you deal with the stress of leaving your home behind. You feel it all—freedom but loneliness. Stronger joy but sharper pain.

Maybe that's the secret to it all—maybe when I'm eighty I'll be full of life, full of memories, full of music, full of stress, and I'll have spent every year prior wishing it had killed me sooner.

But as I look at our group, sitting on that flatbed snuggled together, I know one thing for sure: Wherever I am and whoever I end up being, all I hope is that I'm not alone. I think I can be anything except alone.

FIVE

March 14th — Senior Year

Journal:

Spent almost the entire rest of my spring break alone. The silver lining was that I had the house to myself, so I didn't have to deal with putting on an act for my parents. Mom gave me a standard *we-still-love-you* speech, and during dinner one night, she stage-coughed and asked Dad if he was okay with me being bi. His response, while succinct, affirmed his unyielding support in his own special way.

"Fuck do I care? Use condoms."

I spent the first day recovering from the Lanham Trip: took a shower; listened to my ambiance in the Studio. By day two, though, I took the morning to pace and come up with a plan of action: I needed to talk to Lily about what happened. There were a million what-ifs spinning around in my head—*what if she heard you say 'stop'; what if she didn't; what if she thought you were kidding; what if she's waiting for you to bring it up.* All the conjecture was eating me alive, and task number one was to put a cap on that. I could let my mind go down a hundred horrible roads, but they'd all be hypothetical. As Dad's said a hundred times: "Don't worry about a problem until you've confirmed it's a problem."

So yesterday I ripped the Band-Aid off . . . or, tried to: I asked Lily to go on a walk through the neighborhood. She showed up in my driveway in a gorgeous yellow sundress, same smile as always, and I did my best to act normal. The goal was to do what I'd failed to do on the bus ride home, aka, talk to her about this in a coherent way. My hand shook against hers and I almost pussied out, but I remembered the ache of fucking it up last time, and just blurted it out as we walked: "Can we talk about the other night? In the dorm?"

"Mm. What about it?" she asked, a bewildered little smile on her face. Then her eyebrows perked up. "Oh! I forgot to text you. I got my period yesterday. So it's like I said, nothing to worry about. But I figured that makes you feel better."

"It's not about that," I said.

"Oh. I mean, what else is there?"

Something about the way she said it. . . . It didn't feel at all evasive, but it didn't feel oblivious either. It was this tone of, *I know what you're talking about, but why are you bringing it up?* Everything inside me squirmed around, tossing me back mentally to ninth grade when I made a faux pas every other sentence. What the fuck was I about to accuse her of?

I felt myself getting more worked up, and when I started to hug myself, Lily said, "Whoa, okay, okay. You seem tense. How about we go see that movie you were talking about?"

"Now?"

"Right now, yep." She tried to rub my back but let go when I wiggled away. "I know I said I hate comedies, but if it'll help you feel better, I swear I won't complain."

So that attempt was a bust. For the rest of the week, Lily seemed hell-bent on cheering me up. I didn't meet up with her again, but every afternoon, she dropped off some new gift at the doorstep—a plate of homemade cookies, or a poem about how amazing I am. Her usual whole-nine-yards shit. She started re-posting more quotes on her blog about relationships: "A soulmate relationship isn't only peaches and cream, it's roses and thorns" and "If someone really loves you, no matter what you do, their feelings for you won't change."

All of it made me feel gross, so I just stayed inside and tried to keep myself distracted.

I tried sleeping, but I couldn't do it more than a few hours at a time. I found myself jumping at noises. Not just the usual loud ones, but regular ones too. The doorbell, footsteps, a truck driving by . . . it was like my subconscious thought someone was coming to kill me.

I tried watching porn, only to figure out my dick didn't work. Couldn't stay hard, even when I put on my favorite bookmarked videos. Every time I started thinking about sex, it opened the floodgates back to that night. I spent a day looking at more intense stuff, as much of it as I could find. Anything that could overwrite the movie in my head. Eventually I gave up.

The only options left to fill my days were seeing the group—which, by extension, included Lily—or going to the neighborhood gym, alone.

I lifted a lot of weights.

I started facing away from the mirror when I did it—couldn't look at myself making those dumb faces. If I had to describe the feeling, it was like when you picture a humiliating moment from when you were younger—the kind that makes you squirm and go, *oh my God get out of my head, get it away, ew.*

Ew.

I also got back into writing short scenes. It made me realize how much time I'd spent away from it to hang out with Lily. Last night, I hid out in the Studio—too antsy to sleep—and tried to write a new one.

We open on a shot of GLITTER BOY. . . . Let's take a look at him: a teenage boy in short shorts and a tank top, his hair and face matted with rainbow glitter. He's soft. Sensitive and scared. Whiny and weak. Begging for attention, affection, wanting everything handed to him.

Glitter Boy recoils at the idea of one hard day's work. He depends on all his prescription drugs for his fucked-up head and then when he flies off the handle, he blames the fact that there aren't more drugs in him or more therapists to validate his whining.

Glitter Boy wouldn't possibly be caught BUILDING great things, CREATING great things, HELPING great people, MAKING great changes to the world. Too lazy to get up off the mat. Too soft to ever take a joke. Too scared to ever take initiative. All he does is sit on his phone someone else paid for in the clothes someone else bought and the nail polish he put on to scream his desperation for attention, and he protests the world without ever doing anything about it, and he takes from the world without giving. That's all he does. He takes and he complains when others don't let him take. And if he ever sees that he's not the center of attention in any room he walks into, he opens his whiny little mouth and cloys in his grating little voice until someone notices him.

"LISTEN TO ME!" he whines.

He's not the same as a normal person—how could he be? He prides himself on finding other people just as whiny and just as entitled and just as grating.

I want to scream it: THAT'S NOT ME! Look at my self-awareness! Can't you see it? I see what you see and I'm not him! I'm not helpless. I'm not your bubble-wrapped, sensitive, spineless little bitch. I'm not begging for anyone's sympathy or affection or attention. I just want you to see me as fucking human. I want you to see me as someone who does do hard work and does change things instead of complaining and doesn't beg for attention and isn't afraid to criticize my own people and isn't afraid to admit there are some things you just need to get over. Someone who isn't allergic to earning my way to where I'm at.

I have things that make me smile and things that make me angry and I love my mom and dad and I feel anger I don't know what to do with and pain I wish I didn't have and I'm not who you see when you look at me and I'm not who you think of when you hear the word *victim*. Because how it sounds is nothing like how it feels.

I hit my own kneecap because that makes me different. And I type and TYPE and

I'M NOT HIM! HE WOULD WHINE AT PEOPLE INSTEAD OF HITTING HIMSELF! HE WOULD BEG FOR ATTENTION INSTEAD OF KEEPING IT QUIET! LOOK AT ME AND LISTEN TO ME! I'M NOT HIM!

it hurts.

LISTEN TO ME! LISTEN TO ME! LISTEN TO ME!

SIX

I GET HOME FROM MY FIRST DAY OF GRAD PRACTICE
to find him waiting on the sofa in the living room.

"Why don't you have a seat," Dad says. No greeting; no
acknowledgment of his absence for the past few weeks. Just
marching orders.

I lean back against the wall next to my chair. "I'm fine here."

"Suit yourself." He scratches his face—his hair is longer, and
he has a little more stubble. But otherwise, it's typical Dad. Same
narrow eyes, same bags latched under them.

The ensuing silence makes me feel like I'm supposed to speak,
but I don't have anything to say.

"How're you," Dad finally says in his not-a-real-question
tone. Like I'm a cashier.

I give the floor my ugliest glare instead of answering. This
pretend-I-didn't-fuck-up act is how it always is with him—like
when he hit me, or his episode after the tire blew out. Turner
men don't lay things out. Turner men put on masks and grit their
teeth to grin through them.

"You're pissed at me," he says. He claps his hands on his knees,
making me wince. "That's understandable. But you're going to
be pissed at me with your listening ears on, okay, because there

are some things we need to hash out."

I don't respond.

"When this whole thing started, I did everything I could to be respectful of you and your . . . you know, privacy." He stumbles over the word. I bite back a scoff, which he seems to sense. "I know you don't think that; that's fine. Your mother and I sometimes disagree on this, but it's not my job to be your best friend . . . best pal, whatever."

I take a seat now, not looking at him. We're both staring at our laps—a mirror image reflected across a few feet of hand-laid flooring.

"I hope you like me; that's what I try to aim for, but if you don't, I still don't care. My job description as your dad is such a long list, I couldn't write it down. But if I did, you'd find that 'does my son think I'm a dick or not?' isn't on it. So . . . think whatever you want of me. Fine. But, fact of the matter is, it's my duty to protect you. Situations like these . . . it's out of my control. And you know I just do wonderfully when it comes to that."

He gives a small chuckle to indicate he's joking. My father jokes so rarely—at least in a real way, not his sardonic one-liners—that it's almost a warm feeling when he does. Almost.

He raises both hands.

"You know what my first instinct was after the school told me what happened to you? I wanted to sit down with a pen and paper and have you walk me through the whole thing step by step. Instead, guess what? I took the afternoon—did some searching online. I found that one of the worst things you can do is have the victim re-live the attack, so I nixed that plan. I never asked you for details; I never asked who did it. I wanted to, but that took a backseat to respecting your well-being."

I open my mouth to say, *thank you for saying that*, but that feels a little too weird, so I just mutter, "Thanks."

And he answers, "You're welcome," but cuts off the end, like he feels weird too. I hate how uncomfortable this is. It's moments like these that make me wonder why I wish my father would open up more.

"All this to say." He draws out the phrase. "The numbers are stacked against us. Of every thousand sexual assaults, around two to three hundred are reported. Only forty-six of those reports lead to arrest; and oh-by-the-*way*, only five of those forty-six gets a conviction. The mission here—and it's an important one—is to make sure your case is among the 0.5 percent of times the system actually works." He leans forward in his chair. "I tried to let the school do their thing; I let Sergeant Schmuckatelli go through his motions. But lo and behold, those galaxy brains confirmed that their skills extend to two areas: hemming and hawing. From the get-go, I suspected it would turn into precisely what it turned into—five pounds of shit in a three-pound bag."

He looks right at me.

"But *you* know who did this," he says. "Right?"

I don't know why I don't just lie. But I nod once.

"Okay." Out of the corner of my eye, I see his jaw tighten. "Then we need to pass that along to the state police. That's our only move left."

"No."

"Owen." He sighs, pinching the bridge of his nose. "You are single-handedly holding everything up. How do you not get that, bud; how do you not get that you're holding everything up. Without you giving that info, we can't do squat. I mean, *nothing*. We can't go the police, we can't get more help from the school; we can't sue the school; we can't sue the guy." He crushes his hands together like he's trying to conjure up a better talking point. "You are holding the golden fucking ticket, man. And you're rolling over on it. *Why* are you working so hard to give this person an exit ramp? I'm really asking."

I shake my head at my lap. "I just don't want to deal with this anymore."

"But the *name*," Dad says, his voice straining. He taps on his own knee for emphasis. "If you just give them that, they can take it from there. The school had every reason to want to downplay this already, and then you refused to give them anything to work with. You are *handing* this guy a get-out-of-jail-free card."

I snap my bracelet in silence.

"So now," he says, his face hard, "the questions will change."

(Silence.)

"It's time for us to face reality. What do I mean by that? Glad you asked. It means"—he sighs through his nose—"that as of *now*, you need to disabuse yourself of the idea that turning in the guy who did this to you is in any way *optional*. This needs to happen, okay. And you're going to fight me on it, and I'm going to tell you right now—I'm not going to budge on this. Telling you that *right* now. So we can do a whole song and dance—that's probably going to feel like the better choice for a little bit. Fine with me. What happens next is up to you. If you want to mope and sit here and spend your time *not* doing what I ask, I've got all the time in the world to wait on you. Because this is your one shot. This right here is your freebie. After that, no name? Guess what—we switch to Plan B."

Snapsnap. Snapsnap.

"I'll tell you right off the bat, you're not going to like Plan B," he continues. "And I'm not a fan of it either. It involves us taking away something of yours. And I know what you're thinking— *well shit, Dad, no video games for a month? Sounds doable.* Wrong." He imitates a buzzer. "You tell us who did this, or we take away the Studio."

"Wh—" I climb to my feet. "Wait, *what?*"

"First step would be getting rid of the furniture." Now he's not looking at me—he's muttering to his boots. "After that it's ripping out the flooring, the trim, the drywall, the electrical . . . that structure goes back to being our garage. Now. Owen." He rises to his feet, looking down at me with folded arms. I hold his gaze.

"I *do not* want to do that," Dad continues. "Your mother really doesn't want that—she's fighting me tooth and nail on this. But if you keep holding out, this is what that looks like. By the time you're waving goodbye in August, that space of yours will once again be a workshop, and you'll be SOL. Is that what you want?"

I don't respond to him.

"Of course it isn't. And it isn't what I want either, okay. Took me a long time to build that place. But you cooperate with us on this, or it's going to get dismantled nail-by-nail. You think that's an exaggeration; it is *not*. I've cleared my schedule; I've put all my projects on pause—this is the only thing on my radar now. This *is* my radar. This is what doing things the hard way would look like."

I scratch at my thumb, every muscle screaming with the urge to squirm. I fight it, clenching my teeth.

"*Or*," Dad says to the floor, eyebrows perching optimistically, "we can just grit our teeth and do this. It'll take you two seconds, if you do this. Two seconds, and I'll be out that door, out of your hair, you can go back to your writing, or whatever. . . . I'll never bring this up again. Your mother, either. That's a promise from both of us. I tell you all this, because I need you to think really hard about everything I've just said." Once again, his eyes meet mine. "Now, I'm asking you—and this is a real question, so I want an answer—do you believe me when I say I'll take that place apart nail by nail?"

"Yes, sir."

"Do you believe me when I say I've cleared my schedule for this?"

"Yes, sir."

"And you're getting the sense that this is going to be a lot easier for both of us if you just help the police out here? I've successfully gotten that through your head?"

"Yes, sir."

"Well, there we go. So far so good. Hey—look at me."

My stomach is clutched in an invisible fist. . . . My chest feels like it's about to collapse. Because I see that image of our friend group, reunited after Lily and I patched things up. And I think about all the uncertainty surrounding the incident—who even knows if it'd count as a crime? Who would believe that my tiny, nice-as-could-be girlfriend held me down and did what I'd accused her of doing?

"Hey—*hey*. Look at me," Dad barks. "You don't look down there . . . out there, up there, wherever. For two seconds, for this, you look at me."

I do.

"Owen," he orders, softly. "Tell me who did this to you."

"No."

"Oh, GOD *DAMN* IT!" Dad explodes. Because of course he does. His fist hits his palm, and he lunges in huge circles, pacing like a prisoner in solitary until he swivels on his feet to face me directly.

"So, okay. *Clearly* you don't get what this is. That is *abundantly* clear." He rubs his temples, the veins on his forehead bulging against the scarlet flush of his skin. Then he says, "*Owen*," throwing up his arms. The way he says my name is chilling. It's almost the same tone as, *come on, man*, but with more anger behind it—a loaded warning. An incredulous, *what-did-you-just-say* voice. A challenge.

I see his challenge and I say nothing.

"Owen," he repeats, when I don't respond. "Tell me who it was."

I see his challenge and I say nothing.

"*Owen Patrick Turner.*"

Nothing, nothing, nothing.

SEVEN

THE SHOUTING MATCH STARTS EARLY THE NEXT morning. Dad is in the Studio hauling furniture out into the yard, and Mom is yelling Mom-things at him. She does a lot of talking with her hands. I only catch a few seconds of it as I leave the house to walk over to Lily's. . . . Mom is telling him to come inside. He's not responding.

Lily can always tell when I need a distraction, so she's come up with one: The five of us are gathered in her backyard to turn an old slab of wood into a group graduation mural.

"Can you try not hitting me with that? There you go," Vic says to Austin as he helps move the board to a picnic table. "We're going left—your other left—*other* left—dude, how many days until you get a diploma?"

"Not all of us are going to Hopkins Engineering, *Vic!*" Austin snaps. I try to chuckle but can't quite force it. I'm still thinking about what's being done to the Studio on the other side of the street.

"Are the edges all the same?" asks Beth, framing up the board with her fingers.

"Wh—obviously the edges are the same. It's a square," says Lily. She's dressed in painting clothes—a ratty tank top and pajama shorts—but still has neon socks underneath.

"I know what it's *supposed* to do, I'm just saying it doesn't look straight."

"Hey, O, it's perfect for you," Lily says, at the same time as Vic says, "Great for Owen!" at the same time as I say, "Sounds like my kind of thing."

At least intergroup needling is still alive and well.

"Does it need to be even?" Lily asks.

"It can be whatever we want it to be," Beth says wistfully.

"How many eighteen-year-olds does it take to trace lines," Austin sings, wiping sweat from his forehead with his T-shirt.

"I'm seventeen," I, Lily, and Beth say at the same time.

"How're we picking the squares?" Vic asks him. We all crowd around the slab. "It's your project."

"Technically it was just my hardwood," Austin points out.

"AW, YEAH," the entire group says in a chorus of suggestive groans.

"*I* can pick the squares," Lily says. "Let's get a 'before' picture."

We all gather around it—Austin and Beth holding it up, Vic flashing a peace sign, Lily snuggled against the wood like she's dating it; and me, as always, at the front taking the picture. Then each of us start grabbing at the paints Lily has laid out, trying to decide on our background colors.

"I need to figure out if I want light blue or royal blue for my section," I say.

"You don't want that," Lily says. I've taken my bracelet off to paint, but my fingers reach for my wrist—I know her *trust-me-I-know-better-than-you* voice all too well by now. "You want the writing to stand out, so you should either do white or a light tone."

"No thanks," I say. I look right at her as I say it to remind her of our agreement. She notices, but her mouth is twitching in a *dude, seriously?* smirk.

"Come on!" She pours out a glob of white and grabs a brush, raising it to my section. "Trust me, it'll look good. You'll thank me as soon as you see it."

"Can you stop?"

"Hold on."

"Can you *stop?*"

"Hold *on.*"

"*Hey!*"

Everyone jumps. I claw at my wrist again—shit.

They're all on edge now, wide-eyed, looking at me like I need help with something. Nervous confusion. It's a look I've gotten before, but never from them.

"Dude," Lily says, stepping back with her hands raised. "What's with you?"

Controlyourselfcontrolyourself.

"Personally, *I* don't care about my paint color," Austin jumps in, uneasy. Beth adds in a quieter-than-usual voice, "Yeah, mine doesn't matter."

Vic raises a hand. "I'm sweaty and gross, so I'm going to get water. Peace."

Austin and Beth join her.

Great. I'm the asshole.

Lily turns to me after they leave—arms crossed, eyebrows raised.

"Okay . . . huh?" she asks.

"We talked about this," I say. It comes out more sheepish

than I'd like.

"Huh?"

"The 'no means no' thing. Remember?"

"*Huh?*"

I rub my mouth. "Remember—I said, you start taking no for an answer. You agreed to that; you said it was no problem."

"Yeah, I—for sex stuff! I didn't realize you meant it for like, *everything*—"

"That's not true," I snap. "I distinctly remember, I said, it doesn't matter what the issue is. I made *sure* to say that."

"No, you didn't." She shrugs, then holds it there. "I'm sorry; I don't know what you want me to say. I don't remember that."

I ball my hands into fists, resisting the urge to put them through the slab. I thought we were *done* with this. Reset. And now, as always, that voice shows up in the back of my head: *What if she's right? What if I'm remembering this wrong?*

I pick my battle.

"Okay." I swallow. "From now on, take no for an answer, about *literally anything*. Doesn't matter what it is—" I try to think of different words to use than last time, so she'll remember it. "Just . . . literally anything. Okay? Do we agree?"

"*Yes.* Literally anything. That's fine." She still has her eyebrows raised.

"This is the last chance. Seriously," I say. But it's the same thing I said last time too.

EIGHT

March 17th—Senior Year

Journal:

Still can't sleep. I'm starting to get nightmares and they won't stop.

I'm so full of thoughts about what happened, and I can't share them with anyone. ~~I don't know how to tell~~ I can't tell my parents or friends. Even putting them down here now is such a chore, because it's just me and my keyboard.

~~I don't like revisiting these or unpacking these and I don't know how to do that either!!~~

~~Can't make heads or tails of basic things that used to make sense . . .~~

~~I DON'T KNOW WHAT TO DO . . .~~

P.S. If it sounds like I'm falling apart or something, don't worry about that kind of bullshit with me. ~~I'm no pussy.~~

NINE

THE NEXT TEN DAYS FEEL LIKE THE START OF A NEW
life. There's no school, no studying, and no Studio I'd be able to
do it in. By day I'm going to the senior picnic and grad parties
with the group. But by night, all that joy runs down the drain
as I lie in bed, trying to tune out the sounds of a hammer blud-
geoning wood in the backyard.

Mom tries to talk to me, but I shrug her off. She's not going
to be able to stop Dad, and we both know it. I wonder if she's
kicked him out of their room—he's back to pacing around the
house at night.

I don't like how my graduation robe looks on me. But it's my
favorite shade of blue, so I deal with it.

All the people in the living room—Mom, Lily, and Vic—
applaud when I emerge downstairs. The girls are in their robes
too. Lily has five cords draped over her shoulders for all her extra-
curriculars, and her hair is wavier than normal. Vic, whose cap is

decorated like a circuit board, shakes her robe and points at mine, like, *hey, we match!*

Meanwhile, Mom—wearing a floral dress and armed with a fancy camera—is a bit of a mess.

"Oh! *There* he is," she says, smiling, but she's tearing up. She hugs me and says, "I'm so proud of you, sweetheart," into my shoulder, then, "And Lily! Oh, sweetie . . ." As they hug, Mom says to her, "Thank you for everything you've done for him. And congrats—yay! And Vic! Come here, gamer girl."

"Car in ten minutes, Jen!" Dad barks as he steps into the living room. He looks supremely out of place, dressed in a proper gray suit stretched over his huge chest with a white tie tucked into the jacket. (He stopped wearing his uniform years ago.) He gives me, Lily, and Vic the once-over and says with a thin grimace, "Looking sharp, you three."

I nod back. Dad and I are still on incredibly thin ice, but he's putting on the nice-guy act for today. He gets a point for that, I guess. Maybe half a point.

I hear the storm door open, and Beth calls, "Hi hi!" She and Austin find their way into the living room, Beth in a pink dress and Austin in a white button-down.

"This is weird, this is weird!" Beth is saying in a nervous sing-song.

"What side's the tassel supposed to be on, by the way?" Austin asks, examining his cap.

"I was *just* about to ask that," Lily says.

"I guess it'll either be correct now, or it will be later," I point out.

"Pictures!" Mom says. "Nobody move; pictures! Austin and Beth, do you want to put your robes on?"

"Car in nine minutes!" Dad reminds her. "If you think we're going to get acceptable seats later than that, you are *dreaming*."

The next five minutes are filled with all the expected pandemonium as Mom takes pictures of Lily and me, Lily takes pictures of me with Mom and Dad, then the others join and we start the whole thing over. Eventually my parents head out—thankfully Lily is driving us all separately from the adults, so we can leave for our group's senior week trip right after.

I realize I forgot my tie, and Lily joins me upstairs to grab it. I pick up my best one—it's bright reflective silver. I look *fancy*. I look . . . old.

"Wow," I murmur to myself.

Lily scrunches up her face, grabbing a few other ties from my dresser and holding them up to my head. She says, "Turn your head—oh, nice eyes, yeah," as I rotate so she can better see my face. She does some calculations, then points to a tie on my bed. "Do that one—the dark brown. Goes really well with your eyes."

"No thanks. I like this one." I point to the silver.

She smirks, and my heart sinks. "Oh, dude."

"What?"

"Nothing. It's just . . ." She smiles and nods at me like I'm supposed to finish the sentence. Then, "You can do the silver if you want to look like a middle schooler going to his first dance. If you want to look like a graduate, chuck it."

"No."

"When are you going to trust me?"

"Lily." I give her warning eyes. "Remember? What we talked about?"

"Ohh, the . . . yeah."

"Yeah, that."

"But like, this is *graduation*." She bites her lip. "You want to look good, right?"

I keep staring at her.

"You're still doing it," I say. I'm seized by a rush of anger, the kind that makes you want to shout at someone until you've reduced them to tears.

"Okay, geez." Lily's eyes are wide. "I didn't realize this fell into that category; I'm sorry. I figured it was just clothes."

"Clothes count. Did you really not know that?"

"You want to do this here? When we are . . . moments from going to high school graduation?" she asks. She tenderly touches my arm, rubbing it. "How about this: Right now we focus on getting to the ceremony, then we'll have more time on the senior week trip."

"And we talk there."

"Absolutely. And as far as this"—she points to the tie—"I'm just giving you my opinion, man; wear whatever you want. I'm just saying some people will think you look dumb if you wear the silver. But it's up to you."

I yank the silver from around my neck and throw it back in the drawer.

TEN

March 19th—Senior Year

Journal:

During a night of insomnia, an impromptu zoning session led to me researching hookup apps.

It started with me reading over online discussions about erectile dysfunction in teenagers. That turned into ten more web pages about how sex affects your brain in general. A lot of it was useful insight, but none of it felt like actual answers.

One of the pages mentioned hookup apps, though. Next thing I knew, I had twentysomething tabs open about everything related to those—what to expect from them, how they worked, example screenshots of conversations there.

It stayed stuck in my brain for all of the next day at school.

I wasn't actually looking to sleep with a stranger, of course—that was way too big a leap for me, and it wouldn't solve anything. (To say nothing of the fact that I'd be cheating on Lily.) But what were these apps *like?*

Would people on them talk to me?

Don't get me wrong, I couldn't imagine leaving Lily for someone else. But things with her felt so permanently shot, and we were just walking around school with our bullshit smiles stuck to our faces. She still gave me gifts at lunch—homemade cookies or a card—and re-posted bullshit quotes on her blog. Things like, "At the end of the day, you can focus on what's tearing you apart or what's holding you together" and "I'm not perfect, but you'll never find a person who cares or loves you more than me."

What if I could test that? To see if things feel less fucked up with a new guy or girl I met on an app . . . someone with all the wonderful qualities Lily showed early on, but none of the bullshit?

I downloaded my first hookup app last night.

It was easy, but I had to bullshit that I was eighteen. Four months is close enough anyway.

March 22nd—Senior Year

Journal:

I've met someone new.

We connected on the app. I was smart about inter-acting on there, at first. I ignored all messages asking to meet up, and I set the max preferred age to nineteen. Only that didn't show many profiles, so two days later, I bumped it up to twenty-one . . . that got a lot more. Soon I had to silence the notifications because my phone was buzzing with so many messages of "hey" or more explicit stuff that I ignored.

I reminded myself of my mission: to collect data. "Are there people out there nicer than Lily?"

For a while, I felt sure the answer was no. Every time I got one of those superficial messages, all I thought about was that day she sat next to me on my stoop. *Look at us.*

But yesterday, I found a guy around my age— nineteen—who's named Xavier. He didn't have a face picture, but when I sent him a message of:

Hi there, how's your day been?

He almost instantly replied:

Hiya, thanks for asking! It hasn't been too bad . . . getting nervous for my show next week. How about you? :)

Okay, whoa . . . now we were talking.

I paced around the Studio, sweating and trying to think of the right way to steer the conversation. Then I typed:

I'm great! And what is this show you speak of? I'm intrigued.

I grinned and clutched my phone to my chest until I got a new message a few minutes later.

Great to hear! :) And it's this one-act play I need to do as part of my degree. I'm a total theater dork. Yes, I fit the gay stereotype :P

For the next hour, Xavier and I talked about what it was like to be a freshman in college, and how he was home for the weekend visiting his parents, and how we could maybe meet up sometime, but no pressure if I was uncomfortable with it. And while I didn't say yes, the truth is that I felt more excited than uncomfortable. And beyond that, I was more at peace than I had been since the Lanham Trip.

There *were* other people out there! Nice people . . . hell, maybe even *nicer* than Lily! There were people like Xavier, even though I barely knew anything about him. I would've told him how much our small conversation meant to me, but I didn't want to weird him out. That would not be a good thing to do. Now that I'd found someone who was actually a decent person, I needed to focus all my energy on that.

Eventually he stopped replying, but the next evening—as I sat fidgeting and wondering if I should follow up—he sent a new message:

Super sorry for not replying! Fell asleep last night and practice ran late. How was your day?

Xavier and I messaged the whole rest of the evening. Eventually I ran out of conversation topics, so I just said:

I love your name, by the way . . . is that your real name? I know we all have an air of mystery on this app, haha :)

Then I added:

I apologize if that's invasive! I don't mean it to be.

I fell asleep waiting for his response. For once, no nightmares.

March 23rd — Senior Year

Journal:

When I woke up for school this morning, I checked Xavier's profile to see if he replied yet. He's blocked me.

ELEVEN

AUSTIN'S GRANDPARENTS ARE THE NICEST PEOPLE ON Earth—their house in Virginia Beach is a palace. At least it feels like one. Five bedrooms, basement theater, in-ground pool, balcony overlooking the beach. Plus they're not even here, so we have the place to ourselves.

Despite all the bullshit going on back home, I spend the week walking on air. By day, I lie on the beach in sunglasses while the others swim. (I hate the feeling of natural bodies of water. Too dirty.) By night, we help Beth make nice dinners and have evening water gun fights in the pool. The others even humor me and let me host my annual Batman Night—a tradition where I watch the entire Dark Knight trilogy in one sitting.

The only time I feel uneasy is when I try to go to sleep in the unfamiliar bed. I brought the weighted blanket I use at home, but the pillows are still wrong. I end up spending most of the evenings lying out on the balcony in my pajamas, listening to ambiance and absorbing the night air.

The last evening there, Beth and I make veggie burgers on the grill near the pool while the others swim around. Everyone gets a bit liquored up from the wine Austin smuggled, and two hours later, we're crashing inside while Beth takes a dessert out of the oven.

"Who all wants caramel pavlova?" she calls into the living room.

"What word are you saying?" asks Austin, sprawled out on one of the leather couches in his pajamas.

"I've never heard of it," I say.

"It's a meringue desert," says Vic from the other side of the room. She pauses their video game to take a sip of wine. "Uncultured animals."

"Can you ask Lily if she wants any?" Beth asks me. "She's on the balcony watching the sunset."

"Sure. Will I like pavlova?"

"Hmm—I think so?" She bobs her head back and forth. "It's served with fruit. How do you feel about oranges?"

"I think the person who named them wasn't a hard worker."

She pinches me with her tongs.

I find Lily on one of the beach chairs on the deck, scrawling in her notebook. There's barely enough light for her to see—the sun has completely disappeared at this point. She's still in her bathing suit from earlier today, sunglasses nested in her hair.

"Am I interrupting?" I ask.

"Hey!" she beams. "Not at all. I just finished."

"Beth said to ask if you want pavlova. Meringue dessert."

"I'm good for now." She scoots over in the chair to make room for me. I squeeze into it next to her, tangling my feet with hers.

"You look cute in your swimsuit," she says, leaning her head on my shoulder.

"You too."

"Aw." She squeezes my arm, then her fingers trail south. She lets them rest on my thigh, tucked just under the inseam of my swimsuit leg.

I squirm a little, poking her arm. "Can you not?"

"I'm behaving!" She leans up to peck me on the cheek. "I'm just resting my hand—no, see, what's wrong with resting it?"

"Can you—dude, stop—"

"Relax."

"—Okay. Stop!" When she doesn't, I jump up from the chair, tipping us over. Lily shouts as she hits the deck wood with a *thud*.

"Ow! God damn it, that was my elbow!" She rubs it as she climbs to her feet, scowling. "What the *hell*, O? That really hurt."

I blink at her.

"You're still doing it," I say. I'm too dumbfounded to have a tone—my voice is flat and empty.

"Doing what?"

"You know." I put my fist against my mouth. "You can't not know by now."

"Well. I . . . don't." She makes a fish face at me, like, *haha, I screwed up*. When I don't smile back, she drops it and takes a step toward me. "Look, can you chill? I didn't know the whole 'stop' thing included me literally resting my fingers on you. That's not something most people are thinking about."

"You can't not know by now." I shake my head, not looking at her. My adrenaline is pumping and words are ballooning in me; there are a million things I need to say, but I'm trying to pick my phrases carefully because after all this, even now, I want to make room for the possibility that I'm the one who's out of line.

"I can't not know *what?*" Lily asks.

"That I'm not kidding when I say 'stop.'"

"So, what . . . because of two or three incidents, you think it's this huge deal?"

"How many more times will I have to clarify before it stops

happening? What's the number?"

"This is stupid."

"I agree. What's the number?"

I feel pain written all over my face. How can she not see this? How can she not hear this? How is this rational person—one of the most rational people I know—standing here claiming she doesn't have a clue what she did? What she *keeps doing?*

I let the silence build. *Don't let her dodge this time.*

"I'm missing something here." Lily leans against the deck rail, so she's facing me. "Why is this so important to you?"

"Because you keep doing things after I ask you to stop doing them."

"*Which* is something I'm working on."

"Wh—it's not a fucking art project! There's no work; just *stop!*" This feels so shitty—having to beg her to keep her word on something. Pleading with her to dispense an ounce of remorse.

I try again. "Okay. What goes through your head when I ask you to stop doing something?"

"I think . . . 'Hey, is he serious or not?' Then I remember how important this is to you, which makes me nervous, and by the time I think, 'Wait, I'm screwing this up,' you're slamming my elbow into the deck."

I lean against the opposite rail to look her up and down. Her face is blank, her eyebrows perched . . . like she's still waiting for me to say something important.

Then I ask, "What about that night?"

No answer.

"You didn't seem nervous then," I press her. "So what went through your head? Did you hear me say 'stop'?"

No answer.

"Did you hear me that night?"

"Okay." Lily claps her hands together and holds them there,

her eyes flaring. "Let's get something clear. It *really* bothers me that you feel the need to keep re-living the past."

"I guarantee you that feeling bothers me even more."

"I already admitted I screwed up that night."

"I want to unpack that a little more." I pinch the bridge of my nose. Then I say, in a more strained voice, "Are you even *upset* about it?"

Lily flinches, then scowls.

"I'm *every* bit as upset as you are," she snaps.

"*Really*. So you're—come on. You're not grossed out when you look at the mirror. You aren't having . . . flashbacks."

"*You* don't know! How do you know I'm not?"

"I honestly don't think you get how insultingly insincere you sound right now."

"Answer my question—how do you know I'm not? You're just assuming because I'm not showing that many signs of being upset . . ."

"Let's just be clear; you're not showing *any* signs of being upset."

"Still!"

I karate chop my own hand. "You are asking me to assume. . . . Do you get how it's hard for me to take your word for this? Does that make sense?"

"That sounds like a problem on your end, not mine."

I squeak under my breath, folding my arms against my chest.

"Why are you being like this?" I ask.

"Like WHAT? *You're* the one coming at me with this shit, accusing me of not caring about it . . . thanks for that, *dick*. What, you think just because I'm not curled up in a ball somewhere, that means I'm not upset?" Steam practically leaks from her ears. "What happened makes me sick, but acting upset over it won't do any good. What am I going to—to do . . . dissolve into tears every time I see you? Stay stuck in bed forever? None of it, *none of it*, will change what happened—nothing can. It's DONE!"

"*Did you hear me that night?*"

"O, we've been over this—"

"Lily—"

"—and over this, and over this, and *over this!*" She takes a step toward me, her jaw clenched. "What do you WANT from me?"

"For starters, you never did apologize—"

"Okay, watch: *I'm sorry*. There, did that fix it? Didn't think so. So I'll say again: What do you want me to *do?* Tell me! Go ahead. Give me some, some action item, and I'll do it. You want me to give you all my stuff? You want me to blow you every day? You want my car? I'm *not* kidding right now. Anything you need, tell me."

"Right now, I'd like to leave one conversation with more information than I came in with."

"GOD!" She smacks the table, yells, "OW!" then does it two more times.

I come off the railing, taking a step toward her. I feel a rush from getting her to react, but it's all wrong. What I want is for her to look ashamed, upset—anything to show she gives a genuine shit. I want her to *show* how torn up she was, and is, instead of feeding me bullshit about invisible woes. But all I see in her eyes is confusion, irritation . . . maybe the tiniest bit of concern. My brain, as always, latches onto that: Maybe she's just so ashamed she can't show it. Maybe this is all just a defense mechanism for her. Maybe I'm spouting all this with absolute certainty and I, like so many other times in the past, am *wrong*.

But no. I'm not wrong, and she's not going to lead me down that road tonight.

"I asked you to stop," I say, "and you didn't."

"Oh, that simple?"

"It is *that* simple. I asked you to stop, and you didn't." I take calming breaths, then restart in a more level voice. "Do you get what you did? I mean specifically."

"I know I upset you, if that's what you mean," she says. "But let me ask you this: What about it was so upsetting? Which part?"

"Wh—the whole thing!"

"But *what* about it was upsetting?"

"We're not doing this."

"Why not?" she asks.

"Because I'm sick of having to defend why and how I feel the things I feel."

"I'm not asking you to defend yourself; I'm asking clarifying questions because I don't understand."

"I honestly don't mean to be rude, but if you can't understand why getting assaulted falls into the category of 'upsetting,' maybe I'm not the go-to guy to help you out."

She stares at me while I snap at my bracelet.

"Did you *hear* me that night?" The question burns more each time it passes through me. I feel my eyes prickle, and I swallow a lump of self-pity that works its way up my throat.

"Ah . . ." I think she starts to say "I," but all that comes out is a toneless croak. She closes her mouth, pursing her lips at me.

Don't let up. I change angles, then go in again. "Did you hear me say *anything?*"

"It doesn't matter now."

"Humor me and pretend that it does for a second."

"There's no point in harping on—"

"Can you please, *please* just answer."

"Yeah."

"So do it."

"I just did; that's my answer: yeah. I heard you say . . . what you said."

I squeeze my eyes shut.

"Okay." I swallow. "You told me in the Studio that you *didn't* hear me."

"I . . ." She fumbles again. "What I meant was, I didn't hear it how you *intended* it. What difference does any of this make?"

I bite back the answer that flashes through my brain in a million forms at once:

Because you still aren't stopping.

Because you don't stop doing something if you don't think it's wrong.

Because I think you'd do the same thing to me again.

I'd tell her all that, but I don't think it's enough to convince her of the thing she's apparently not already convinced of, which is that this behavior falls under the definition of the word deliberate—which in no way excludes people who have shut themselves off from their own shit, and then gleefully kept doing it.

This fight isn't worth it.

I unclench my fists, open my eyes, and deflate.

"Fine. Forget it," I say.

I'm starting to turn away when she says, "Are you going to be pissy about this later?"

"I don't know; I don't control that."

"I just don't want you to be angry on the last night of senior week."

"That's not a scenario I'm thrilled about either."

"*And* I don't want to deal with pissy-Owen. Am I going to get pissy-Owen?"

I swivel back around to face her—she's got her hands on her hips. God, she knows how to make people feel small. It's never enough for her to win the argument—you have to lose on her terms too. Once she gets what she wants, it's another half-hour of her explaining why this was obviously the fair outcome, and how she helped you by shining a light on how wrong you were.

It's like she'd shatter if she ever came face to face with what she was really making you feel. So you had to smile after you lost, or you got in even more trouble.

"Forget it," I say again. Even smaller this time.

"You know, this happened to me too."

I stiffen. "What?"

"This happened to me too." Her words are tentative, but her face is gnarled in anger. "Not just you. Both of us."

I mull that over. Then I shake my head. "No."

"What?"

"You're just wrong. It didn't happen to both of us."

"*Okay*," she says, in an aimless voice. "That's screwed up of you. Because this is, it's—"

"You did this."

She falters. "What?"

"You did this," I repeat, my breath heavy. I step toward her until we're right up in each other's face. I force myself to look at her. "It's no one else's fault; this was you, *all* fucking you—"

"O—"

"Your decision, your actions!"

"Stop yelling."

"*This was all you!* All y—"

I never see it coming: Lily's grip locking onto my arm, bending it shut and wrenching me backward to slam my elbow onto the deck handrail. *Thud*—"*OW, fuck!*"

I stumble sideways, jam my hip into the table corner, and topple to the ground with a pained grunt.

Lily's eyes are wide.

Lily's hand is covering her mouth.

Lily's head is shaking back and forth.

Lily tells me, "I'm sorry."

But she's walking away before she's even done saying it.

TWELVE

LILY BOOKS IT UPSTAIRS AS SOON AS WE GET INSIDE. I try to follow, but I don't get far.

"*Hey*. What was that?"

An anvil slams into my chest—Vic's voice. I freeze and swivel around to find all three of the others still sitting in the living room. Each of their faces—Vic's scowl, Austin's wide eyes, and Beth's pursed lips—screams the same message: They saw.

I make a beeline for the stairs, but Vic stops me cold. "Hey— *hey*. Owen."

I press a casual hand to my throbbing elbow.

"What was that out there?" Vic's eyes have enough anger in them to ignite the ocean.

"Nothing, *noth-ing*," I plead, my voice cracking. "Please, guys, just—"

"Okay . . . dude?" Austin cuts me off. "We saw that."

"Come sit," Vic says.

"I don't want to. Seriously—"

Beth disappears into the kitchen and returns with a bag of frozen peas. She presses it to my elbow; the cold shocks my skin, and I shout, "*FUCK, Beth!*" I slap the bag to the ground, and a million frozen peas scatter over the entire room's hardwood.

As I start to tear up pathetically at the sight, Austin just says in a small voice, "Well, it's a rental."

I wait for Beth to scamper away or curse me out. Instead she puts a hand on my shoulder, guides me to the front door, and says, "Let's go somewhere."

The beach is dark and empty except for the four of us. I sit across from the others with my toes digging into the sand, the nighttime ocean to my right and the lights from the boardwalk to my left.

Vic leans back on her heels, arms folded. "How long has that been going on?"

I raise an eyebrow at the sand. "You sound pissed."

"I am. That's abuse, dude."

"This was the first time." When she scowls at me, I roll my eyes. "I can tell you don't believe me."

"Well, about two seconds ago you were ready to tell us you got that mark on your elbow from falling down the stairs or something, so."

"I was actually going to go with 'tripped in the shower,'" I say, wiping my nose on my arm. "Figured that would sell it more."

"So *that's* what you were doing in the shower earlier," Austin says, raising a finger in an *ah-ha* gesture.

"No, then I was masturbating."

"Ah, of course. Hey, it's a rental."

"*Guys*," Vic snaps. "You *swear* that was the first time she's done anything like that? What about when you guys broke up?"

"Will you get off my ass? We didn't break up; we had a fight," I say. "Which we resolved, then got back together."

"Yeah, if you ask me, you shouldn't have done that."

"I didn't."

"You didn't get back together with her?"

"I didn't ask you."

Vic stares me down. Austin and Beth pretend to play with the flashlights on their phones.

"Listen," I say, carefully—I need to sell it. "I appreciate this. But everything is fine; things just got out of hand. I promise."

"Things have been bad between you guys for a while," Vic says. I realize it isn't a question, and she adds, "Lily tells me things. We're best friends. Or, were."

"Were?"

"She's been kind of bitchy lately."

"Like, this week?"

"Like, the past year. I mean, I love her, but . . . I don't know. We could all tell you guys were having trouble."

"How?"

"Lily's sent screenshots, you've sent screenshots . . . I know what your fights look like. And you two say some . . . awful shit. To me, that was the first red flag."

I try to muster a scoff. "I guess we bring out the worst in each other."

Vic leans toward me and says, hotly, "You should say that with more concern."

"This isn't black and white."

"Okay, two things: One, yeah, it is. With hitting, *yeah*, it is. Two—"

"This is stupid."

"*Two*, why did you guys break up as soon as she found out what happened to you on the trip? Was that really just a coincidence?"

They all wait.

Waves crash.

This is my window. I'm being given a moment on a silver platter; the opportunity I've been waiting for . . . *tell them. TELL THEM.* I latch onto Vic's urgency, and I picture unloading that whole night onto them. Their shocked looks, strong hugs, their sympathy, their support.

But there's still that same barrier as always—the permanence of telling them this thing they could never be untold. What if they reported it to law enforcement, got Lily arrested? What if the local papers printed stories, and there was a trial where I had to share that whole night to a room full of strangers, and only then would I realize I'm not even right about this—that she actually didn't do this thing, and I made the most colossal misreading of a situation in my life?

I try to hold on to all the images I just planted in my brain out on the balcony, but they're all blank. And I circle back to the only thing I know for sure: that however miserable this is, it's a price worth paying to preserve my daily life. It's not ideal, but it's a trade-off I've weighed and chosen knowingly.

"It was coincidence," I tell Vic. "Lily just had a lot of feelings about the Lanham thing because she's the one who helped me come out then."

"It's funny you bring *that* up," she says. Her voice is darker now.

"Vic," Beth says.

"A couple hours before then—" Vic starts.

"Oh, come on, don't—" Austin is saying.

"—she told us you were bi," Vic finishes.

I freeze.

"What do you mean, 'told you?'" I ask.

"Exactly that."

"You're such a liar."

Austin sits with his head in one hand, adjusting his glasses with the other.

"Dude," says Vic. "Why would I lie about this?"

"Why would she?"

"She said she wanted to make sure we were all cool with it ahead of time," Austin says to his lap. "I'm sorry, man."

"Okay." I chew on my lip, relieved to have an excuse to latch onto. She had a good reason; of course she did. "That's not a crime. That's fine."

"Are you kidding me?" Vic says. "You're saying this doesn't bother you at all?"

"Of *course* it does; will you stop fucking with me?" I snap. "She's not, like, this cartoon villain who's scheming to ruin my life—"

"I didn't say that, and I don't think that," Vic says. "What I *am* saying, and what I do think, is that she could steal a baby, light it on fire, punt it at your fucking head, and you'd write a poem about how great she is for trying to keep you warm. That's what I'm saying."

I can't help but smirk at how Vic-ish of an answer that is.

"Fine," I say. "*I'm* saying it's complicated, and you don't get it. She and I aren't . . . we're not a normal couple."

"I don't know what that means."

"This stuff usually looks like red flags, but it's not for us, because we have a different way of doing things."

"I don't know what *that* means."

"We're the exception."

It's clear from their faces that they aren't buying it. This is exactly why I don't want to talk about this with anyone. They weren't there for those moments in the very beginning. They don't know what it felt like that night Lily and I emailed for the first time—how she plucked me out of the crowd. So of course they wouldn't believe me when I say this is complicated.

Hell, Vic hasn't even dated anyone before—by her own admission, people annoy her too much. So how could she understand all my tangled thoughts?

"No one's trying to tell you what to do. But if you do break up, there are other . . . you know." Vic flings a stick at the water. "Fish in the sea. Like, it *will* be okay."

I laugh into my hands.

"What is it?"

"I've seen what's out there," I tell her. "I—no, *trust* me. I've seen."

I think back to all those nights I spent on hookup apps a few months ago. The evenings I would be upset in my bed because some guy blocked me or said some shitty thing, when my phone would buzz with a text from Lily:

Hey there! I hope you had a great day :)

And I'd think to myself: Yep, nothing will ever come close to this.

"Trust me," I repeat to Vic. "Those people make Lily look like Florence Nightingale."

"Bud, there are 7.8 billion people out there, and every one of them is a gender you're attracted to. You will find another Florence."

"There are other people, but they're not *this* person."

"You are tantalizingly close to getting the point."

"What if she's the person I'm supposed to be with?"

"You're seventeen."

"I know. And look at where I'm at."

"We are."

I don't respond to that one.

"*I* have a thing to say," Beth pipes up.

I wait.

"Just so you know. Because I think it's important." She picks up a fistful of sand, letting it drain through her fingers. "Whether you were dating Lily or not . . . we were never going anywhere, you know. We never had one foot out the door."

"What're you talking about?"

"I'm talking about the way you always sit on the floor at hang-outs so everyone else can have the nice chairs. Or how you always buy our favorite snacks and bring us food when we come over."

"*Or* how you always volunteer to be the picture-taker," Austin adds.

"I like doing that stuff."

Beth shrugs. "If you say so."

"Why else would I do it?"

"Because you always thought we had one foot out the door." She looks hard at me. "You feel like you need to make it as easy as possible to spend time with you—like if our job is to do anything other than show up, we won't. So I'm just letting *you* know . . . in case it needs to be stated. We were always going to show up, dude."

"Absolutely," adds Austin.

Vic taps me on the knee with one finger. "You hear that, right? Lily or not; we weren't going to stop showing up. Ever."

I look out to the ocean, shaking my head with a smirk. "Four years to tell me this, and you're doing it three weeks before we move away."

"Well, life's full of disappointments." Another Vic answer. She leans toward me. "We're just letting you know, for when you're at college making new friends. People are going to show up for you. *You.*"

That gets a real smile out of me. I can't believe how much I love these people. All three of them on their last night of vaca-tion, and this is how they're spending it.

I really don't know what I'm going to do without them.

"Question," Beth says, half-raising a hand. "Do you want me to talk to Lily?"

"*No.*" God, no.

Vic: "Do you want any of us to talk to her? Send her a text?"

"No."

Austin: "Muster an army of locusts?"

"We'll keep that one on the table."

THIRTEEN

I CAN'T SLEEP, SO I GO OUT TO THE BACK DECK WITH
my writing notebook. The ocean roars in the distance, but the
night is completely clear.

I sit at the picnic table and stare at the paper.

It's impossible to concentrate—I keep replaying the group's
conversation from earlier. I'm kicking myself for not telling them
everything. Imagining how different their reactions would've
been . . . How much more horrified they would be if they knew
it wasn't just my elbow.

Vic's voice turns around in my head.

That's abuse, dude.

God, that word makes my skin crawl. It feels totally mismatched with my situation. Like I'm detracting from cases that
are more serious, more real.

"Plenty of abuse to go around, folks," I murmur aloud to the
dark, empty air.

That can't be what this is.

I set down my pen and pull out my phone. A few keyword
searches lead me to a chart called the Power and Control Wheel.

I pull at my bracelet as I read some of the items.

- *Using intimidation – Making her afraid by using looks, actions, gestures.*
- *Emotional abuse – Putting her down. Making her feel bad about herself. Calling her names. Playing mind games.*
- *Isolation – Controlling what she does, what she wears, where she goes.*
- *Minimizing – Not taking her concerns seriously. Saying the abuse didn't happen. "It's all in your head."*

I sigh into my fingers.

"Fuck."

Okay.

I want to un-read the words. All this ugliness bubbles to the surface with them. Memories, like when I told Lily I wanted my first kiss to be special and planned out; then the next day she grabbed me and kissed me on the bus because now I wouldn't have to worry about it anymore. Or when I decided to silence my phone for a night after an argument, and she showed up in my yard to shine a light in my eyes through my window until I responded to her.

I pick my pen back up and try to get back to my sketch.

(Blank page.)

I start to write Caesar, the twisted game show host that Lily and I created that night we emailed.

(Blank page.)

Caesar laughs and claps.

"We have a winner, folks! We asked one hundred people the question, IS THIS ABUSE, and survey says yes! Congratulations . . . what will you do next?!"

I squeeze my eyes shut.
Everyone is waiting.

"Oh gosh." I cock an eyebrow, putting on my best sarcasm face. "Do I have to choose, Caesar?"

"Hahaha! Well, of course you do."

I dial up the charm. "Come on, I'm bi. You know we hate choosing."

Laughtracklaughtrack!

"Oh, you thought you were out of the woods when you solved the riddle, didn't you? Didn't he, folks?!"

LAUGHTRACKLAUGHTRACK!

I lean against the table, cradling my head in my hands as my lip trembles. *Whatever you do, don't fucking cry.*

"What are my . . . options?"

Options.

"Now we're talking! Don't worry; we've got lots of help for you!"

Help.

"Let's ask our first audience member—the wisest woman in the world!" Caesar hands the microphone to MOM, who waves nervously, blushing among the cacophonous applause. But her face turns serious when she answers, echoing words she told me when I was twelve.

"Buddy: I just need to tell you that you are the most wonderful boy in the world, and anyone who can't see that isn't worth your time. Don't let anyone hurt you in a way you wouldn't want someone to hurt me. Make it important to love and respect yourself as much as I do."

I grip my pen until my knuckles go numb.

"Well, what do you think about that?" Caesar asks me.

I shake my head, wiping my eyes.
"I don't know." My voice rattles.

"You don't know?" Caesar balks at me. And no sooner has he taken the microphone back than Lily appears, grabbing my mother's elbow and slamming it into the concrete wall behind her. A sharp cry of pain. Mom is knocked to the floor and out of sight among the cheering crowd.

"Stop it! Stop it! STOP!"

I write on the page in front of me:

JUST END THINGS WITH HER, YOU FUCKING IDIOT!!!

"What other options—let's ask this guy right here!" Caesar walks right up to a boy: seven-year-old Owen, who has racecar pajamas, a stuffed panda bear, and a black eye.

"What happened to your eye, buddy?"

The boy looks away shyly. "Daddy hit me."

"Oooh," the crowd purrs.

"Well now, that must mean he didn't love you much. According to that nice lady over there."

"That's different—he can't help it."

"Says who?"

"That nice lady over there! She told me we need to make sure it doesn't happen again, but not give up on him."

I write.

MAKE SURE IT DOESN'T HAPPEN AGAIN, BUT DON'T GIVE UP.

Now the crowd starts yelling all at once.

"Boys will be boys!" cries a woman in a cross necklace.

"SITFU, you pussy!" yells an old man to a boy with my face and no limbs.

The boys from elementary school yell and throw rocks at the rest of the audience members who laugh as they get hit because they're eager to be included.

A tiny man in the back row slams together cymbals made of human faces.

I write a third option.

Suck It the Fuck Up, PUSSY.

It's barely legible. I stand up and my knees give out almost at once—I fall to the deck floor with a grunt.

"We've heard from lots of great people . . . time for you to make your decision!"

DING DING DING DING!

Lily appears next to me, blushing and giggling in the same outfit as when we met. She stands on her tiptoes, kisses me on the cheek, then kicks my legs out from under me.

The sign explodes in Technicolor above Caesar's head: APPLAUSE!

APPLAUSE!

APPLAUSE!

The ocean erupts into cheering.

"What will you do next?!" Caesar yells again.

PLENTY OF ABUSE TO GO AROUND, FOLKS!

I try to pick myself up, but my shoes are glued to the floor. I try to remove them, but they're made of my skin. I look down at my torso and realize I'm completely naked. The crowd jeers and points. White light flashes everywhere as they take pictures. I try to conceal myself, but my arms won't move. My motionless body is covered in bright red Sharpie—Lily's signature is scrawled all over my skin.

(Blank page.)

The crowd takes Caesar's chant, clomping their shoes and clapping their hands. "What will you do next? What will you do next? What will you do next?"

Options.

A SPOTLIGHT erupts over the stage . . . a crimson beam of light.

Help.

WHAT WILL YOU DO NEXT? WHAT WILL YOU DO NEXT?

I roll over so I'm lying on my side. And the chant burgeons on all sides as I clamp my hands over my ears.

WHAT WILL YOU DO NEXT!
WHAT WILL YOU DO NEXT!
WHAT WILL YOU DO NEXT!
WHAT WILL YOU DO NEXT!
WHAT WILL YOU DO NEXT!
WHAT WILL YOU DO NEXT!

FOURTEEN

March 26th — Senior Year

Journal:

I'll admit I paced for hours trying to figure out what happened to screw things up with Xavier. First I searched online to see if any glitches were occurring with the app I was using—maybe he hadn't meant to block me. If he did, fine, but it just didn't make sense. Maybe he deleted his profile? But that wouldn't explain why it was still showing up, grayed out.

All I wanted was an explanation.

I pored over my last message to him. I studied the wording, running scenarios in my head. What could I have said to scare him off? Maybe the thing about his real name? I tried to tell myself that if he was someone who'd block me over that, then good riddance. He was the weird one in that situation, not me. But I didn't care who the weird one was. I just wanted our conversations back.

I moped for two days, then took my name off my profile.

I hate how much I understand Dad now. For years, he's had this ugly poison inside him . . . frustration and fear and invincible anger at everything that moves. I swore that would never be me. But I look inside myself now and I'm starting to see that same poison, too.

March 31st—Senior Year

Journal:

Hookup apps are murder on my ASD. I bought some weed from Austin to try to keep my nerves down, but even that only helped so much. I was still spending hours at a time fixating on messages I'd sent, pacing around the Studio and wondering if this would be the one that ruins things. There were so many rules about how to talk to people. All this ghosting, half-talking bullshit . . . the definition of vapidity. I didn't get it, I didn't like it, and I sure as hell couldn't emulate it.

But earlier this week, I think I found the trick. I call it Window Shopping. Here's how it works: Instead of sorting by people who meet your criteria, you sort by who's online *right now*. You pick one and message them. Something explicit, to get their attention. Then you get talking—you don't swap info; you don't swap greetings—the only thing you swap is dirty talk. Then you both get yourselves off, close out the app, and go back to your lives. No investment, no letdowns, just the chat equivalent of porn.

It works.

Reliability has become key to the persona I've put together: By day, I hang out with the friend group, putting my bullshit smile on and pretending nothing is the matter and trying not to squirm and feel slimy when Lily and I hold hands. But then, by night—or, rather, the minute I get home from school—I'm back on the apps, washing the slime off with something else. All these messages from people, mostly pictures, some pickup lines. Your run-of-the-mill creeps who get too persistent, so I tell them to go fuck themselves and block them.

I've been window shopping every night this week.

P.S. Lily finally stopped getting me *Owen-feel-better* gifts. I guess she figured out they weren't working.

April 1st—Senior Year

Journal:

I've written a new scene piece.

It starts with

RIGHT-BOY—teenager, mild-mannered, in a simple solid-color T-shirt and faded jeans—standing in a boxing ring, even though he isn't dressed for the occasion. His opponent is his mirror image: an identical boy, mild-mannered, in a simple solid-color T-shirt and faded jeans. Except everything about him is flipped. His head tilts the wrong way, his zits are on the wrong side of his face, and his bracelet is on the wrong wrist. Completely identical yet completely wrong—a carbon copy. This person, we quickly realize, is the piece of garbage from the last write-up: Glitter Boy.

Right-Boy is supposed to hit Glitter Boy, so he does. SMACK—right across the face, hard enough to bruise knuckles. And ZIP—an electric burst of firecrackers as every color of the rainbow explodes from the impact. A dozen florid fireflies. Right-Boy smirks—that looks cool. And Glitter Boy's face is blank. That didn't hurt, it seems to say. You can do it again if you'd like, he seems to say. So Right-Boy does it again—this time, harder. CRACK! Even more light—what beautiful colors! CRACK!

The harder he hits, the more light explodes, and the whole time, Glitter Boy's face remains expressionless. Even when he falls to the ground, bloody and trembling and still taking blows. Nothing gets to him; maybe he even likes it. We can do anything we want! We can make all the colors on Earth that we want. And what beautiful colors!

See how much beautiful light this wrong boy can make!

CRACK! CRACK! CRACK!

BEAUTIFUL! BEAUTIFUL! BEAUTIFUL!

FIFTEEN

LILY DRIVES EVERYONE HOME FROM THE BEACH HOUSE
the next morning. Nobody says much during the ride. When I
get dropped at my house, Lily and I don't kiss.

I'm walking up my front steps when I see it: the Studio couch,
sitting along the side of our house draped in a plastic tarp. That's
the first red flag.

Piles of broken wood are strewn throughout the backyard.

I recognize my desk first—it's sawed into several sections,
and the corner joints have been smashed with a hammer. Next I
notice the side table Dad built me, disposed of in the same way.
My chair and coffee table lay in a separate pile, pinning down the
rolled-up area rug. Cardboard boxes full of my desk possessions
are lined up next to the porch.

The empty Studio gapes out at me.

Dad's on the ground. He's grasping at the wall and grunting in
pain—trying to get up, but his knees are too wobbly. He falls back
onto the floor, where a patch has been torn up to expose old concrete.

234

When he sees me, all he says is, "You were supposed to be home an hour ago."

"Where's Mom?"

"She drove down to D.C. for the immigration reform rally this afternoon." He tries again and manages to stand, groaning through his teeth as he does. Then he repeats, "You were supposed to be home an hour ago."

My eye catches Dad's tool caddy on the Studio floor. "Where did . . . why do you have a reciprocating saw?"

"Sectioning the drywall." Dad leans against the wall, panting. "Makes it easier to rip off."

He's bluffing. Power tools—anything more than a 20-volt drill—are the enemy. That's how it's been since the dawn of time, with both him and I. Neither of us can handle the noise.

I look at the pieces of my desk. Numbness.

"You didn't have to get rid of the furniture," I murmur.

Dad gives me a *what-can-you-do* shrug. "Got no use for it if there's no Studio."

"Okay." I compose myself. "Listen to me."

"Sure."

"You don't need to destroy the Studio. Why do that, right? I mean, you built it, it works well . . ." I start grasping at straws. "You, you can keep it! Do that, yeah. Just keep it, go ahead. Use it for something. But just please don't . . . tear it up. Just, whatever you do."

"I didn't build it for me, okay," he says with another shrug. "I built it for you. I explained to you why I'm doing this. This is not about me taking things from you to give to myself, or somehow benefiting—"

"Take the stuff! Take all of it—I don't care!" I chew on my lip, digging my nails into my skin. "You built it, so take it—"

"I built it for you," Dad repeats.

"*Don't destroy it*, seriously!" I stare at the desk, the pristine mahogany stain. Dad's initials carved into the back corner. "Do *not* get rid of anything else; we can figure something out—"

"I don't want to be doing this," Dad says, crossing his arms and coming off the wall. "You remember I laid all this out, right? We went over all of this. There's a very simple thing I've asked you for, which you've insisted on blocking at every turn. This is how it's going to be if we go down that road. But we don't have to. I don't want this, you don't want this. So come on, man." He leans forward until he's almost down to my height. "Just tell me who did this to you. Come on. One conversation, and all this goes away."

I close my eyes against a million images. Faces. Lily, Luke, Principal Graham, Dad, me.

All this goes away.

All this.

Go away.

(All this.)

"Tell me or we're going to gut the entire structure."

"You can't use power tools," I say, my eyes still closed.

"Tell me."

"You can keep the stuff."

"Tell me."

My lip trembles under my teeth. I want this to be over. But what does that look like? Who wins? Lily is hell-bent on holding everything together, and Dad is on a mission to blow it wide open. Two paths, opposites but leading to the same destructive place. And me. Me . . .

I want this to be over.

I open my eyes, fixing them on his chest. I take a deep breath. "I—"

"Yeah?" Dad's eyes light up as he shifts his weight back and forth, a hand pressed to his mouth. "Come on, bud; hey, listen, we do this—you do this—and I'll put all this back. Right now, I promise!" He licks his lips. "I'll put everything back exactly how it was, and we even . . . you can even pick out new furniture, if you want. Why don't we do that? You just tell me this, we do this *one thing*, and everything will go away, okay. I'll fix up the Studio like new—better than new!—and keep it that way so you can visit whenever you want when you get back. You just need to tell me this. So come on, man."

I stand in silence, reaching for words that aren't there.

"Do you need time? Take your time. Come on. Or, or . . . how about this? How about I go get a paper and pen, and you can just write it down. No need to say a word about it at all. Should I do that? I can go get it right now, you can just write down who it was, and that'll be it. All over." When I stand there unmoving, unresponsive, Dad's eyes dim. The panic in his voice climbs. "Or how about this? Would you be more comfortable telling someone else? You could tell your mother, or a friend, and they could just let me know. Or, hell . . . cut me out of the process altogether. You could tell the police directly! I'd never need to know who it was. However you want to do this, get it reported; this is your show."

Dad is sputtering and shaking and we both stand there in the Studio, the exposed concrete between us, our arms tight to our chests.

I close my mouth,
Open it,
And close it.
And shut my eyes.
And shake my head.

SIXTEEN

THE CLASSICAL MUSIC IS GONE. INSTEAD DAD BLARES death metal at the speaker's maximum volume. Shredding both our ears. He has earplugs in his tool kit, but he doesn't let either of us use them. He makes me jam a crowbar into the baseboard trim, holding it in place while he hammers—*CLANG, CLANG, CLANG*.

(Steve Turner, the Destroyer.)

With every earsplitting hit, he and I both grunt, wince, jolt. Still we don't stop. His huge shoulders scrunch, agony written all over his face as he fights the urge to reduce the noise. I yell at him to turn the music off. He yells at me to tell him who did this.

We rip the trim off, cracking it down the middle and tossing it into the grass. Next we resume pulling up the linoleum floor, jamming our tools under the groove and twisting to pop it off. Dad's knees start to give out again. When he tries to get up, he yelps in pain and stumbles into the wall, hugging it for support.

"Dad—seriously!" Jesus Christ, he's going to kill himself.

"Tell me," he spits.

"Stop, just fucking stop!"

"Tell me who!" He's doubled over, the death metal hammering him, his hands on his head. Cowering from invisible torturers.

"Who was it, Owen? Tell me."

"NO!"

He says, "Motherfucker," at the same time as I yell, "Mother-fucker!"

Just stop.

Tell me.

No. Stop.

(Just tell me.)

No. Stop.

And then:

"WHAT THE HELL ARE YOU DOING?"

My mother's voice has never made me jump like that before. The crowbar jumps out of my hands, and I wheel around to see her standing on the other side of the yard. She's dressed in a T-shirt that reads *No Human Is Illegal*, and her eyes are huge and horrified.

"STEVE!" She screams it at the top of her lungs as she marches toward us, stopping to press pause on the music. My ears ring and burn against the new empty air.

Dad sits back on his knees and resumes hammering at the piece of drywall in front of him.

Mom ignites.

"*What the hell is wrong with you?* HE'S A *CHILD*, STEVE! This is your *son!* Look at you—look at what you're *doing!* Steve, you stop right now and look at me. Steve. STOP!"

The hammer hits, hits, hits.

Mom grabs me by the wrist and pulls me back, holding me away like I'm a toddler and Dad is a dangerous stranger. I struggle against her grip. "Mom—"

"Owen, go inside. *Inside*, now!"

The hammer hits, hits, hits.

My hands clamp over my ears. I feel like I'm seven again;

the drywall is flying in powdered pieces, my father is yelling, the hammer hits hits hits; I'm scared and trying to figure out what to do and my mother, who's never cursed in front of me before, is screaming, "You put that fucking hammer down; Steve, you look at me *right fucking now!*"

The drywall, flying in powdered pieces—

The hammer hits, hits, hits—

And my father bellows at the wall, "*Tell me who it was!*"

"Owen, I said go inside!"

"Mom!" I don't know why I yell for her—she's right next to me. I start to ask her if I should call the police, and her head whips back and forth urgently as she says, "No no, *don't* call the police! Steve, you listen to me. If you keep going, you're not coming back in the house."

The hammer freezes.

Holds.

"I mean it," Mom says. Her eyes are brimming; her face, twisted in fiery adamance. My calm-in-a-crisis mother is, at long last, no longer calm.

Dad looks up and puts a rattling hand over his rattling mouth.

And says, "I'll stop when Owen says who did it."

Mom's grip on me tightens. I don't answer.

Dad stares at us, expressionless. Then he stands, limps to the other side of the Studio, and brings the reciprocating saw over.

"Steve, I swear to Christ." Mom takes a step back. "I will call someone to come change the locks. I will put a suitcase full of your shit on the front lawn. You turn that on, and you're out. I mean it. *Stop*. Ste—"

She's still saying his name when the saw roars to life.

SEVENTEEN

April 2nd—Senior Year

Journal:

I was in the middle of window shopping on the apps today when I got an email from Dad.

Owen—it looks like rain tonight. Good chance to practice wet driving in the school parking lot. Be ready to go by 1900.

We'd practiced at the school a few times before, but this was the first time doing so in the rain.

"Just remember: steady movements, easy on the gas," he said. "We're going to go to the second-to-last parking space on the right, loop around past that bush, and come to a full stop."

As always, I loved how clear his directions were—he never got nervous; he always knew exactly what to tell me. I felt safe with him as a guide.

He had me try pulling around to the back lot, and I was just easing into it when he said, "Hold on. You see that on the ground?"

I squinted at where he was pointing, about fifteen feet ahead.

"It looks like a boot," I said. "I can go—"

"WHOA, stopstopSTOP!"

I squeaked and slammed on the brakes. Dad wrenched the wheel out of my grip. The brakes jackhammered under my shoes as the anti-locks kicked in, and we slid to the side.

"Hazards on!" Dad barked.

"Wh—"

"Do it now." When I fumbled with it, he leaned and punched the hazards button with his fingertip. Then he got out of the car—T-shirt and ratty jeans and all—into the downpour. I was fumbling with what to do when I saw him waving at me to join him. I shut off the car and got out into the rain, yelping at how thick it was. Dad hollered at me through cupped hands, "THERE'S A BLANKET IN THE TRUNK!"

"Huh?"

"THE *BLANKET!* GET THE BLANKET!"

I ran to do as he said, finding an old white throw quilt under a stack of cardboard. I used it to shield my head as I ran back.

"Hurry!" Dad said. He was hunched over the boot, and I was about to ask what the hell he was doing when the boot made a noise, and a head poked out of the opening.

"Oh," I gasped. "Oh my God."

I couldn't tell if it was a kitten or a small cat. Either way, it wasn't in good shape. Its fur was clinging to its face, soaked, and one of its eyes was halfway closed. It was looking right at Dad, who—I did a double take—had eyes as big as saucers and was pressing a hand to his mouth.

"Oh my God. Oh my *God*, look at you." His voice was an octave higher than normal. He was in pieces. "Owen, here, give me that . . . there we go. No, hold on! Don't touch her."

"Are we leaving her in the boot?"

"Calm down. We're going to cover her, use the blanket to keep her steady, and carry the bundle to the car." When I stammered, "Al-alright," he said, "Come *on*, bud!"

Five minutes later, I was sitting in the passenger's seat with the bundle tucked securely on my lap. My father, dripping water everywhere, was back in the driver's seat.

"You keep a firm hold on that, okay," he said.

"Are we going home?"

"Emergency vet. Don't dick around with the GPS; I know the way." He was still panting like he'd just escaped a burning building. "Hold the bundle tight, just hold it. It's very important that you do what I say right now."

I reaffirmed my grip on the blanket. I kept waiting to get yelled at, but Dad spent the whole drive talking to the boot.

"Shh, sweetie, it's okay," he said, when we heard a small noise come from it. It was the softest I'd ever heard him speak in my life. When we got to a red light, he leaned down.

"You're okay, sweetie," he whispered, a lopsided smile on his face. "Shh. Oh my God, look at you. Such a pretty girl. Keep those gorgeous eyes open. Shh. You're okay."

"How do you know she's female?" I asked.

"The genitals are saddled right up against the anus. On a male cat it'd be farther apart, okay."

(I don't have the first fucking idea how he knew that.)

Dad reached gingerly into the boot. I heard a small

noise, and my father dissolved.

"Oh my God, I'm sorry! I'm so sorry, sweetie. Shh, oh my *gosh*." His eyes were still enormous. He said in a splintered voice, "Owen—uh, bud, you're going to have to be the one to bring her inside. We'll be there in a minute."

We didn't even park—just pulled right up to the curb, and I rushed the bundle into the e-vet to hand off to the people there. Dad took care of the paperwork once he'd pulled into a space. Then he collapsed into the chair beside me, his head in his hands, the boot and blanket in his lap.

"Christ, poor thing—they think she has a damaged spine," he said.

The two of us were the only ones in the waiting room. We both pretended to watch the HGTV show on the screen in the corner.

"How did that happen to her?" I asked the TV.

"Fuck do you think? Someone threw her out into the road, bud."

I didn't answer.

"What a cutie, though," he said, shaking his own head like he couldn't help himself. "Captain Boots."

"Huh?"

"Well, that's her name, okay," he said, like that was obvious. "They called her a brave little soldier when I asked how she was doing, so I was thinking her name would be Captain. But then I wanted something with more character, right? And I was just looking at my lap here, see, and at first I thought Captain Blanket, but what is this, a wuss? Nah, this is a tough cat. What did that teeny little head pop out of? A boot, okay, *so* . . . Captain Boots."

Who the hell was *this* guy? The man who calmly asked

for details when he learned that his own mother had died, brought to his emotional brink by a cat.

"Hey," Dad said to the receptionist, after fifteen minutes. "What's the status?"

"No info yet, I'm sorry. Are you the owner?"

"I—what, yeah, yeah," he said.

She gave him a weird look, and he clarified, "We're going to be, after this."

"It doesn't quite w—"

"Whatever it costs, doesn't matter. Money is no object here. Give her the best treatment; call in goddamn Sanjay Gupta if you need to. I want you to *try* to spend too much money here, understand."

He began pacing throughout the lobby.

"Uh," I said, then tried again. "Uh. We're adopting her?"

"Well, yeah," he said. "What do you think they'd do with the poor girl otherwise?"

"What if Mom doesn't like it?"

"Oh, hell," Dad just said, waving off the idea. "How could anyone say no to that little face?"

The poisonous, pissed-off Dad gradually resurfaced over the next two hours. He started asking for updates every ten minutes, then every five, and finally a vet came out to give him some info: They were working on it, but it looked like Captain Boots had at least partial paralysis in her back legs.

"And it's still touch and go. She's not as strong as we'd like," the vet added.

"Whatever you need to do. You hear me?"

"We'll let you know."

From there Dad kept pacing around the waiting room

and talking. He talked about how he was going to build Captain Boots a wheelchair, and it would be lightweight and stylish and easy for her to use; "the best a kitty could ask for."

He grinned at me and rubbed his hands and told me how he was going to keep the boot she was found in, and we could put it in the spare glass case on our living room shelf, and it would be a reminder of how she came into our lives.

He was going to research the best food and the two of them would watch TV together while she healed. "Like your grandma used to do with this old tabby we had growing up."

He rubbed his face and talked about how good these folks were for taking care of her, and how good I was for swerving out of the way. As I sit here in the waiting room, writing this journal entry to kill the time, I keep looking to my father. And all I see is the joyous grin of a man I'll never understand.

April 3rd — Senior Year

Journal:

Captain Boots died just after nine o'clock. When the vet gave us the news, I waited for Dad to scream or curse or throw a fit. But the only time he got upset was when they gave him shit for wanting the body back, since we weren't the owners. I expected him to give some huge monologue, but he just paid the cremation fee and quietly drove us back.

In a wobbly voice on the way home, Dad talked about Captain Boots like she was the family member we never had. He told stories about how they would've snuggled together when he went to sleep, and she would've clawed up the carpet, but he still would've loved her and given her extra catnip anyway. He talked about how "so many people have something waiting to piss you off," but there was nothing disappointing about Captain Boots. Not her, never her.

Wordlessly I followed him around back when we got home. The ground was wet, but the rain had stopped. Dad got a shovel from the shed and started digging a hole in the backyard, ignoring me when I reminded him there was no body to bury. When he started to have trouble with it, I took over even though I didn't know why we were digging. Maybe we were digging to dig.

We worked until we were both covered in bug bites and had a hole in the ground the size of a pillow. Then Dad crouched down, and I realized he had the boot in his arms.

I watched as he examined it under his head lamp, turning it over in his hands like an artifact. And as he ran his eyes over the holes and chewed-up laces, my father said, "Fuck," tucked the boot under his arm, and started to cry. Not ugly uncontrolled sobs, but soft and stone-faced and for himself.

Eventually he lowered the boot into the hole and mumbled in a hoarse whisper, "You were a good girl, okay." Then he slid the mountain of dirt over the whole thing.

When we went to our rooms that night, Dad just said, "Thank you for your help today."

And despite how incredibly taxing the evening was, I found myself smiling as I fell asleep. I thought about how my father saw Captain Boots—this wounded creature—and just helped her. He didn't yell at her. He didn't blame her. He helped.

And I thought about how we did this together, buried something together—"thank you for your help"—and there was no yelling, no steamrolling, no rudeness. My father changed tonight—I'm sure of it. And that change is here to stay. I'm sure of that too.

EIGHTEEN

DAD SWINGS THE SLEDGE AGAIN AND MOM KEEPS YELLING TO COME INSIDE BUT I CAN'T LOOK AWAY. I DON'T WANT TO BE HERE BUT HE SAYS THE SOONER WE DO THIS THE SOONER I CAN GO INSIDE BECAUSE IT'S LOUD. IT'S TOO LOUD. THE SAWS ARE GOING AND THE DRILL IS GOING AND THE HAMMERS ARE SMASH-ING INTO EVERYTHING, WE WORK FOR HOURS AND WE DESTROY THE DRYWALL, WE DESTROY THE SHELVES, WE HAMMER AND IT'S TOO LOUD BUT HE SAYS HE DOESN'T CARE UNTIL I TELL HIM WHO IT WAS SO I JUST KEEP SWINGING UNTIL THERE'S NOTHING LEFT; ONLY THE BARE STUDS AND THE CONCRETE WALLS AND THE TORN-DOWN TABLE AND THE TORN-DOWN SIGN THAT READS *OWEN'S STUDIO*. AND I WANT TO GET UPSET BECAUSE THE STUDIO IS GONE, BUT I'M JUST RELIEVED WHEN IT'S OVER BECAUSE EVERY-THING IS TOO FUCKING LOUD.

NINETEEN

I WASN'T SURE IF SHE WOULD, BUT MOM REALLY DOES it. When Dad and I emerge from the garage hours later and try to get inside, we find the doors have already been fashioned with new locks. I wait for Dad to throw a fit, to pick up the power tools and saw his way into his home. Instead he picks up the suitcase lying on the front lawn, loads it in his car, and drives off.

Not a word.

I'm still staring at his empty spot in our driveway when Mom comes rushing out and hugs me. She whispers how sorry she is; says a bunch of Mom-things. When I ask her when he'll be allowed back, she gives me a tearful talking-to about how this is for my own safety and it should've happened sooner.

At first, I'm sure that one of them is bluffing—that he'll be back with apology donuts and we'll bullshit our way back to normalcy. But when he's still not here for my eighteenth birthday two weeks later, it sinks in that this may not be temporary.

My present turns out to be a used car—specifically, Mom's used car, which she's replaced with a newer model thanks to a promotion at work.

"Do you want to have your friends over?" she asks me that

night as we eat the brand of ice cream cake I have for my birthday every year.

"We're celebrating next week," I say.

"How about Lily? How's it been with her lately?"

I feed her the usual BS. In the weeks since the argument at
the beach house, Lily and I have mostly stuck to seeing each
other at group events—movie nights at someone else's house or
going swimming at the neighborhood pool. The group is set to
disband the first week of July, aka six days from now: Beth is
going on a family road trip, Austin is moving early to stay at his
brother's place, and Vic got into an honors program that starts a
month before the semester.

So I have a new mode: *Hold on. Hold on until the group dis-
perses, until it's just you and her left. Then break up with her, and
it'll just be you.*

Mom and I watch home videos from my first ever birthday
party while we eat our cake. Her request. We end up leaving it on
for an hour, playing through the first three years of my life . . . tiny
me, going from crawling to walking to talking. Mom is holding the
camera in most of them, but in one, Dad is doing the recording.

I watch as he approaches toddler-Owen, who's on the floor
with a sketchpad and crayons.

"Owen!" says Dad—a younger man; more fun and less
pissed off—in a singsong. Then he growls, in a mock-scary voice,
"What're you doin' down there, huh?"

Toddler-Owen giggles and holds up his drawing, beaming
proudly for the camera. The picture is of two stick figures, smiling
and holding hands under a lopsided sun. One—whose shirt is
made of green and brown—towers over the other. The poorly-
scribbled caption:

Me + Dada.

Dad laughs—(laughs!)—and says, "Did *you* do that! *Wowww.* I'm going to put this up on the wall so I can look at it every day!" Then he laughs again and says, "I'm very proud of you . . . you're *so great*, bud."

(You're *so great*, bud.)

When the video finishes and Dad's voice leaves the air, the house is quiet again.

Mom tries to compensate by making more small talk. It reminds me of the days back when Dad was deployed, when she and I would do things like this to distract ourselves from his absence.

Neither of us addresses the ugly part, though: that he's not overseas serving his country this time. Instead he's alone up at his cabin, cut off from everything he used to come home to.

TWENTY

April 5th — Senior Year

Journal:

I've just scheduled my first hookup. I suppose I'm still
processing that—I didn't start out with that intention. I
was sitting in the Studio, browsing through group pictures from senior prom the day before. I'd just smoked the
last of the weed I bought from Austin, and I decided to do
some window shopping.

The thing is, today's person deviated from the script.
For one, they initiated the conversation with a polite
message:

Hello, how are you today? :)

So, a step up from the usual.

I typed a response back and made some small talk to
warm him up. I checked out his profile, which had three
things listed: his name (Dewey), his age (eighteen), and
his bio ("bi, shy, and ready to cry"). It's the type of thing
that would've charmed me if I were new to the game, but

I knew how this worked by now. First rule of the app: No one who seems nice up front is immune to being a dick. Full stop.

It wouldn't have gone any further than that, but then he went off-book again: When I tried to start the usual dirty talk, he shut it down. His message read:

Hey, would you be comfortable meeting up in person instead of doing this over text

It's completely fine if not. I just can't stand this interface.

I closed out the app. Useless.

But then he sent a follow-up:

Will you be at the pride festival this weekend?

This time, I replied.

Isn't pride in June?

His answer, a few minutes later:

Yeah, this is a festival being hosted by the county library system. I think they want to have it in the spring so more students can go. I'm helping run the library booth, so I'll be there all day. We could meet up then and see where things go from there :P

For a while, I didn't type back.

I had to resist the urge to call him out for his false politeness . . . that nice-guy act these assholes always pulled until you didn't give them what they were after. I wanted to tell him to go fuck himself, just to watch that courteousness crumble and buckle to a bunch of profanities and playground insults.

But the thing was, I wasn't sure I wanted to tank this right away. Part of me wanted to meet one of these gray squares in the flesh just to see what it was like.

I'm still not entirely sure why. But I told him fine.

He couldn't resist another peppy reply:

Great! Let me know when you arrive, and I can meet you at the front entrance. And we can play it by ear from there :)

I set down my phone without answering.

TWENTY-ONE

OUR GROUP'S FINAL HANGOUT ALSO SERVES AS MY belated birthday celebration—combined at my request. The best gift they could give me was the free rein to plan out our final day together. They all know that; so that's what they do.

Technically it isn't everyone's last day. . . . Vic will be around for another week, and Beth and Austin will be back for a few days separately in August. But none of it will overlap, so I asked that this be the last time I see them before leaving. I want a clean break, a clear moment of farewell with all three of them at once. I want an *event*.

And I get one: The five of us spend the entire day together, and we do everything on my list. Breakfast at the local diner, just like on senior skip day. Swimming at the pool and having a water gun fight like we did two summers ago. Packing a picnic lunch and eating it in the bed of Austin's pickup truck. I even allow for a surprise deviation where they drive me to the gas station across the street so they can watch me buy my first scratch-off ticket. It wins two dollars.

I take pictures throughout the day, and we eventually end up doing an entire group photoshoot down by the playground. We capture a dozen different pairings: Austin and I doing finger guns, the three girls leaned against each other, cute ones of the couples, jokey ones of all five of us in sunglasses.

"Shit, I blinked!" Austin yells for the last one.

The last leg of the day is spent in the spot where it all started: roasting veggie burgers and s'mores at the fire pit. I try to take in the feeling as everyone starts to reminisce . . . talking about the days when we'd watch *Judge Judy* at Beth's house after school, or the time Austin donned a full snowsuit to kill a wasp in Vic's basement. Eventually we run out of memories, so we devolve into the usual banter.

"I want to grow a tail someday," Austin tells us matter-of-factly.

"No you don't," Beth says, shuddering. "Ew!"

"Oh hell yeah I do. We'll be back for Thanksgiving and I'll be swatting people all over the place with that thing."

"Ooh, just picture how that would spice up sex," says Lily.

"Ew! I don't want to picture that! No, *stop!*" Beth screeches as Vic tickles the back of her neck with a leaf. And even though I laugh, there's a sadness to it as I stare at the flames and think one thing over and over: *I miss these people already.*

Eventually thunder rumbles and rain rolls through, so the five of us pack up our stuff and cluster under the pavilion. I'm afraid we're about to disband, but we stay talking for almost another hour. Our conversations are unimportant—stupid stuff like what gives rain its smell or how often our future roommates are going to shower. But I feel the impending goodbye growing with each second, and I think the others do too.

The thing about goodbyes like this is that they don't take their toll in an immediate way. No one is dying and no one is disappearing for good. But this moment—the quiet, cataclysmic shift happening *here* and happening *now*—is always what marks the beginning of the end. It's not like you're going to stop seeing each other; but from here on out, you'll see each other a little less, bit by tiny bit. It's scary how subtle it is. Slow and soundless. Then one day years from now, it'll dawn on you that those people have found their way out of your life for good, and you'll realize how right you were to be sad on that rainy day under the pavilion in the first place.

"Alright, guys," Vic eventually says. She looks us over. "I've got to head back."

"Same," says Austin, wiping the fog off his glasses.

It's the same exchange we've had a hundred times before, but this one has a different ending.

"Wait," I say, scrambling to my feet. "Beth, what classes are you taking again?"

She gives me a sad little smirk—she knows what I'm doing. "You already asked me that."

"Wait!" I repeat, more urgently. But Beth just steps toward me, takes me by the shoulders, and looks me right in the eyes.

"Owen," she says . . . gently, but with a tough-love edge. "Hey. It's time."

"No it's not." I grimace like I'm joking, but my throat is closing up.

"Yes it is. Come here—yes it is. Come here."

I start to cry as she hugs me. Then Austin, who promises he'll visit. And all the while, I look over to the spot where we had our first bonfire. *There we are.* The five of us laughing, bantering, and me . . . me, I know with everything I am that things are *happening*—that this is exciting, and new, and the start of something that will scoop up my whole heart. And little-me might be barely fourteen, but he already knows to fear the day when that goodbye comes. Because when it does, no matter how much you've braced for it, you still find yourself in frantic search of a loophole—the same way you try to stay asleep in a blissful dream when you know you're waking up. The moment always comes when you open your eyes and you're grabbing onto your sheets just like you knew you would be, because no matter how hard you try or how much you want it, this system can't be hacked. This is here, this is happening, and it's time. *Listen, now, because it's important to understand: It's time.*

Vic's hug is the last and longest. As we hold each other, she says into my shoulder, "Remember our talk, yeah? People will show up for you."

And I fill up with so many things I can't tell the group because I don't want to make it weird—things like, "Thank you for being nice to me when you didn't need to." "Thank you for that night at senior week." "Thank you for my life and every day you were in it." So instead I dig out three copies of a goodbye letter I wrote them last night and tell them to read it later. And as they promise they will, all I add is, "I'm never going to meet people like you again."

Lily puts her arm around me as all the others swap hugs too, and they say all the standard goodbye phrases like "we'll video chat all the time" and "see you at Thanksgiving." We're at the ugliest part now—the part where we've said all we need to say, wringing every meaning we can out of this separation. Everything we came to do here is done, and all that's left is to let go of that too.

And then it's finished, just like that. Like all those countless nights that the five of us said, "Alright . . . 'night, guys!" and walked our separate ways back home. Austin Lambert, Vic Parmar, and Beth Lieberman all shout, "Bye!" and "Later!" and squeal as they run off into the rain.

And I'm about to turn away when suddenly I yell, "WAIT!" and chase after them, gesturing for Lily to follow. They halt in their tracks and Austin is in the middle of saying, "Dude,

I really need to run—" when I pull out my phone and ask for a picture.

"Move in a little closer—that's good," I say, and I snap the picture of the four of them standing by the playground, arms around each other.

"Wait, dude, you're not in it!" Beth says.

"I don't need to be," I remind her.

TWENTY-TWO

LILY OFFERS TO WALK ME HOME FROM THE PAVILION. It's dark outside and I'd prefer to be alone, but I tell her yes because I can tell she wants to.

Now's your perfect chance. Just do it, dude.

I practice the words in my head: "I want to break up." But my mouth doesn't match it.

Do it before you get to the house.

"So—" I start.

"Oh, before I forget." Lily pats my arm with two fingers. "Can you gerbil-sit for two weeks in August? Like a month from now."

"Huh?"

"Dad and I are planning a trip to my grandparents' place in Milwaukee—our last family time before I leave for college and stuff. So I was just wondering if you could, you know. Sit on my gerbils."

Shit. How am I supposed to answer? Say no and raise suspicion, or say yes and then break up immediately after?

"You can do it, right? Please?"

"Sure," I blurt out. *Shit.*

We're at my house.

"Are you okay?" she asks.

"I'm fine," I lie. "I just want to be alone."

"It doesn't look like it." She grips my arm. "I'm not leaving you alone like this. Why don't we do something?"

I don't want to do something right now.

"No thanks."

"Come on—we're doing it."

IwanttobreakupIwanttobreakupI—

I head around the side of my house.

She calls after me as she follows, clearly confused. I keep walking, slowly even though we're getting wet in the rain. I navigate around the piles of debris in the yard and lift our garage door open. I step into the structure that was once the Studio—open and empty, except for a few bags of trash.

"Whoa," says Lily. "What the hell?"

No more drywall—bare studs. No more linoleum floors—just the grimy, cracked concrete. All the pretty topcoats scraped away to expose the rot underneath.

So much destroyed.

I slap my own arm, listening to the echo.

"Can I ask you something?" I say. "And I promise I'm not trying to be a dick. I really want to know this."

She raises an eyebrow. "Okay?"

"Why do you do this?"

"Do what?"

I shake my head. "You listen to me sit here day after day, and I ask you to take no for an answer, and you don't. I explained why it's important to me; I think you know that, so . . . what goes through your head when I ask you to stop doing something?"

I don't want to discuss this. I don't want to have this same fight again and get shoveled the same bullshit and—

"I don't know what you mean," she says.

"I'm not trying to yell at you, or blame you, or whatever, I just . . ." I rub my palms together, trying to start a fire between my wrists. "I'm *asking*. I'm trying to figure out how you think."

"I don't need a lecture right now, dude."

"It's *not* a——" I pull at my bracelet. "I'm not trying to lecture you; I want to know. I just want to know."

"What are you trying to say right now?"

"I'm not trying to say anything! Shit!"

"Can you not yell at me? Can you manage that and not be a fucking child?"

I try to open my mouth and unleash verbal fury; to tell her that I'm not yelling, I'm not lecturing, I'm not implying, I'm not stating, I'm not accusing, I'm not attacking, I just, JUST am asking because I want to know; that's all, that's it. I want to know because I'm sick of having to defend goddamn reality. But as I open my mouth, I look at her and I think about all the words boiling inside me, how they're just new versions of all the same things I've said to her a hundred times, how no one who couldn't understand me before would suddenly understand me if I said it *just one more time*, and all that ends up coming out is a tiny tight-lipped whimper, and I fall back against the bare wall, poised in grim acceptance that this is how things are.

(This is how things are.)

Then I say, "I think you don't want to stop, and I think you knew what you were doing."

"Wh——God. Wait."

"Sure."

"What do you mean, I knew what I was doing?"

"I think you knew it was wrong. While you were doing it, I think you knew it was wrong."

"Are we talking about what I think we're talking about? Again?"

"You said it was complicated, but how, how could it be

complicated? It couldn't, right? Because it—"

"Jesus Christ—"

"—it shouldn't be complicated; if someone is doing something like that, you tell them 'please *stop*; you are hurting me,' and if they care, they'll stop; but you didn't, because you don't."

"Oh—yeah, okay." Lily grabs her own head in the darkness. "And you don't think there's *any* chance it could be more complicated than that, no? Just . . . you've got it all figured out, done?"

I feel so stupid for how I started this. The way I tried to give her the benefit of the doubt, to make an earnest attempt to understand her. Because every time it happens, it's like seawater for thirst—all you want is some relief, but each time, it just makes you sicker and leaves you worse off.

"Nothing I'm saying is unreasonable," I say, softly. "Stop treating it like it is."

"You want to know what *I* think—"

"Not really."

"—*I* think the problem is on your end. I love you, but pretty much anything gets you worked up, and this is why—let me finish, please—see, *this* is why I keep suggesting you look into stuff like exposure therapy, because it can help you to stop getting hung up on things that aren't worth getting hung up over."

"You never, ever fail to somehow take the astoundingly low bar I've set and find a way to curb stomp it."

"*I'm not saying* your feelings aren't valid; but clearly you're upset about that night at Lanham and I think you could be a lot happier if you worked harder to—"

"Stop."

"Stop what?"

"Stop bullshitting me. Please."

"Stop bullshitting you?"

"Please."

"Wh—O—"

"You do this all the time." I come off the wall, stepping toward her. "You say things that sound like they're supposed to help me, but really are to get you off the hook. There's nothing we can discuss that's going to make me okay with the night at Lanham. I think we need to break up."

"That's *rich*." Lily scoffs. "You lecture me about not giving you a choice, and now you want to just make a unilateral decision that affects both of us, with no input from me. Not everything can be your way, O—that's not how a relationship works."

"*Fuck* this." I turn away from her. "I want you to leave."

"Seriously?"

"Seriously. Go home and yell all this shit into a brown paper bag—it'll do as much good then as it is now."

"I want to talk about this."

"No you don't. You want to explain to me why I shouldn't be feeling the things I feel, so you can justify why you haven't done anything wrong." I draw strength off my own voice, my conviction. "I don't owe you a conversation anytime you want to have one."

"*I think you do.*"

"That crushes me."

"Fuck off with your sarcasm."

"Goodbye."

"Hey!" Lily steps toward me. "I am *not* leaving."

"I'm asking you to."

"That crushes me."

Don't let up now; no, keep going, keep going!

I work my mouth, trying to use my momentum to load the next round into the chamber. But nothing comes out, because I'm just so, so sick of all this. The feeling of groveling for good-will that isn't there and never will be. Then you recharge just enough to think you're ready to go again, and it knocks you down just as it did before. Oh, the hoops you'll jump through for the slightest bit of deference toward you. And they know it. It's a whole delicious dance for them wrapped and tied with a fucked-up bow. God, why does it need to be this way? I spend half the time agreeing with my own actions, and the other half wanting to throw last week's version of myself down a flight of stairs and yell, *"You goddamn idiot! Of COURSE it wasn't going to change!"*

For the first time since the conversation started, I try to make out Lily's expression in the darkness. I'll say this: She looks exhausted. Almost as drained as I feel. There we stand, the two of us, the rain cutting through the wind to my right. To the left— stillness and silence and dead air.

And I say, softly but without hesitation, "I want us to stop doing this."

"Doing what?"

I don't blink. Simply, "This."

"Yeah, can you be a little more specific? I don't know what you mean."

"Yes, you do."

"Wh—no, I don't. O—"

"You know exactly what I'm talking about."

"I *don't*."

"Yes, you do." I keep my voice level. "You know exactly why I'm upset; you know exactly what I mean right now, and I'm telling you I don't want to do any of this anymore. I don't want to keep doing this same goddamn routine where I try to talk to you about a problem, you find a way to throw it back at me, then promise it'll stop, and I fall for it. I don't know what you call this—this fucking cycle. I don't know if there's a word for it. But I'm calling it this. And I want us to stop doing this."

She blinks at me, bleary-eyed.

"There is a word for it, O; it's called a relationship."

"It's not. But I think you know that too." I take a deep breath. "I think you know a lot of things."

I'm not sure how to describe the war on her face. It's not that her expression dims, exactly . . . it's more like a tight realization, tinged with relief. Like a bank robber who sees the police sirens in the window. Someone who's run out of rope and is at least a little bit relieved to stop running.

Then: reload.

"So, just to be clear," Lily says in a harder voice, "you think that everything I say is bullshit."

"It doesn't matter anymore," I say.

"In other words, I just have to deal with whatever accusation you make of me. I have no options."

"Acknowledge it or don't. You have two options."

"Well in that case, we shouldn't be in a relationship."

"Okay."

"*Okay?* That's what you have to say?"

Yeah—for once, it is. And God, it feels good.

"So, what I'm hearing is you don't care at all about us," she spits.

"Okay."

"Any of it. Not about me, or my feelings, or anything you may have done to cause it. All that—right out the window. Just gone. You don't care about anything you personally may have done to hurt someone you're supposed to love. That's pretty messed up, don't you think? That's what you're saying right now. You're saying that you don't care if you hurt other people. Am I wrong? Correct me if I'm wrong, but that's what I'm getting from this."

"Okay."

"I just want to get that on record."

"Okay."

"Say something else! *Christ!*" She shuffles toward me, both arms outreached like she's coming to wring my neck. I stare at a tree in the distance, a silhouette shivering in the storm. She starts hitting me in the arms, then in the chest.

I let my eyes go out of focus and keep them there.

She grabs my shoulders, digging her nails in. I bite down on my lip to keep a noise from slipping out.

"O," she says, her voice wobbling, "you're making a *mistake*."

I say, "Fine."

"What?"

"Fine—maybe I am. Maybe in ten years I'll be sitting in some bar remembering this and I'll think, *You idiot, you threw away a perfectly healthy relationship because you're a dumbass.*" I size her up. "Only I don't think that's what I'll be thinking in some bar ten years from now. I think I'll be thinking, *Holy shit, why did I put up with that and how the hell did I do it for so* long?"

"You *need* me. Do you remember what it was like before you met me? You were *fucking* helpless."

I don't answer. She's found my weakest spot.

"*One* more chance." She's panicking now. "O, I'm sorry for everything, but please. Things will be different, I swear."

I feel her words worming their way into my head.

This is the narrative, isn't it? *Man, if only you'd given things ONE more chance, this would've been the time it shaped up!* But that was the narrative six chances ago. There will always be a "one more time," but there won't ever be a change. So now I'm the asshole for pulling the plug on things.

"I don't think I'm wrong about this," I tell her. "But if I am, I still don't care."

Lily lowers her arms.

Instead of answering, she walks over to the center of the room. Lays down under the skylight. At first I hear a noise that

I think is the wind, but then I realize it's her—panting for air, hyperventilating.

I kneel down next to her. She's trembling. I ask what's wrong, and she stammers, "Panic attack," and next thing I know, I'm holding her and we're rocking back and forth and I'm whispering that it'll be okay the same way she's done for me before.

"I'm sorry," I murmur in her ear.

Idiot.

"Forget what I said. We'll figure it out later," I say.

Fool.

Lily stops shaking and rolls over onto her back, wiping her eyes.

I lie beside her under the ethereal glow of the moon—our fingers almost touching but not quite; our free arms lodged under our necks. I watch the rain eat at the glass pane above us, imagining it bursting and flooding the whole room. The two of us suspended in all the weight of the water. I play Brian Eno's "Ascent" in my head . . . the song I was listening to when Lily's hand touched mine for the first time.

I blink twice. Two blinks—I'm back at that day when she and I laid on this floor after losing our virginities and watched the sky before it was inked out by this ugly gray. How hilariously young we were . . . everything so simple and genuine. No fighting. No hurting each other or staying up until 3:00 a.m. wondering if I can keep doing this. Just bright, blissful existence of being.

The hand that takes mine is cold, but I pretend it's hers. Not the girl beside me—the girl from back then. I pretend I'm the boy from back then. I imagine that I can blink us back in time, to that era, to the covered-up concrete and the sameness of our hearts.

Beneath the moonlight, the girl beside me says, "Tell me what you're thinking."

I wonder if intentions can change who we are.

I wonder if everything I've ever felt will drain out of me someday.

"Why couldn't you just stop?" I whisper.

She turns her head to frown at me in confusion.

"Do you want me to say sorry again?" she asks. "Is that what you want me to do?"

I shake my head, eyes sealed shut. "I just want to sleep."

"Will an apology fix this?"

"No."

"What will?"

"Nothing."

I feel her eyes on me, but I don't open mine.

"You know," she says. "Every day since I met you, I've spent half my time wanting to kill you and the other half wanting to hug you."

"I know."

She tries to hug me. I don't let her, so she hits my shoulder instead.

And there we lie.

"When I was younger," I say slowly, "starting probably when I was around ten, I started going to sleep thinking about what it'd be like to be somebody's boyfriend. I'd listen to slow songs and picture someone to dance with." I snort. "Sometimes I'd grab my pillow—the big one—and hug it, pretending it was a person. There was even this one time, I held my own hand and I acted like it was someone else's."

The girl squeezes my fingers and gives a small sound that I think is a laugh.

"And eventually I'd need to let go of the pillow or my hand or stop the slow song and there was this comedown that was just so lonely. It was like a reminder that this would never actually happen."

"And then it did," she whispers.

(And then it did.)

"What did you think?" she asks.

"When it happened?"

"When it happened."

I lean away from her. "I kept thinking it was too great to be real."

"That doesn't make sense."

"I guess not."

"What do you want, O?"

I stay silent, listening to the rain and the night noises around us. Feeling my achy bones and the enormous cavern in my chest—a hole where my heart feels like it was hacked away months ago.

"At this point, I just want something to turn out the way I'm picturing it in my head," I say.

"That's no fun, though."

"But it's predictable. And safe."

"Nothing is predictable or safe."

I wait a long time before voicing the next thought that comes into my head. The one that's been lingering there for a while.

"This used to be," I tell her. *You used to feel safe.*

And what I almost add, but don't: I feel even more alone now than I did in my bedroom as a kid. Because at least then I had someone to wait for. A fantasy girl instead of some shattered illusion, splintered and skewed by the harshness of knowing unknowable things.

I feel a hand—hers—come to rest on my chest, just above my heart. She keeps it there, applying pressure so light that her fingers are almost floating above the fabric of my shirt. I inhale for as long and slow as I can, then exhale as long and slow as I can.

I think of those two little kids lying on the ground, and I

want to exist Nowhere and Everywhere at the same time. I feel the overwhelming urge to be alone, but I can't stand the thought of not having someone next to me. I picture what it would be like to leave this whole body. Pulled out of it until I've separated from every drop of blood and piece of bone. Lifting me through the roof and the rain until I'm Everything and Nothing at the same time. Tinier than a molecule but all around in the air and the clouds and the stratosphere. A sky soul. Nothing. Everything. Nowhere. Everywhere.

I open my eyes and find Lily staring back at me. Not upset, not smiling, not brimming with a single unspoken thought. Just locking her empty eyes with mine.

Finally she whispers, "Look at us."

I do. And this time, I'm looking down at the children on the concrete. They look just like us. They're smiling at each other— laughing, teasing, discovering life—searching for their future with wide-eyed wonder. And I feel so fucking sad for what they'll find.

STORY THREE

PPP

ONE

April 12th — Senior Year

Journal:

Our town's pride festival was held at one of the local parks. The parade was the day before, but this was more of a low-key event with booths, food vendors, live music, games for kids . . . stuff like that. Mom was thrilled to drive me over, but I told her I was meeting up with Lily and the others. I waited until her car disappeared to pull out my phone and message Dewey that I was at the main entrance.

I pulled at my bracelet as I waited for him, thinking over all the logistics. Where were we going to do this? I'd checked the park map, and they had single-use bathrooms on site, but I didn't know how clean they'd be. Who was going to do what? And all this was assuming this dude was even 1) real and 2) here.

I looked up from my phone and noticed a guy about my age staring at me from the park entrance. I was pretty sure it was him, but he wasn't moving. Then he sighed to himself, like he'd just made a command decision, and started walking in my direction.

I took a second to size him up. He was around my age—a Latino boy with neatly combed black hair and wide brown eyes behind a set of thin-rimmed glasses. Between his face full of acne and awkward slouch, he wasn't exactly cute, but not bad either. His fingernails were painted a metallic blue, and he wore a white V-neck that read *Choose Books Not Bigotry* in rainbow text. As he got closer, I saw that he had a bi pride flag drawn on his right cheek with face paint.

Definitely him.

He was a few steps away, typing on his phone, when his foot caught a stray tree root on the ground. His march devolved into a stumble as he was sent careening right in my direction, barely catching himself before he ate shit.

I was trying to figure out whether I should say something when he held up one finger and said to the grass, in a mortified voice, "I meant to do that."

As I blinked at him, he turned his phone to show me a message he'd been typing in our chat thread:

I'mmm heeere!

I turned on social mode. "Hey, careful not to trip."

"That's my second time today, believe it or not," he said. He had a nice voice—a little soft and subdued, but with an upbeat edge. Like nothing could ruin his day. "I was carrying a box of books the first time, though."

When I didn't respond, he said, "Should I ask if you remember me?"

"Huh?"

"Okay, didn't think so." He chuckled. "I live in your neighborhood. I'm the guy in the green house, like one street over? We had a conversation in the locker room one time about autosexuality?"

"Oh. Oh, wow." I looked him up and down again. His hair was different than before—the mop was chopped off, and his glasses had changed—but now that he'd pointed it out, I put two and two together.

"I recognized you while I was walking over," he said. "Good to see you again. Thanks for making the drive here."

"I was dropped off, but yeah."

"Ah. Still."

"Where are we doing this?" I blurted out. For some reason, I trusted him even less than before. Had he been stalking me? It felt like he was trying to cover something up. I wanted to get this over with.

"Oh." He blinked, clearly thrown. "Is it okay with you if we walk around for a few minutes? Just so I can make sure you're not a serial killer or anything. Sorry if that's weird."

"Any serial killer could pretend they're not one for a few minutes," I pointed out.

I could tell from his face that this was not the right thing to say, so I just told him fine.

As we made our way into the park, I got absorbed by trying to take everything in. A stage was set up near the center of the park with a live band singing a Lady Gaga cover. Food trucks and pride gear vendors lined the paved pathways, which snaked all the way around a lake. It was late in the afternoon, so the sun was out but hidden behind the trees. The air smelled like spring. Clusters of all types of people—families, couples, groups of friends, organizers—were all over the place, most of them decked out in pride gear. Suddenly I felt out of place in my plain blue T-shirt, but the vibe was so electric, I didn't even mind.

"Is this your first pride event?" Dewey asked, noticing the look on my face.

I nodded.

"Neat! Same here." He jumped on that, giving me finger guns. "I've been manning the library booth for most of the day, though, so I haven't gotten a chance to walk around yet. This is nice."

I didn't respond.

"Do you mind if I ask if you're like . . ." He glanced at me, lobbing his head. "Gay, or bisexual, or . . . ?"

"Bi."

"Neat! Bi-five." As soon as he held up his hand for a high-five, he cringed at himself and lowered it. "Oh my God. Ignore me. I'm already regretting that. Sorry."

"You're fine." Once upon a time, this awkwardness would've had me falling head over heels. Now, though, it just pissed me off. *Nice try, but I've seen this shit before. I'm enlightened to the fact that no one hauls out their real face at first. I know what you're doing and I know how this works.*

I tried to get us back on track.

"So what's our plan?" I asked him. We looped around the path, so we were walking parallel to the lake. "Where did you want to do this?"

"Hm. Right here!" His voice went higher. "No, I'm joking. Actually, do you mind if we talk a little longer first? Sorry. I really don't mean to, like—"

"It's fine."

"Well I mean, I can tell you're kind of annoyed, dude. And I appreciate you working with me." He fiddled with his glasses, drifting a few inches away from me as we made our way past a pack of college kids. "I don't want to be one of those guys that talks a big game and says, 'Yeah, let's do this!' then flakes for no reason."

"Can't stand that shit," I said. "Why does *everyone* do that?"

"You know, I have no idea. I think about that a lot." Dewey's face scrunched up. "I mean, the answer is because we're on an app to interact with strangers. There's that weird sense of entitlement when you're behind a screen. Right? I know I sound like I'm forty, but isn't there?"

I just nodded. He stopped to grab a smoothie from a nearby vendor, and we plopped down in the grass near the stage.

Get this over with.

"But yeah, I'm not on any social media," he continued. He held out his smoothie. "Want a sip?"

"I'm good. You don't have *any* social media?"

"Absolutely none, nada. If someone wants to say something shitty, they need to either have my phone number, or else say it in person. Which isn't much better, but—"

"I think it is," I cut him off. "If someone's going to do that, I prefer in person."

"Oh, I disagree. If someone yells at me in person, that's like . . . oof." He thumped himself in the chest. "Just the worst feeling on Earth."

"But texts stay there," I pointed out. "You can look at a text an hour later and it's like you're re-experiencing it."

"This is true." He nodded. "But I think in person is worse because then they can really have a *tone*. You know? That leaves more of an impression on me, anyway."

"People are just assholes."

"Which people?"

"People."

He scoffed, playing with his straw. "And yet, you and I and a lot of other folks download those apps, and talk to the assholes, and give the assholes the time of day . . ."

"I didn't say it was a working system."

"No, I mean, I'm as guilty as anyone with this, right? When I was younger, if pretty much *any* cute stranger was nice to me, I'd just want to throw everything at them and be like . . . fix me! Hey. Do it now. Did you do it yet?" He gave an exaggerated, hammy smile, then dropped it. "So you try to make it work because hey, you got this far. Sunken cost fallacy and all that."

"I don't know what that is."

"Oh—sorry. I guess an example would be what my dad did with his old jeep. The thing was probably worth, what, like . . . five thousand bucks? But if you look at the past ten years, he's probably spent twice as much on repairs to keep it running. Why would he do that, right?" He answered his own question, leaning back. "It's because each repair on its own is only, like, a few hundred bucks. So you get in this weird position where you've put all this money into something when you would've been better off in the long run just junking it. Hence the name, ta-da: sunken cost."

I chewed on that.

"Anyway." He fought off a mouthful of brain freeze, then stood. "Sorry for getting philosophical. I know it really sets the mood."

"I don't mind," I said. And I realized that I really didn't. Even if I still couldn't pin down what I thought of him.

He leaned to toss his cup in a nearby trash can, pumping

his fist when it landed. "Hey, I need to run some of our booth supplies back to the library at five . . . so basically, now. Do you want to just come with me? It's just up the road. I can run us back here afterward."

"Isn't the library closed on Sundays?"

"That's why I'm asking—I have the key to the building, but it'll be empty. We can maybe . . . use the bathrooms there? Or . . ." He cringed. "We can figure it out from there. Is that cool?"

I still couldn't figure out this guy's deal, but I didn't see a better alternative. So I told him sure. We made our way to the library booth, and I hung back awkwardly while he helped a few other volunteers pack up supplies. He hugged them goodbye, brought a stack of boxes over to me, and we hauled them to his car along with leftover reward pizza.

The walk was long, hot, and humid.

"I apologize in advance if I smell like sweat," Dewey said, as we pulled out of the parking lot.

"You and me both. Also, aren't there security guards?"

"It's a county library, not the Lenin Mausoleum. No cameras in the main area either . . . there's this big debate about customer privacy. We're all set." He cranked up the air conditioning, then his radio. I almost asked him to turn down the volume because it was too loud, but I didn't want to be that guy.

Instead I asked, "What group is this?"

"Isn't it good? Love these guys. This is Fleet Foxes." Dewey leaned back in his seat, grinning at the windshield. "Have you heard of the singer Father John Misty? His real name is Josh Tillman, and this album—*Helplessness Blues*—is the only one to have his backing vocals on it.

I started listening to them a couple years back. 'Mykonos' was the first guitar cover I learned. Yes, I'm one of those guitar douches. That should say a lot about me."

I didn't respond.

"Though I don't play at parties," he assured me. "I mean, I could, but I don't."

"Maybe that's how Josh Tillman started out."

"That's a good point! Very true."

We pulled onto the main road, trees blowing by us overhead. Dewey cracked his window, drumming the steering wheel to the beat of the music.

I bit the bullet. "Can you turn it down a little?"

"Oh, sure. Sorry about that."

"I'm just over-sensitive to sound. I'm on the spectrum."

I don't know why I told him—I hate telling people about it. It feels like I'm trying to score sympathy points. But I guess he didn't strike me as the type of person who I had to worry about that with.

"Just making sure, you mean the autism spectrum, right?"

"Yeah."

"Got it." He paused. "Sorry . . . I don't know what the right thing is to say to that? Like, I didn't want to be like . . ."

"*Congratulations!*" I said in an exaggerated game show host voice.

Dewey laughed, high-pitched and squeaky. "*You're the lucky winner!*"

"One time I told a teacher; I had this teacher, Mrs. Pettrey, and I told her about it, and she said . . . here's what she said: *Oh . . . I'm sorry.*"

"She's like, *I sincerely apologize for this unfortunate incident.*"

"Right? I wanted to be like, *Why are you apologizing? What, did you personally give me autism?*"

"Just gave it to you wrapped up in a gift box and everything."

"You can return it if you don't like it."

"I stapled the gift receipt to the card!"

"Man, that secret Santa is a BITCH."

"We said a FIVE-DOLLAR LIMIT, Mrs. Pettrey!"

I couldn't stand how much fun I was having.

Dewey was fighting for air, one hand on his chest as he laughed himself silly. "Holy shit. Listen, I'm so sorry if any of this is like, over the line, or . . ."

"Don't worry about that around me."

"Worry about what?"

"Hurting my feelings with what you say. You're not going to."

"Noted. I also got made fun of in middle school a lot, so I just want to be careful of that."

I scoffed at him.

"What? What's funny?"

"I don't know." I tried to come up with something that wasn't dickish. "I thought I was the only one who got made fun of in middle school. I wouldn't have thought you were."

"Oh, yeah, you kidding? First of all there was all the racist Mexican bullshit. Most of it wasn't even directed at me, but it was just like, stuff kids would joke about to each other. Super, right? And then I got called Lover Boy from . . . I want to say, the middle of fifth grade all the way until we left middle school. Yeah, it lasted a while."

I made a face. He made one back, his cheeks boiling.

"Should I ask why you were called that?" I said.

"I mean, there's not a lot to the story. It was my first crush. . . . I think I was ten. And I kind of wanted everyone to know I liked her? Yeah, I don't know *what* I was thinking. Maybe I was just an attention whore." Then he raised an eyebrow and said, "And now I'm being . . . a different kind of whore! So anyway." He staged an awkward cough. "So I started just telling people I liked her."

"You told her?"

"No, that's the thing; I told everyone except her. I mean, she obviously found out. But my classmates made fun of me forever for that."

"Did she like you back?"

"Who, the girl? Of course not."

" . . . oh."

"Yeah. I have a real problem with impulse control. Telling people . . . not a great decision."

"Well, at least you also got nothing out of it."

He laughed again, giving me a conciliatory nod. His casual vulnerability was so strange to me. From the moment I met Lily, she knew exactly who she was. This guy had confidence, but it was so unassuming. He owned how unsure of himself he was, and somehow that felt stronger.

A new song filled the car now. The best way to describe it was . . . dreamlike. A lot like my ambiance songs. There were lyrics, but they were spaced between this ethereal background chorus. Melancholy, but softly wistful. We sat there with our eyes forward, watching the road as the sounds and sunlight washed over us.

"What's this song?" I asked.

"The group is called Beach House—they're easily in my top three. The song is called 'PPP.'"

"Huh?"

"Literally the letter P three times. Unless it's pro-nounced *pppppt*." He blew a raspberry into his palm. Then, "That's what I like about it. They don't tell you what the letters mean; it's up for interpretation. Some fans think it stands for 'Piss Poor Planning' and is about a failing relationship. The band said it never stood for anything. It was always a placeholder, and it's just PPP . . . it means whatever you want it to." He looked to me for a long second. "That's a good theme for today, right? Just letting it be whatever it wants."

"It could be, 'Pretty Philosophical Pride.'"

"That's good. I like that. How about you? What does it make you think of?"

I closed my eyes and thought about it.

"Victor Hugo," I told him.

"Is that an ex?"

I winced as I remembered that first email conversa-tion with Lily. "He was an 1800s French writer. He had this quote: It says, *'A writer is a world trapped inside of a person.'*"

"Oh," Dewey said after a long beat like, *is that it?* "So what does that mean?"

"I . . . don't know. No one's ever asked me that before."

"I'm just picturing that as one of those quotes you'd Photoshop over a mountain range or something, but it doesn't mean all that much. I'm not an author, though, so ignore me."

"No, it's . . . I guess I just like the idea that everyone has their own world in them. And we express it in differ-ent ways." I gestured with my hands, then let them drop. "I don't know."

"No, that's valid," he said. "I'm going to tell you a secret and say that this isn't my first time sneaking into the library after-hours."

"Oh."

"The reason isn't sketchy or anything," he assured me. "What you said just reminded me of that. There's this sitting area with a penny fountain where I can listen to music and stare at the water . . . calm myself. The whole place kind of feels like my world when I do that. I don't know. But I also feel like—I'm going to get philosophical again for a sec, sorry—I feel like we're going to get more of that control as we move out and get older? Like we can pick our house and our job and which people we surround ourselves with. So in that way you're in tune with your life, and now *you* feel good, and everything's dandy. Does that make sense?"

I nodded. "This is going to sound weird, but I like talking about this sort of stuff."

"Dude . . . you're really weird!" he said, wide-eyed, but his face gave way to a grin. "Just kidding. Also: Can I ask you something I probably should've asked sooner?"

"What's that?"

"I was trying to think of a good way to bring this up, but. I realized earlier." He grimaced. "I don't know your name."

"Well . . . shit."

"That's a weird name."

"Har har." I rolled my eyes. "I guess it's only fair that you know mine since I know yours."

"Huh? You don't know my name," he said. "Why, did I tell you earlier?"

"No, it was on your profile. Dewey, right?"

He laughed. "Dude, you're supposed to use a made-up name. That's just what I call myself on there. Because of the library. Books, Dewey Decimal system, yada yada."

"Wait. Hold on . . . so your name's not Dewey?"

"Nope." He shook his head. "Sorry, man, that like . . . didn't even occur to me. No, my name's Lucas Delgado—people call me Luke. Good to meet you."

"Owen. Good to meet you too."

We pulled up to the rear entrance of the building, and ~~Dewey~~ Luke directed me on where to put the boxes inside. It was strange seeing the library like this—silent and empty, with all the lights off. Once we finished unloading, we plopped ourselves down at a table near the circulation desk and munched on our pizza.

"So," Luke said politely, between mouthfuls, "are you graduating this June too?"

I nodded.

"Insanity, isn't it?"

"I'm dreading it."

"Dreading? Why's that?"

"I've been dreading it since ninth grade." I faltered, gauging how much to share with him. "I'm . . . I have a tough time with things changing. So going to college is going to be a big shift. I have this friend group . . . they're like my family—"

"I know who they are," he cut me off in a level voice, nodding. "I've seen you guys. You look like you're really close; it's sweet."

I looked away. I waited for him to bring up the elephant in the room: that Lily had tried inviting him to hang out before she met me. That he could've been our sixth member, but he was the boy who never waved back.

"Which school are you going to?" he pivoted. "If you don't mind my asking."

"Lanham."

"Ah. Well, that should be fun too, right? Like, you'll probably make new friends there, but you're still a comfortable distance from home."

"It just feels like part of me is getting . . . left behind, I guess."

"Hm. What do you mean by that?"

I studied his face, trying to get a read on whether he was making fun of me. But his smile was the same as before—serious and earnest. He really was curious about this, and that was that.

"I don't know," I said. "It's the whole 'next chapter of your life' thing. I figure everyone worries about that."

"Hm. I don't, but I'm also doing community college for two years, so I'll be staying put."

"Are you doing something with music?"

"I would *like* to. My dad's making me do something with STEM, because money, so I'm majoring in Computer Science. I figure that's close to music tech, which I guess is what I want to do right now. I'm reminding myself that the lead guitarist of Beach House started out with a degree in Geology." His face scrunched up again. "Do you know what you want to study?"

"Something with writing," I said. "I thought my parents might make me do STEM, but they've been pretty supportive. My mom cried when I got my acceptance letter."

"That's sweet." He smiled. "My parents have this weird way of being supportive, but also strict. Like, they'll expect me to get high grades, but then they'll still be all 'oh my gosh that's so great!' when I do."

"My dad does something similar," I said. "He's supportive and stuff, but starting when I was in elementary school, he'd tell me, 'Always remember: You're not special.'"

Luke frowned. "Oh. Ouch."

"He didn't mean it in a 'you're a failure' kind of way," I clarified. "I think he just didn't want me to get a swelled head about stuff."

"Hm." He considered that. "I think it should be a balancing act. Personally. I don't mean to be a downer here . . . but, like, okay. I've written four of my own songs, my grades are decent, and I got a job at the library at sixteen. And on one hand, that's pretty awesome—like, that's a *solid* resume. But I guarantee there are a bunch of other teenagers out there who write music, or get good grades, and have probably just as many accomplishments as me. But on the other hand"—he took a breath—"if you get too self-conscious of that, then your brain just shuts down. You know what I'm talking about? Like you say to yourself, 'Why the hell am I writing this song? So many other people write songs every day.'" He shrugged. "I think my parents did a good job of that—praising me but also keeping me in check. It's probably one of my favorite things about them."

I didn't have anything to add to that, so we ate the rest of our pizza in silence. Soon the windows darkened and we were covered in shadows all over. The only light source was the blue emergency glow strips that ran along the floor. It reminded me of a movie theater.

Stop getting comfortable.

I stood. "Not to be rude, but what's our plan?"

"Right—not rude at all; I've kept you waiting a while. Let's do this." Luke stood too, clicking his tongue and surveying the empty library. "The question is . . . where do we go?"

"We could do it in your car."

He wrinkled his nose. "Uh, there's a lot of stuff back there."

My phone buzzed with the usual evening text from Lily:

Hey, I hope you had a great day! I love you :)

As I typed back a

You too!

I told him, "Let's just use the bathroom, then."

He didn't seem sold on that idea either, but neither of us had a better one.

The bathrooms were single-occupancy, so we were able to shut ourselves into the small space. We stood shoulder-to-shoulder, facing the mirror. Luke was only an inch or two shorter than me.

"Autosexuality," he said with a nudge, trying to reference the old joke. I jumped at his touch and swiveled myself around so I faced him instead of the mirror. My whole body started to shake like I was freezing—I bit down to stop my teeth from chattering. This was it.

Stay calm. Stay in control.

It was just us and way too little space and way too much silence, until Luke tilted his head and tried to look at me and said, "You're cuter than I was expecting, by the way." He did his best to make it sound sexy, but he squeezed his eyes shut and said, "Sorry, that . . . sounded like a compliment in my head. I realize it didn't totally translate."

Control.

His *aw-shucks*-awkwardness wasn't cute anymore. I didn't want his distractions and I didn't want his jokes, so I didn't respond. Instead I put my hands on his jeans and moved them to the right places.

"Oh," he said. "Just checking, your profile said no kissing, right?"

"Right." I tried to sound authoritative, but my voice was unstable. I only realized now how wildly unprepared we were—aside from the condom in my wallet, we had no supplies; no plan, no prior discussion of how far we wanted to go or who would be doing what. But I was hell-bent on powering through this, breaking through these goddamn obstacles, so I started undoing his belt until he backed away a half step and said, "Are you feeling okay?"

Don't screw this up; almost there, don't screw up.

"Do you want to sit back down?" he tried again.

I told him I didn't, and I almost had a hold of myself again when something slithered across my skin, and I stiffened. Luke's fingers were tentatively wrapping around mine.

I closed my eyes, trying to ignore it, but—nope, I didn't like this. The images were changing now; my wrists being held down, Lily on top of me; Luke on top of me; stop, stop,

"Stop."

"Oh." Luke's hand sprung open, untangling itself from

mine. "I'm sorry—shit, okay. That was stupid." He said it bluntly, sounding flustered. "That was stupid of me."

"You're fine. I'm being weird."

"No, but, okay. . . . That's not weird, is it? You barely know me, and I just . . ."

"Got the impulse?"

"I . . . was thinking about doing that for a while, actually. If I'm being honest." He clapped his hands together and pulled them apart into two fists, lips folded. "Listen, I'm thinking we should do this another time."

There it was—the letdown.

Knew it.

(No one is honest.)

"It's not that I don't want to do this." He was trying to meet my eyes again, clearly concerned. "You just seem kind of—I don't know. I think it's best we hold off."

"You don't have to lie," I snapped. "You don't want to do this; that's fine, just don't feed me some bullshit about why."

"I—fine." He looked irritated by that, and I felt a surge of satisfaction . . . now we were *finally* dropping the act; leveling with each other.

"I'd love to keep hanging out here." Luke was still trying to make eye contact. "We could stay as long as you want and talk some more. I was enjoying that. But if you want me to run you back to the park, your call."

"Would hanging out more increase the chances of you wanting to hook up tonight?" I asked the sink.

"I'm not going to say there's *no* chance, but—probably not, sorry." He shrugged. "I don't want to lie."

"Yeah." I scoffed. "Okay."

He got the hint. "I'll drive you back."

We left the bathroom. I slammed the door behind us as hard as I could, wincing at the sound of my own strength. It's rare that my plans are changed on the spot in public, but when they are, those outbursts are always the worst.

I watched Luke waddle over to a sitting area and collapse onto one of the couches, rubbing his face and telling me he'd be ready in a second. I couldn't stand the brutal thoughts brewing in my head—images of me grabbing his hands, holding him down and telling him I *knew* he wanted to do this, we *said* we were going to, so we were going to. I wanted to put a fist through all his politeness, take total control. The past few hours had been some of my favorite ones in a while, but I'd felt these butterflies before—with Lily. And seeing this headed south in the same way made me want to nuke the whole night.

I blinked the images back.

"Just give me a second and I'll be set," Luke repeated.

I shuffled over to the sitting area. The couch sat facing a small penny fountain—a simple stone basin about five feet in diameter and a few inches tall. Water trickled to the gentle hum of a pump. A neon exit sign hung above the door beside us, bathing the entire area in blended light: green from the glow above our heads, blue from the floor strips under our shoes.

I collapsed onto the couch beside Luke. We both stared at the pennies beneath the surface of the water.

"Before we go, I wanted to say sorry again," Luke said. He turned toward me. I could only see part of his face, but it was filled with regret. The pride paint on his cheek was smeared. "I really did come here wanting to do the stuff we planned. But this is also my first hookup, ever, at all; which you could probably tell—"

"Yeah."

"Pretty obvious, right? And—I'm just going to preface by saying this—I'm *not*, at least, I don't *think* . . ." He showed his teeth, his eyebrows perched. ". . . very good at this."

"I don't know what you want me to say."

"You don't have to say anything. Let me just—okay." He raised both hands. "Here's why I'm here. Not to over-share, but the short version is I've been dealing with really intense social anxiety for . . . I want to say at least five years now? So like, let's say I'm working the front desk over there . . . I'm helping out customers, and I'm a-okay. It's great, it's good, it's all peachy. But if someone were to walk up and invite me to hang out, my brain would just . . ." He mimed crushing his own head. "Right? And the frustrating thing about that scenario is like, people are going out of their *way* to try to include me, and . . . if I'm being honest, I don't have a lot of friends? And it's because of *this*; like, I swear I'm not a—"

"Serial killer?"

"Right. Exactly!" He shrugged and held it there, his eyes darting back and forth. "And I'm not. But you remember I mentioned earlier that I have problems with impulse control, which has led to stuff like that Lover Boy incident, or me blurting out stupid shit. So any time I get the urge to do something, my anxiety shoves that right out the window; it's like, 'get out of here, we don't want you back here.' Even if I'm just getting asked—'Hey, come do this thing! We won't hurt you!'—I just, I *fucking* freeze, dude. I catastrophize, and I avoid; because at the end of the day, it feels so much easier to isolate and just stick with . . . you know. Doin' me. And I don't think being alone is necessarily a bad thing. *But.*" He dropped his shoulders, really looking at me now. "It's *very* tough to come out of that."

I thought again about the day Lily waved to him when we were younger. Or the time he tried to start a conversation from nothing in the locker room. The ignored invites. All the assumptions.

"We're all just people," Luke continued, gesturing to all the color around us. "Doing our people thing. You know? Everybody poops. And I got sick of feeling like I couldn't ever *move*, so—to *finally* get to my point here—that's what got me proposing meetups with a stranger on an app, all of five days after I turned eighteen. No I didn't think it through; no I'm not a smart person; yes, I feel over my head right now. No offense, it's nothing to do with you; but this was a mistake on my end—add it to the list, right? Throw it right on there. There are *so many examples* of why it's better for me to just *not* do these things, and I shouldn't have . . . and I'm aware none of this helps you. But I'm sorry."

The water in front of us trickled and hummed.

I'd been spending this night treating Luke like an unknowable box—a faceless gray square. And the longer I lingered on his words, the more they unlocked a new impulse in me: the urge to unmask myself the way he just did. To let him know how alike he and I were—both feeling like prisoners of our own circumstances. Each of us itching to make the life change we *knew* needed to happen, but too scared to leave the safety of the status quo. So instead, there we both sat . . . kicking ourselves for pinning our hopes on an unplanned night, face-to-face with the empty result. Unmarked pennies in an unchanged fountain.

I thought about how we all retreated to our own worlds: Luke to the library, me to the Studio, Dad to his cabin. But as peaceful as these places were, we were all alone in them. Luke had been alone his whole life and wanted to let others in. Dad had been to other continents and just wanted to shut everyone out. And me . . . I just wanted someone to rule my world with.

And as Luke and I sat facing the empty library, I pictured two thrones instead of two cushions, and gates instead of doors, and for just a second, I felt unconquerable.

Tell him.

I couldn't. The words burned inside me, but they wouldn't come out. There was no way to bring it up, even though I was sure he wouldn't mind if I just blurted it out.

Luke leaned back, propping his sneakers on the edge of the fountain. I did the same.

"Dare me to stick my feet in," he finally said.

I did.

"Well." He slipped off his shoes, then his socks. "Since you dared me . . ."

He wiggled his toes, pretended to gasp, then dipped them into the fountain water. He tapped one of the pennies with his big toe, saying, "Boop."

He dared me to next, and even though my brain was starting to abdicate my body's motions to autopilot, I played along and joined him.

"Can you imagine if we did this during the day?" he asked. He looked right at me when he laughed, like he was trying to get me to join in. When I didn't, he cleared his throat and asked, "Do you ever get thoughts like that?"

"Huh?"

"Intrusive thoughts, I think they're called? Like when you're sitting in an exam and you think, 'What if I just screamed really loud right now?'"

I grimaced, then nodded. "Do you?"

"All the time."

Grabbing my wrists.

Stop.

Grabbing his wrists.

STOP.

"What about screwed-up intrusive thoughts?" I asked, more softly.

His puzzled expression made me look away, dirty and ashamed all over.

"Hey. You alright?" he asked.

I didn't answer. The two of us leaned back, sinking into the couch with our heads turned inward. We sat there, face to face—nearly nose to nose. Breathing each other's air. I could barely make out his eyes in the glow of the light, but I could see the rest of his face—his reassuring smile—clearly. Every cell in my brain was roaring at me to be on the defensive: *Remember to keep your guard up!* But just like Lily, Luke was making me forget what that angry voice sounded like. Everything about him was disarming—his earnest expression, his harmless demeanor. Raw vulnerability. I didn't know much about him, but I knew I'd never met someone more easy to talk to.

And I needed to talk to someone.

Luke poked me in the shoulder. "What're you thinking about?"

"You have no idea. So much."

"Well, like what?"

I looked from the lights,
to him,
to the lights,
to him.

And I asked, "Can I tell you about something that happened to me?"

"Is that something you want to do?"

"Not really. But I think I should anyway."

Luke listened.

I don't remember exactly what words of comfort he offered once I finished, but I remember they were generic and kind. He asked me if I wanted to keep talking, and I told him yes, but I was exhausted and my parents would be expecting me home, so we should call it a night.

The drive home was quiet, but comfortable—like he understood that I wasn't up for any more deep conversations at the moment. So we just put on some more music— "Should Have Known Better" by Sufjan Stevens—and he made small talk about how much it was going to suck getting up for school tomorrow.

As we approached the neighborhood, he said, "So. Should we talk about what we're, like . . . where our heads are at?"

"We don't have to," I said. "Not if you're uncomfortable with it."

"*I'm* not uncomfortable talking about this. Personally. I mean . . ." He stared at the road, selecting his words. "Like, we *should* talk about it, right? You don't really know me; I don't know you, and . . . I don't want to make this awkward. But like, in terms of when we see each other next, if we see each other next. . . . What's the plan, Stan?"

"My name is Owen," I said in a mock-angry voice.

"Hey, you know . . ." He shrugged. "I had a great time tonight, and I just—it would be a very *me* thing to ruin it at the literal eleventh hour."

"You're not going to do that."

We pulled into the neighborhood.

"Well." He tapped the steering wheel. "I think taking it slow is the important thing. It sounds like we both have stuff we need to get a handle on, so maybe we . . . take care of that first? I work on being more of a person of action; you work on getting out of your relationship, then we figure out how to go from there?"

I stiffened.

"What is it?"

I kept my eyes on the playground as we passed it. "I don't know how to say this, but I'm not . . . going to get out of my relationship."

I felt the car slow as it approached my street. Luke put it in park and turned to me.

"Um," he said, in a slightly softer voice, "why?"

"It's like I told you, there's no choice."

"But . . . after what she did?"

"You're not hearing me; like, I *don't* have a choice. I'm stuck."

"Okay." He paused. "I don't want you to think I'm trying to be a homewrecker because I like, want you for myself or whatever, because that's not it—"

"Dude—"

"Are you safe? That's what I'm getting at."

I scoffed at the dashboard. "She's my girlfriend, not a criminal."

"Actually, she's both."

"I'm good." I felt his eyes on me, so I repeated "I'm good" with more force.

He didn't respond.

"Listen," I said. "I'm tired now, and I need to get home, but I'd like to talk to you again. Can we just leave it at that and see each other later? I'll give you my number, here. We can text."

I could tell he was in that same mode he was in earlier tonight in the bathroom—unsure. Quietly doing his own calculations. But he put in my number, then held out his arms for a hug. "Until next time, friend. It's been a night."

I said it back to him as we hugged. Then I said into his shoulder, "I really can't tell you how much I needed this."

"Same exact boat."

And we just looked at each other as we broke apart, both silently saying, *I've been there, and I know that no words can express this. So we both have to properly trust that we're thinking the same things and don't need to say anything at all.* And we were. So we didn't.

I feebly raised a hand.

"Bi-five," I said.

And now I sit here in the Studio hours later, still remembering how his smile filled out as he high-fived me back. I keep re-reading the conversation above—the part where I told him I was going to stay with Lily—and I'm already kicking myself. What the hell was I thinking? Why did I, after this whole entire *night*, still have that thought and why did I share it?

I hate my own head sometimes. Of all the things the ~~incident~~ assault took from me, this seems like the cruelest: the inability to trust this person in front of me, despite them giving me every reason to and no reason not to. I want to know what Luke is like; I want to lie with him and listen to him ramble about music and ambition and all these things he has thoughts on; and I'm so angry that it's tinged with this suspicion. A dread at what's under the surface; the fear of flying too close to the sun and waiting for the day it all turns to dust.

All of it gets put to rest tomorrow. Tomorrow, I'm going to make a plan to conquer this; to learn to trust again and start to rebuild. But until then, I'm just left sitting here, coming off the high of tonight. Remembering the last sounds of it . . . me shouting for Luke to never tell a soul what I confessed to him; and him promising, in a shaky voice, that he wouldn't.

STORY
FOUR

THE MEN MADE OF WAR

ONE

I LEARN ABOUT THE GRAY ROCK TECHNIQUE THROUGH an online forum. The most common topic is for people who want to get out of their relationship but aren't able to break up with their partner. The Gray Rock technique is where you make yourself as uninteresting as possible—you don't respond more than you need to; you don't express yourself any more than is necessary to keep the peace. It takes a while, but if it goes on long enough, you become so undesirable that your partner will end the relationship themselves. Theoretically.

I stay in Gray Rock mode for the rest of July.

A week into August—exactly one month after the group said goodbye—Lily comes over to give me the key and instructions for gerbil-sitting. She joins me in my room, where boxes are starting to fill up with my belongings.

"Just text me if you have any questions," she says. "I got you peach ice cream as a thank-you—I know that's your favorite. It'll be in the freezer, so, help yourself."

Alright, I tell her. *Thanks.*

"Oh, I meant to ask! Did you get your housing assignment yet? Which dorm hall are you in?"

Patuxent, I murmur.

"Ugh—I'm all the other way on the other end of campus. I'll have to kidnap you a lot." She looks at her watch. "I should finish packing. Want to video chat tonight? Assuming my grandparents get signal."

Sure. If I say no, she'll ask why not.

Lily puts her hands on my shoulders, trying to meet my eyes. "Hey, are you okay? You've been off lately. Is it just all the . . ." She gestures to the boxes. "Emotions?"

I nod, smiling enough to sell it.

This is the crux of Gray Rocking—under no circumstances should you take the bait to try to fix things. It's a position I never understood until I was in it: that it's easier to play dead. Because if you try to speak up, or explain why you're not fine, you get another helping of all the shit from before. The pushback. The lectures about why you're wrong and need to be the one apologizing.

Not only is it insulting to have to ask for more, but it's doubly painful when they explain to you why you're wrong for wanting it. It's an unsolicited reminder of how small your voice is and how stuck you are.

No, it's so much easier to bury it. It hurts less, ruins your day less, if you just hang your head and accept this as the norm and work with what you've got from there.

It's the fixing that's tough. The fixing is so tough it's just plain not worth the fix.

I take my driver's test the next morning and pass with a perfect score. Mom encourages me to take the car out, but there's nowhere to go.

TWO

THE HOUSE HAS NEVER BEEN SO QUIET.

Mom and I spend the entire last two weeks of summer doing the purple cramps routine every morning. It doesn't feel like I've earned it, but it's obvious she's trying to spend as much time as she can with me. Given the circumstances, I'll admit it's a mood booster. Mom has always understood me perfectly—she knows what topics I like to discuss, which distractions are helpful.

She and I treat my last evening at home casually. We eat pizza as though it isn't the last meal I'll have at the table until Thanksgiving. We watch TV in the den as though I won't be living somewhere else by this time tomorrow.

I leave to do my last gerbil-sitting at Lily's house a little after it gets dark. (She's getting back tonight, but it'll be late.) On top of the pet stuff, she's asked me to water the "leaf children"—aka the plants in her room.

I've been in Lily's bedroom a hundred times, of course, but almost never without her there. It's tidier than usual. All her stuff is packed into boxes the same way mine is. I turn to look at the wall closest to her headboard, which is her version of a memory wall. There are a few photos—most of us, a few of her and her mom—but below that, she's turned the wall into her own personal diary, etched in with permanent marker.

I look at an entry from sophomore year that I helped her write—

HAPPY NEW YEAR!

And another—

Let's see . . . sleepover, then breakfast with the group. Good day? I think so.

And another—

No matter what happens, I will always keep moving forward . . . seeking to learn, teach, inspire, and give back. Because of my friends, I'm a better person. Because of them, I will help create a better world.

And another—

A day of adventures, an endless windy stream . . . —July 2

And the biggest one, toward the foot of the bed—

Anyone confused? I know I am.

I draw closer to the wall, entranced.

"Lily." I say it into the empty air. Just her name. "Lily."

Then I look further down and see a picture frame tucked between her mattress and the wall. I realize I recognize it—a piece of notebook paper is framed inside.

Mountains wander among their filthy corduroy pineapples.

It's the original. Not some phone picture or photocopy, but the original notebook page from that day when we were fourteen.

I stare at her wall, at every etch and curve of the handwriting. I touch my finger to the surface. I'm desperate to glean something; to get a shred of insight about what goes on inside that head of hers when she sees me, talks to me, listens to me.

(Look at this wall.)

I think of that vicious cycle of making up, vowing to do better, then seeing it dissolve all over again . . . knowing that things are torched, but handcuffed to the hope that it can still be made to work—that a Hail Mary will make things right. You keep convincing yourself that you *need* to get rid of this person, and then that goddamn cycle comes around, and somehow you get roped back in—by some really good night among all the ugliness, or a beautiful memory wall among all the heartache. And all the while you're certain that no one else can ever know what it's like to be stuck this way. Locked in the cage of your own life.

(LOOK AT US!)

I want to kick myself for letting myself end up here. I'd hear about toxic people when I was younger, and I was sure I'd be able to sniff out their bullshit from a mile away. Just watch out for the vapid, self-centered assholes who act full of themselves; the popular pricks who only pretend to give a shit about others and spend every minute obsessed with their own status. Watch out for the dickhead who only texts you when it's convenient, or the partner who's embarrassed to be seen with you in public.

No one says, "Watch out for the kindest person you've ever met." No one says, "Watch out for the girl who wore sunglasses to Homecoming with you." No one warns you about the friend who frames your magnet poetry.

God, why would they?

THREE

I DON'T TAKE LILY'S THANK-YOU ICE CREAM FROM her house.

Instead I drive to the frozen yogurt place down the road and get a peach cone from there. I worry that Mom will miss me, but she sends a text, telling me to enjoy my "last night of freedom" and pointing out that we've already spent a solid amount of time together.

I sit on the curb in the parking lot and eat.

My phone buzzes with the nightly call from Lily a few minutes later. For once, I silence it instead of answering. The screen goes blank, and I bask in the summer air as I feel the weight shift off my shoulders a little.

A foot taps the curb beside me.

At first I jump, certain that it's her. But then my eyes trace up to the shirt—a baby blue polo with the library logo on it.

"Sorry," says Luke, hands raised. "Scaring you is the thing I was trying to not do."

I blink.

"What are you doing here?" I ask.

"I walk here after work sometimes," Luke says. He points, and I see the library peeking through the trees on the other side of the road.

Goddamn Town with Two of Nothing.

Luke heads into the shop. At first I think that's the last I've seen of him, but he emerges with a mini-sundae a few minutes later and approaches again.

"Hey," he says, tilting his head with an awkward grimace. "It's cool if not, but can I join you?"

I shrug, then nod. He seats himself on the curb beside me, and we both rotate so we can see each other better. Then he sighs, like he knows this may be a loaded statement, and says, "It's good to see you."

No answer.

"I figured you'd have left for college by now," he says.

"Tomorrow."

"Oh, wow." He taps his cup with his spoon. "How're you feeling about that?"

No answer.

"Okay, different question: Do you have any desire to finish our last conversation?" he asks. "About what happened, I mean."

"What do you care?"

He looks pissed at the question. "Because I have a brain?"

I knock my sneakers together.

"I didn't trust you when I first met you," I tell him.

"Oh yeah?" Luke says, his brow knitting. "Was I acting weird?"

"Not really."

"So you're just suspicious of everyone you meet, or . . . ?"

"As a matter of fact, yeah." I glare at the pavement, wanting to say more. I want to tell him how I trusted people, until I didn't. And once you fuck that, it never gets un-fucked up. It's just *gone*, and it stays gone, and people like him who had nothing to do with it are stuck dealing with it.

Instead, I just wave in his direction. "Trust doesn't come back.

I wish it did. I wish it was like your, your . . . spleen or whatever, where if you damage it, the organ re-grows—"

"You mean your liver?"

"Which organ re-grows?"

"Your liver."

"Then that's what I meant."

He smirks at his lap. I wait for him to look at me for the next part.

"I decided to trust you even though I didn't think I should." I shrug. "Don't ask why. I don't know what kind of . . . magic you worked, or whatever, but I thought, 'You know what, maybe this guy isn't that bad.'"

"And then I completely blew that up," Luke says. "Yeah. I get it."

"But you *don't*." I lean toward him, framing up the air. "You were *it*, dude. When I got home from the library, I was all set to cut ties with Lily. I was an inch away from being out of the woods. Then you did what you did, and turned out to be *exactly* what I was afraid of. So I stayed with her—I put up with another thousand pounds of bullshit, and that's what I'm pissed about. *That's* the part you don't get." I rub my forehead, my voice strained. "You were the silver bullet, man. And you *fucked* me."

We both blink at the pavement for a while.

"Well," Luke says, still soft, "you're right. I didn't know any of that, and yeah. Of *course* that's going to feel awful; I can only imagine."

"Yeah."

"I reported it to the school because I'm an idiot," he says. "That's the short version. The long version is that I was scared for you, and—as I may have mentioned one or two or a million times—I have serious problems with figuring out when to pull the trigger on something."

"Scared?" I laugh. He doesn't.

"I'm serious," he says. "We were all set at the end of the night, and I was like, 'Heck yeah, we're good.' Then you said that thing at the end about staying with your girlfriend because you—quote—'didn't have a choice.' And this *can* be a gray area, right? It's a big ol' mess. But we'd just said all that stuff about me not listening to doubt, and I was all turned around. I literally thought *because* I was scared to do it meant that I should; and by the time I decided, *hey, maybe I shouldn't*, I already had."

"That was a mistake."

"Yeah, no *shit*, dude!" He spits out a scoff, grabbing his own head. "Do you have any idea how it felt when you texted me later that day, and I realized I'd undone . . . I mean, everything? For it to turn out exactly like all my other screw-ups—but about you, and about this—*dude*. I'll say it any number of times you want: I *fucked* up. And the only reason I'm even still bringing it up is because it's important to me that you know I thought I was doing the opposite. And I'm sorry."

Now it's my turn to take that in.

The two of us finish our ice cream in silence. He throws away my napkin for me afterward.

"Can I ask you something?" Luke says.

"Yeah."

"You called me a silver bullet earlier."

"Yeah."

"Why does there have to be one at all?"

"Because I need one." I shrug at him. "Simple as that. I can't pull myself out of this shit without one. I'd need to . . . tell more people what happened, and I'm too much of a pussy to do that."

"Have you tried to?"

"I appreciate what you're doing with the devil's advocate

thing here, but trust me when I say there's nothing you can suggest that I haven't thought of a hundred times before."

He repeats, more gently, "Have you tried to?"

I purse my lips, squeezing my eyes shut. I can't look at him.

"Alright." Luke scoots a little closer to me. "Hypothetically. *If* you were going to get out of this. Where would you start?"

"I'd tell people what happened."

"But which people?"

"Someone who could do something about it."

"Who would that be for you?"

My eyes are still shut.

Until I pull out my phone, shakily type a text message, and hit send:

Can I come see you tonight?

Dad's reply, almost instant, is simply an address.

I wipe my nose on my arm.

"Side note," Luke adds. "I'm clearly not good at advice, so take all that with a big ol' grain of salt."

"Oh." I wave the phone at him. "Too late. You should've told me thirty seconds ago."

"Well, there I go again." But he pats my shoulder and says, "I hope it works out."

The two of us stand.

"What happens now?" I ask him as we amble toward the car.

"What do you mean?"

"I don't want this to be the last time I talk to you."

"It doesn't need to be." Luke shrugs, his face scrunching up. "But I want to let all this . . . marinate. I think that'd be good."

"For what, a few days?"

"Mm . . ." We reach my car, and Luke stops so he can face me.

"I'm thinking more like a few months."

"Is that . . . negotiable? Can I text you?"

"Sorry, man." He shakes his head. "This is what I want."

"I'm not mad at you anymore."

"But that's the thing—you should be, right?" He smiles at me, but his voice is serious. "I appreciate you hearing me out, but I'm not going to pretend I was right to do what I did just because you're okay with it. Like, don't get me wrong, I'd love to. But you just told me how much I screwed up your trust—a lot, it sounds like—and I'm hearing you, and I want to make that right. So I'm not comfortable just . . . magically fixing things in one conversation, like, 'woohoo, we're good!' Like, I *actually* wouldn't be comfortable with that. I'm right there on the path with you, friend. This is me; this is you . . ." He holds up two hands. "And we're going like this." He moves them upward, side by side without touching. "We might want them to do this"—he rubs them together—"but they can't do that until they get way the heck over here, right?" And he lifts his hands all the way above his head. Then he drops them with a shrug. "Maybe that's me being a stubborn asshole."

"A little."

"A little, for sure. What else is new, right?"

I watch him say all this. And I think about how he's treated me: always listening, asking how I'm feeling, never judging me or making me feel wrong for liking the things I like. It's so easy to breathe around him. And I ache with how much I wish that day back in ninth grade had gone differently—what my life could've looked like if I'd ignored Lily's wave just like Luke did to her; and if I'd approached Luke just like Lily did to me.

I want to say all this.

I want to say, *You gave something back to me that I thought was gone for good.*

I want to say, *God, the things we could've been.*

(God, the things we could've been.)

"Tell you what," Luke says, clearly seeing that I'm disappointed. "Here's what we'll do. You go do your thing at Lanham, have a good semester. Then when you're back for winter break, if you want to get coffee or have another night in the library . . ." He taps the emblem on his shirt. "You'll know where to find me. We'll pick this back up then."

I open my mouth to push back. But I hear the sureness in his voice and I see the victory in his eyes, and I can tell this is the way forward . . . not just for me, but for him too. He's finally taking hold of his own behavior: action without impulse. A proper plan.

I swallow a lump, knowing it's time to leave now—I have a drive ahead of me.

So I say, "I'll hold you to that."

"Good. Sounds like a plan, Stan."

"My name's not Stan."

"I know it's not." He looks right at me. "Take care, Owen."

"Don't tell me what to do," I say in a voice full of fake, indignant anger. But we're already hugging.

FOUR

I LEAVE FOR DAD'S CABIN DIRECTLY FROM THE parking lot, just as the sun sets to touch the highway. It's the longest drive I've ever made on my own—eighty-two miles.

I start out choking the wheel in an iron grip, keeping my eyes on the road and my mind fixed on breathing slowly. I feel myself gradually relax mile by mile, owning the fact that I'm still moving, still here, still safe. Putting pavement behind me and moving myself through unfamiliar towns.

A warning light appears on the dashboard about halfway through the trip, but I realize it's just the low fuel indicator. My first instinct is panic, but I beat it back and adapt. Pull off the road, refuel, pull back on, and continue. I decide I want strawberry milk, so I run inside the mini-mart and buy some.

I can do that.

(Still moving, still here, still safe.)

The whole trip takes just over an hour and a half. The road disappears for the final stretch, giving way to gravel and dirt. Another mile of darkness, and then I spot it: a tiny little light at the top of the hill. The incline feels too steep to drive, so I park at its foot.

I shut off the car, letting go of the wheel and leaning back.

My hands hurt, but my chest is lighter.

(Eighty-two miles.)

Made it.

It washes over me the instant I open my car door: overwhelming silence. Absolute absence of all stimuli; stillness in all directions. No cars, no horns, no lights, no footsteps, no music, no noises. Total tranquility.

I'd always pictured the cabin as being in the middle of a thick forest, but I find that this is the opposite—the hill overlooks nothing but open field, an endless expanse of land. Moonlight etches odd patterns over the ground, sending skewed shadows in every direction. And to my right, lying in the grass as I march toward the cabin: hand-built bookshelves. One, then another . . . *another.* Dozens of them, enough to fill a library; all tossed in an enormous pile like a stack of broken toys. Polished wood weathered by rain and snow and sleet. I recognize my father's craftsmanship as I run my hand over several of them; all are nearly identical save for the tiniest, almost indistinct differences between each. A decorative notch placed half an inch higher than the others. A crosspiece angled at forty-six degrees instead of forty-five. A whole mountain of imperfect iterations—a hundred failures.

(*Builder.*)

Every last one of them is riddled with bullet holes.

(*Destroyer.*)

He didn't get them perfectly spaced, but he tried.

(*Dad.*)

I send a warning text as I approach the door. A wooden sign is mounted on it, the cabin's name burned into the grain:

Valhalla

I knock twice, then try the knob—it's unlocked. Light spills onto the dirt under my shoes, climbing farther and farther as I swing the door open.

I'm standing in the Studio.

The room in front of me is laid out identically to it. There's a copy of everything, even down to the area rug. On the right, an old TV is bolted to the wall. Hanging beside it are a dozen photographs of our family, as well as uniformed people I don't recognize. Below that, a sword mounted to a polished wooden plaque that reads 0341. On the left, a leather couch and handmade coffee table, seated directly beneath a square skylight. And sitting in my chair at a writing desk identical to my own: my father.

He lifts his head from his phone—my text on the screen—and I meet the gaze of a man who's aged fifty years in five weeks. His face is falling off; drooping, pale. Where there was once a pristine buzz cut, his hair is grown out—stringy and more matted white than silver. His stiff hands, weathered with blisters, rest limply on a polished wooden walking cane. His eyes are gaunt and gray, dimmer than before. Wearier.

He's the world's tallest walking corpse—chewed up and spat out by a war that never wanted him. Tiny.

He says my name like it's a question.

I don't answer.

He gets up with a grunt, leaning on the cane and limping to usher me into the next room. The cabin is larger than it seems on the outside—just off the living room is a little eating area, complete with a wood-burning stove and freestanding sink. A handmade table sits with two chairs along the wall, where I spot the old drawing of mine hanging up:

Me + Dada.

"There's Kava tea on the stove if you want some," Dad says.

"What's that?"

"It's made from the roots of the *Piper methysticum* plants in the garden out back. The kavalactones in it help ease the mind."

"I thought you couldn't stand gardening."

"I can't."

"So why do it?"

"It's how you get the best tea."

The ensuing silence makes me realize a contemporary classical tune is playing gently from a turntable in the corner. Max Richter, I think.

I nod toward his cane. "What happened? Did you hurt your knees?"

"Yeah."

"When?"

"About twelve years ago. It's just now that I'm doing something about it." He taps it on the ground. The polished handle has elegant carvings etched below it.

In a steady voice, I tell him, "Please sit down."

The entire ocean empties out of my chest, giving me the ultimate rush as I murmur the order and—incredibly—he obeys. I seat myself across from him at the kitchen table. For a moment we just look to each other . . . utterly drained, the both of us. So *spent*. Worn away and whittled down into these feeble skeletons.

There we stay.

(Until.)

"Please pass me that," I tell him, gesturing to a jar of pens on the table. Then I ask him to get us pieces of paper. Once again, he obeys.

"What is this?" Dad asks when he returns to his seat, arms folded.

I take one of the papers and pens and tell him to do the same.

"What is this?" Dad repeats.

I look at him, wielding the pen in my hand like a weapon and say, "I'm going to tell you what happened. And you're going to tell me too."

"What *is* this?" Dad repeats.

"I'm going to write down everything that happened to me that night. And I know there are things that happened to you too that you can't say. The shit that made you hit me that time when I was little and put bruises on Mom's arms while you were asleep. So I want you to write those too. Don't leave anything out."

"Owen." Dad is speaking in a new voice now—weaker, but more agitated. "I'm not going to do that."

"You need to."

He doesn't blink. Neither do I.

"You're right," I finally say. "I don't need to know; I get that. But I want to."

"You do *not*; Owen, please, I promise you. There is a *reason* I've never told you this shit, okay. Your mother, either. You don't know what you're talking about."

"You don't know what you're talking about with my stuff either."

"That's fair."

"I want us to."

"Owen."

"I want us to know what we're talking about. I want us to talk."

"I'm asking you. Please."

I stare at him until he looks away.

"There's something important I need you to understand," I say. I reach for words and find them. "You asked me over and over again who did it. And I didn't want to tell you."

"I know."

"I'm here now because I do. Not because any of that shit you did actually worked. And not because I'm trying to get some apology out of you."

"Owen." Dad shakes his head like a child who won't eat. "I don't want your forgiveness, okay. That's a thing that's earned."

"I'm agreeing with you—I didn't come here to forgive anything. I came here to talk," I say. "We've *never* talked. Not in the real way. I want us to be people who talk about everything; that's what I want." I take a breath. "And I came here to tell you what happened on my terms, not yours. So that's my counteroffer; that's what I'm asking. I'm asking you to share your shit since I'm sharing mine. If you don't want to, fine—it's not like I can force you. But I'm asking."

He looks to me, then to the roof.

I look to the roof, then to him.

He shakes his head.

And picks up his pen.

"I'm going to start writing now," I say.

Dad keeps perfectly still save for the sharp, quick tracing of his pen over the pad. Ink striking paper.

I rub my eyes as I start to write. I pause, trying to tap into the words that could embody everything stirring in my head, as I start to write. I think of Lily—wincing, wading through all our memories and making little noises—as I start to write. I think of my classmates—all the rumors floated about the incident—as I start to write. I think of my father as I start to write. And I start to write.

FIVE

The Story.

SIX

WHEN I FINISH READING MY FATHER'S WORDS, I STAND and begin to pace with my hands over my trembling mouth—willing myself to not get sick.

When my father finishes reading mine, he does the same thing.

The two of us eventually collapse into chairs in the living room—me on the sofa, him in a seat dragged from the kitchen. I fold my arms, but he stays like he was—hands frozen over his mouth. Failure written all over his face.

"Oh God." Dad shakes his head. "Owen. Oh my *God*."

I don't answer. Images are running wild in my mind—grotesque scenes of horror and hell painted by my father's words.

I wait for him to ask me questions, to offer condolences, to say he loves me, to sit in stoic silence. But instead he says, simply, "I can't imagine what that was like for you."

"It's nothing by comparison," I say. I tuck my arms close, trying to cast out the images. "What happened to me is nothing compared to what happened to you."

"You were younger."

"Why does that matter?"

"It matters," he says, like it's non-negotiable. Then, "And more to the point: I made the choice to enlist, okay. I signed up for the violence."

"So?"

"You didn't. You didn't."

"What does 0341 mean?" I point to the wooden plaque on the wall.

"In the Army and Marines, each job title is identified by something called a MOS—Military Occupational Specialty code. 0341 was mine."

"But what does it mean?"

"It means I was a Mortarman."

"Oh. You never told me that before."

"I guess not."

"Why are you now?"

"You asked."

My arms are still squeezed tight to my chest.

"What's it like?" I murmur.

"War?"

"War."

He purses his lips. "A lot of it is predictable. In a good way. There's something nice about the order and routine of life on base—no matter what country you're in, it feels familiar. It's boring—a lot of downtime—but it's consistent."

He can see that I want more.

"Thing is, though, it's consistent until it's not." His voice is more hoarse, lower, but still steady. "Hours, days of playing golf, writing letters, shooting the shit . . . until suddenly your best friend's on fire and you're running for your life. You think your last thoughts. It's not too long until you learn to always sleep with one eye open. That's the kind of thing you take home with you."

I swallow, sitting forward. "What else?"

"Guilt. *Plenty* of that to go around," he says. "You're in the type of place where people get hurt because of your actions, or lack of action. Sometimes both. They die and they die badly. And you watch."

"The stuff that happened to you and the others—" I cut myself off, pointing to the paper. "That wasn't your fault at all."

"It was."

"How?"

"It was." Dad folds his arms, mirroring me. "So you take that home too. When you hug your wife, you picture that guy who won't hug his wife again. You replay the situation, and you wonder why you. What the hell brought you back when it struck down all those other devils worth ten of your rickety ass?"

"God?"

"No God." He spits it. "This isn't God's world, man; this is all us. Every awful thing was done and made by us. And there was no part of God in anyone over there. There was no part in them and there sure as shit was no part in any of us."

My father speaks so vividly—I can't believe how many experiences live inside him. It's like a car accident: I don't want to hear any more horror, but I feel myself hanging on to every word.

"How could you stand it?" I ask.

"The adrenaline gets you through it." His voice wavers slightly. "You either make it out or you don't, right? No time to think."

"Right."

"It's the after-war that no one's trained for, see," he says. His gaze is on the floor now, his mouth tight. "No one teaches you how to come home. Not in the way you need to be taught."

I feel my heart twist—not for the images anymore; but for the fact that anyone, let alone my dad, would need to be taught how to come home.

He covers his eyes.

At first I think he's recollecting himself. But then I see his shoulders shake, and the wetness pressed through his fingers, and realize he's started to cry.

"I miss the war," he admits. Then in a panicked, wobbly whisper: "Some days I miss it so much I swear it's going to *fucking* kill me, man."

And as he sits there crying, I realize I know what he meant earlier about how our experiences aren't so different, at the core. My life and Dad's are nothing alike, and our burdens are our own. But we were both awakened to the same sickening truth: that there's nothing other people aren't capable of. We each know what it's like to be upended by our own harrowing experience. The kind that suffocates your soul if you don't know better than to let it—building to the moment when all your wide-eyed wonder turns to dust, and you wake up to a colorless world. And the more you move forward, the more that cynicism festers until it's become a part of you—baked into your bones and poisoning your heart.

Dad sniffles and murmurs, so softly I almost don't catch it: "I miss Captain Boots."

Now. Now, he and I are talking.

"You helped her," I say.

"I tried."

"You took care of her."

"I tried."

I lean forward, my hands rattling. And I feel bold enough to ask the question.

"Why not me?"

He uncovers his eyes. Blinks away burgeoning pain.

And he says, "I tried."

"No," I tell him. "You tried to fix. But you didn't try to help."

No answer.

"You *helped* her," I say. I wrestle with my own voice. "Why not me? I just want to know the reason. There has to be a reason."

"She was easy to care for."

"Whereas I'm not."

"People aren't, Owen." He looks at me seriously—not sad, just serious. "People aren't."

Our eyes stay on each other.

"The love was there," Dad says. "I hope that's clear. Everything I did for you, it was out of love."

But, I think to myself, *that isn't how it works*. The plants in his garden wouldn't feel the most love if he flooded them with water. A baby doesn't feel the most love if you hug them so tight that you crush the air out of their lungs. At the end of the day, it's easy to convince ourselves we've done right by someone. We fixate on all we've given them—gifts, effort, intention. But in doing so, we often shut ourselves off from the most important part: that the trueness of the love we give is measured by how it feels for the person we give it to.

My father showed the least love because he made me feel the least loved. He found it convenient to pretend he was doing something else . . . something productive; something useful. Something for me. But I know it wasn't; he knows it wasn't, and it wasn't. It wasn't love because I didn't feel loved by it.

Dad drops his head and covers his face again.

I want to tell him I see a man stripped of all masks and

sardonic one-liners, all his height and scars and silver hair and I just see a person; someone like me, just a guy with his head in his hands trying to figure himself out. Someone worried about what's in front of him grabbing at every piece of experience and past knowledge and thinking about his fuck-ups and wanting to make amends but worrying how to do so; worrying about how that rawness changes him, changes this. Itching to apologize but afraid it'll look like he's bullshitting. Oh, I've seen bullshitting before. I've seen people break down in front of me and cry, pretending they don't want to be let off the hook, when that's all they're after. I've had my naïveté, my blind willingness to take things at face value, peeled off layer by layer until it was gone for good. I'll never get that back—Lily took it with her, replacing it with a cold disposition that will always assume the worst about everything in everyone. But now, seeing my father dissolving in his own world inches from my own, I don't see any of that. I just see him.

"You did a lot of things right," I say.

He lowers his hands.

"I grew up in one of the nicest neighborhoods in the state," I continue. "I had health insurance. I had the Studio; I got my driver's license, I was admitted into my dream college, I never had to worry about who I loved, and I know how to turn a wrench."

Dad swallows. "What's your point, man?"

"That you did a lot of things right." I hold his gaze. "I'm leaving the house with my head on my shoulders. That's not a small thing."

"I should've done better."

"That's true. But what I'm saying is true too."

"Whole thing's a balancing act," he says. "No parent gets it right; I sure as shit didn't. My dad was stricter with me—any screw-up, no matter how small, meant beatings with a switch.

Can't tell you how relieved I was to get the hell out of that house."

"Did you ever talk to him about it?"

"Afterward. Years later. When he was in the hospital and we exchanged our goodbyes."

"What did you say?"

"I hugged him around the shoulders and thanked him for every goddamn day of it."

The two of us are standing by the window now, him leaned against his cane. Hills stretch all the way back to the tree line. I had another question for him, but I can't remember it now.

"You should go home," Dad says. "Spend your last night with your mother—you owe her that. She's done more for this family than you'll ever know. And she gets lonely."

"She said it was okay for me to do my own thing tonight."

"That's what she'd say no matter how lonely it'd make her."

I draw a tiny bit closer to him.

"You should come with me," I say.

"No." He raises a finger to the glass pane, tapping it. "I've done enough running from this shit. Wouldn't be proper to come home before I've had some time to straighten it out. My VA case manager helped me find a guy about half an hour from here that specializes in counseling for . . . that stuff. Been doing weekly sessions with him, and he referred me to a second guy who's going to start me on EMDR treatments."

"What's that?"

"Something I should've started a long time ago."

I don't respond. He turns to me.

"It helps," he says. "Therapy. Once you get settled in on

campus—doesn't have to be tomorrow, but within your first week—I want you to go to their counseling center. I won't ask questions; I won't pry. But promise me you'll book an appointment and stick to it."

I tell him I will.

"As for coming home, I'm not saying it won't ever happen," Dad says. "But it needs to be a while. Your mom has put up with my BS for long enough."

"She loves you."

"Then she'll still be there when I get back."

I steal glances between him and the window.

"Almost everyone you meet in life is going to try to sell you a bill of goods," Dad says. "It's important to me that I not be one of them."

"I know."

"I'm not going to pretend I was right to do what I did, okay."

I snort. "You're the second person to say that to me tonight."

"Hm. Who was the first?"

"A guy I really like talking to."

"Someone special?"

"We're not dating or anything," I say. "Not right now, anyway."

"But is he special?"

I smile at all the warmth that comes with thinking of Luke's face. And I think about how my father probably spent years in search of someone who could give him those same lost pieces. I imagine the agony of finding and marrying that person, only to watch it all be overtaken by unhealed wounds. And suddenly Luke's plan to take things slow makes more sense, and Dad staying up here makes more sense, and Mom's years of living in home movies makes sense too.

And I answer Dad, "I think he's the most special person I've met."

"That's good. You deserve that," Dad says. Then: "You deserve an amazing life."

"So do you."

"I've got one."

"So do I."

Dad walks me back to my car, all the way down the hill despite his bad knees. Our goodbye hug is fast and formal, but it feels proper. It's a shared understanding that we aren't okay yet, but we'll be ready to put in the rest of the work when the time comes. Someday soon we'll return home and finish figuring out what we need to. But for now what I need is to be on my own, and he knows that. So all he says is, "You're ready."

I'm about to open my car when I remember my question from earlier.

"The stuff that happened to you," I say. "Did you get nightmares afterward?"

He looks away, then nods.

"Did you?" he asks.

I look away, then nod.

"I'm sorry," he says.

"Do they ever get easier?"

I watch my father as I ask it . . . his figure tiny against the backdrop of the night. His cane digging into the cracked earth; his eyes, gray ghosts.

"Christ, I hope so," he tells me.

SEVEN

MOM REACTS TO MY STORY THE SAME WAY DAD DID.

I have her read what I wrote for him, so I don't need to re-tread it. After she's finished pulling herself together, she spends a lot of time hugging me and crying and asking me the same question over and over: "What can I do?" I can't think of anything, so she makes me promise to let her know. Then I ask her to dial it back, so she kisses me on the head and watches TV with me until it's time for bed.

I want to go to sleep too, but this is my last night here. So instead I finish packing.

I've saved the toughest part for last—the boxes in the garage full of my desk items. I find them still shoved in the back corner on the concrete floor, stacked beside a trash bag and covered in cobwebs.

I sit down, tear the flap off of one, and wedge it under my knees. Using my phone as a flashlight, I dig my way through the first box: mementos. Mostly old photographs, the ones I'd printed out to tape to the wall. There are a lot of the group, and, of course, a lot of Lily. A few of them make me cringe, and most make me smile.

I look at all the photos of Lily and me—countless memories

from when we were just little kids—and I let my eyes rest on her smile. It feels like it belongs to a stranger. *That is a girl*, I think. Then it properly hits me for the first time: *This person is gone. You aren't going to see her again. You'll never hear her voice or laugh at each other's jokes or hold each other's hands.*

I sit back on my heels and flip through the pictures. Our first selfie—the two of us at freshman year pep rally, with me squinting and sporting newly-sprayed blue hair. Us at our first Homecoming, slow dancing in sunglasses. And so many of her just hamming it up for the camera, making funny faces with me. I pause on the one she and I took after our first Friendsgiving in ninth grade. I'm in an old sweater that's too big for me, and she's in a green blouse with her leg kicked up like she's in a movie. She's clutching my arms, her chin on my shoulder and an enormous grin on her face.

All this living we did.

I wipe my nose with my arm.

A beautiful girl. *God*, she was a beautiful girl. Impossible not to love, once. And I did love her, once.

Even though she hurt you.

Yes.

That's screwed up.

But you didn't know her. The things she did for me. The way she gave me my voice.

Without ever listening to it.

No.

Yes.

Stop.

She didn't.

I know. But shut up and let me look at her. Not her, the person who hurt me. I mean Her—the sweet ninth grader who befriended the boy with the broken arm and invited him to things because he seemed lonely. The person who looked out for me, and loudly loved me with all her golden heart.

I thought it was that simple, once.

But then that love unmasked itself bit by bit, gradually—across *years*. Lily was the girl who had my back; who let me find my words and helped me share them with others. But there was always that ugly imbalance under the surface—an immunity to loving me in any way other than her own. She became someone whose currency was control: She secured it, hoarded it, and always made sure she had enough to spend when needed. And the one night she couldn't have it, she took it because she could. A simple theft that sent me into the worst kind of limbo—the kind that taints everything good, bleeding your daily life dry of all its joy. Plunging you into an ugly, insipid gray.

Once, I knew a girl. Let me tell you about her: Her name was Lily Caldwell, and she was the author of all my joy. She was a girl who teased me when I couldn't finish my smoothie without brain freeze. Someone who got excited over cute dogs on the street. A poet who had a name and wanted to sign it all over a forgetful planet. A person who seized the world by all its stars and saw every one of them for what they were. She was a girl—my classmate and my first crush; my first love and my first friend. And God damn was she a great one.

But she was also everything after. I'll never know where the schism started—where one girl morphed into the other. All I know is I'd give anything to see that first girl one more time. Why can't I have that? Just for a few minutes . . . enough time to thank her for finding me on my front stoop and asking me about my arm. To tell her I love her and let her know I'll carry a piece of her with me wherever I go. To wish her well, thank her for my childhood, and give her a hug goodbye.

But this is what I'm left with instead: pretty pictures and skewed memories. Grieving someone who's still alive—

a mangled, unrequited catharsis. Because there are no two girls out there, conveniently split so I can love one and turn my back on the other. There is only this one girl. And there will be no tender goodbye between us . . . not tonight; not ever. There's letting go, and that's all.

I reach for my bracelet, snap it one last time, and pull it off my wrist. It sinks into the trash bag with barely a sound.

Lay your memories down and put them to rest. They aren't going anywhere; not tomorrow and not ever. No one can change them or undo the fact that they got made. But it's time to let them rest, now.

I nod.

Find a way to live with that.

"Okay," I say, softly. And I will.

It's time to let go now.

"Okay," I say, softly. And I do.

Before I go to sleep, I take the story I wrote for my father earlier tonight and put it on the ledge. I scrawl a quick sticky note to put next to it.

Mom—please give this to Mr. Caldwell.

EIGHT

I SLEEP FOR A LONG TIME.

I'm woken up by my mother, who gently knocks on my room and peeks her head in. She's wearing a Lanham sweatshirt even though it's August.

"Hey, college man. Just wanted to make sure you set an alarm."

I groan and sit up—I hadn't.

"Ready for the big day?" She perches herself on the end of my bed, then shakes her head at me. "*College*. I can't even believe it."

"Me neither," I say, rubbing my eyes. Per my request, she isn't coming with me to help move in. I want to make the last drive myself.

She clears her throat. "I went over to the Caldwells' place about an hour ago and did what you asked."

I wait for her to tell me how everyone reacted, but she doesn't say, and I decide I don't want to know. All she adds is that we both got an email from Dad, who reached out to Lanham's guidance office and started the process for an NCO.

"No-contact order," Mom clarifies. "He said you can cancel it if you want, but I think it's a good idea. It'll take some doing, but when they say no contact, they mean *no* contact. Not in classes, dorms, emails, texts . . . she even *looks* at you funny, her academic status is toast."

"They can do that?"

"They can do that. So you'll be safe."

Safe.

"I got you light bulbs for your dorm." Mom can always tell when I want a subject change. "I ran out early this morning and found them. These are special ones that sync with your phone—you can use an app to dim them. I'm assuming your roommate will be okay with it."

"Oh, thanks. And yeah, I don't know." I shrug, yawning. "I'll ask him today when I meet him."

She shakes her head at me again. "You're going to have so much fun in college."

"Hopefully. Thanks for letting me go alone."

She smiles and says, in a gentle voice, "It's time for you to get away from here."

We nod to each other.

"You had an awful thing happen to you," she continues. "There was no reason for it. And I think getting away is what's best. It's amazing what people can do once they get a hold on us. When you love someone, you pull yourself open for them and trust them not to rearrange your pieces. And sometimes they do anyway." She runs a hand through my hair, her eyes etched with seriousness. "But here's the thing: No matter where those pieces of yours end up or who's done what with them, they all still belong to *you*. This goes for college and everything after. Other people can do great things for your life or they can take a wrecking ball to it. But neither of those things makes it belong to them either. Because the one thing no one else can ever do is live our lives for us. That's a job for you and you alone, so take the time to do it."

I tell her I will.

"Will you be okay?" I ask her.

"Me? Oh yeah," she says, giving me a thumbs-up with pursed lips. "How could I not be, right? I'm the luckiest mom in the world."

"Every mom in the world says that."

"Every mom in the world is wrong."

"Except you."

"So I *did* teach you something. See how lucky I am?"

"Pretty lucky," I agree.

"Pretty lucky."

I take my last home shower and eat my last homemade breakfast. And soon it's time—really time. The trunk is packed, my room is double and triple checked, and all that's left to do is hug my mom goodbye.

She does it in our front hallway, holding me tight and rocking back and forth and apologizing for tearing up. She says, "Remember what we talked about," and I give her a thumbs-up. Then she adds, "When you make that drive, keep your eyes forward for me."

I can't tell if she's offering more existential advice or nagging me with a driving tip, but I don't ask.

We swap I love yous, I promise to text when I get there, and then I'm out the door. Walking to my car; starting it up, swallowing hard.

Then I look across the neighborhood, to the houses on the other side of the street, and I see her sitting on her front stoop: Lily, eyes drenched, head bowed. She looks up and sees me, and I see her.

She purses her lips in a grimace, raises a hopeful hand, and waves.

I put the car in gear and drive away without looking back.

NINE

To My Dear Friends in the Neighborhood:

By the time you read this, we'll have all finished our last hangout in this place. Most of you will have packed up and moved away already, and when I go, that'll be the end of our time here.

Obviously there's a lot of emotion with this . . . remembrance; hurt. It's easy to think back on all the moments that took place here. I could spend pages just listing them out—all our walks to the neighborhood gym, talking about our day. Getting midnight McDonald's on a snow day after a movie night. Our infamous all-nighter where we still aren't sure why the couch got moved. Countless game nights, countless jokes, countless captured pieces of life. To anyone on the outside (and maybe even to you all) it all looks so unnotable . . . a couple of young people who had a few fun years together. A group of ordinary folks among ordinary houses doing ordinary things. But to have lived it—to watch our paths align knowing it wasn't going to be permanent—makes that borrowed time all the more precious to me. It makes me wonder where it all came from. How did we create this? Something so simple, yet so loaded with joy . . . what did we do right and how the hell do we do it again?

I could spend pages unpacking the nostalgia, all of which would circle back to the central point of it all: how very, very much I love you. But . . . you know this. And the thing is, despite all the feelings that seem so big now, this was such a tiny piece of our lives. We've grown out of it, plain and simple. Each step we take now will be another step away from all this; time will chip away at those images until we feel like spectators to what was once the snapshot of our daily lives. And this is proper. It hurts—unbearably if you think too hard about it—but it's a proper type of pain. All of us are moving on, taking steps into those new places to repeat this same old cycle. More ordinary people will fill these ordinary spaces and make them extraordinary, just as we once did.

You all know me, and I know you're aware of how tough this is for me. All I want to do is hold on to this place, because most days it feels like I won't have any direction without it. And I'll admit, that's a tempting idea. It feels like the thing to do. But there's an even higher nobility, sometimes, in laying moments to rest. Letting them go becomes the ultimate act of love. And while there is that sadness, there's also everything after. The next chapter is here, and it's every bit as beautiful as this one was the second before we stepped into it.

I need you all to know I will never forget this group, these days, this extraordinary little era that you gave to me. And with that, I let it go.

Long live Old Friendship.

TEN

THIS IS IT—THE MOMENT I'VE BEEN PICTURING FOR four years. The car is moving; my house is shrinking. Then I make my turn onto the road, and it's out of view for good.

Keep your eyes forward for me.

"Okay," I say to the empty air, drumming my hands on the wheel as I drive through the neighborhood. "Okay."

I'm passing by moments now—there's the spot where the group had their first game of capture the flag. The mailbox that we duct taped Austin to on his fifteenth birthday. The pavilion where Lily and I discovered magnet poetry. Tiny memories, but all beautiful and all mine.

"Doing great," I murmur as I pass the playground and turn left out of the neighborhood. "Doing great."

Now I'm at the plaza. The first place I pumped gas. The site of Dad's panic attack.

Next, the library. Luke.

Eyes forward.

My GPS pops up with a notification: "Do you want to save nine minutes via an alternate route?"

"No," I tell it. Instinctively, I wait for Dad's voice to berate me on how I should learn to take the efficient route instead of the familiar one. Instead, the prompt shrinks and closes.

I smirk at it.

"Keep the route *exactly the goddamn same*," I add, for good measure. Then, "Actually, look up fast food places."

It reads a few to me. Wait, where do I want to go? I wasn't really serious. Except . . . food sounds good.

"Add option one to route," I say, grinning. When I get to a red light, I turn on the radio. An upbeat tune begins to play. Do I want it louder?

I decide I do, so I use the thumb controls on the steering wheel to crank the volume up. Then down again.

Loud.

Quiet.

LOUD.

Quiet.

Green light.

No one is stopping me. I'm still moving forward.

I laugh like a maniac, invigorated. I have such a *long* way to go, don't I? There's more out there of what I had here— new friends I never thought I'd meet and old friends I never thought I'd lose. God, I'm young. I bet my dad looked like this when he was my age. I wonder if he had a drive like this when he left home. I wonder if he listened to music the way I am now.

I lost. That's a fact. Everything I fought so hard to hold on to—my group, my girlfriend, the Studio, my whole life back home—is in the past and anchored there for good. It should be a crushing defeat, but it doesn't feel that way. Instead I feel bulletproof. All my greatest fears have come to pass, and here I still am. So instead of lingering on the loss and pain I felt in the final days, I want to take all those scars and saddle them up in the backseat of my brain. To focus on everything ahead—

shedding all the shit from my past and stepping into my new self.

It's so easy for this to feel like an irreparable downgrade; like I'll never find another Beth or Austin or Vic. *There will never be another like this place, and the joy we found in it with each other. There is nothing else out there that will sweep me off my feet and electrify my life.* But then I remember that I was filled with that same feeling before I met these people. There was nothing like this group, until there was. And there is nothing like the group I'll meet next, until there will be. And there will be.

I don't know how long it's going to take, but I'll find others—more friends, more relationships, more homes. More chapters of my life. Eighty years ahead against the eighteen I'm putting behind me. And someday when I'm old and my whole life is laid out, I'll have an entire collection—bunches of friends and neighborhoods and relationships and chapters. And I'll be able to look back on this one and say, with a sated smile, "I've still never forgotten you. How could I, when you were my very first?"

This story is coming to a close now, but I'll tell it to others. I'll tell them about how, on one rainy afternoon, five friends hugged each other goodbye under that pavilion, then went home to their new lives and didn't come back. I'll tell the story of how so much love happened here, in my tiny little Town with Two of Nothing. And as I speed down that highway with my windows open, I know with everything I am that all of it will stay with me. Because it's the story that made me who I'm leaving as now: a man who lost all he held close to his heart, but finally won his war.

At the next red light, I raise my head and stare at myself in the pull-down mirror.

For once, I don't flinch.

Instead I revel at where I'm at. Hell, six months ago I couldn't even drive. And now here I am . . . facing the open road with my life packed in the backseat and my hands on the wheel. Alive and unshackled and full of love. Laughing until I lose my air, smiling so hard it hurts.

Look at me.

ACKNOWLEDGMENTS

FIRSTLY TO MY SUPERSTAR AGENT, ALLISON REMCHECK, I would simply say the same thing you told me when you learned I was on the spectrum: "Thank you for being exactly who you are."

To my editor Lauren Knowles, my publicist Lauren Cepero, my copy editor Heather Taylor, designer Julia Tyler, and the rest of the incredible team at Page Street: Thank you for believing in my words, for helping me use them, and for all your patience as I found this story piece by piece.

To my fellow authors, reviewers, and friends in the publishing industry: There are too many of you to name, but thank you for providing me all the support, guidance, and community that you have for these past few years. And to all the titan authors who gave me the time of day to lend their support—particularly Angie Thomas, Laurie Halse Anderson, Stephanie Kuehn, Brigid Kemmerer, Bill Konigsberg, and Caleb Roehrig—thank you all for treating me as a complete equal even when I was a complete unknown. I won't ever forget it.

An abundance of thanks are in order to those outside of publishing. Mom, Dad, and Jackie: for your unwavering support and love. My high school crew—Phil, Andy, Kevin, Paige, Callie, Emily, and Allison: for all the joy I couldn't even come close to capturing in this book, and an unforgettable senior week. My amazing mental health care team, particularly Jeff Taulbee,

Eddie Lomash, and Yael Schreiber: for helping me navigate my own explorations of life, love, and the ever-elusive world around me. Michael Rowley: for being the person I spent my first Pride with, and for forever revolutionizing my music library. (That flag is still on my desk and always will be.) My neighborhood crew: for creating lightning in a bottle, and for the best Halloween party ever. Brodie Spade: for the magical night we met, and every day since. And Emily Rittenour: for so many things, but in particular for the idyllic era of our final days of high school. Thank you for the snowman we built, our movie theater in the woods, our forest escapades, our adventures at the Square, watching shooting stars the night before we left for college, and for every other chapter in our story. No book I write will ever come close to its beauty.

Honorary shoutout to second book syndrome, COVID-19, health anxiety, and all the other blights of 2020: for infusing this project with more headaches and misery than I could ever quantify. Words cannot express how overjoyed I am to forever escape your vile presence.

Finally and most importantly, to all my readers: for every fan letter and thank-you message you've shared with me about how my writing helped you. My wall is full of your kind words, and this book wouldn't exist without them.